CW00665964

WALK
IN THE PARK

A brand-new utterly hilarious and
heartwarming summer romance

CHARLOTTE BARNES

Choc Lit

A JOFFE BOOKS COMPANY

Choc Lit
A Joffe Books company
www.choc-lit.com

First published in Great Britain in 2024

© Charlotte Barnes 2024

This book is a work of fiction. Names, characters,
businesses, organizations, places and events are either
the product of the author's imagination or are used
fictitiously. Any resemblance to actual persons, living
or dead, events or locales is entirely coincidental.
The spelling used is British English except where fidelity
to the author's rendering of accent or dialect supersedes
this. The right of Charlotte Barnes to be identified as
author of this work has been asserted in accordance with
the Copyright, Designs and Patents Act 1988.

Cover art by The Brewster Project

ISBN: 978-1781897478

To Benji Barnes, my wild-haired, open-hearted boy,
thank you for all of the walks.

PROLOGUE

Owen

Collie and I hadn't had much interest in Christmas — though we'd upheld our usual Grinch and Max role-play, ignored my family as much as we could and eaten too much. We were, however, every bit interested in this, our glory day: the opening of Green Fields dog park. It was going to be . . .

A veritable mud bath. I surveyed the landscape from its fringes. I'd thought we were early, but the place was already riddled with dogs and their owners, all of them making idle conversation and admiring the scenery that the cynic in me thought probably wouldn't last. What was the council thinking, opening a dog park in the middle of winter? But, still, it gave us both something to look forward to and something to do on what would have otherwise been a quiet Sunday in January. And from the rate that Collie was tearing her way through the paths, past the bushes and sniffing in among the winter-flowering buds, she seemed as happy as she'd ever been, which was pretty much the only thing that mattered.

It wasn't long before the idle conversation caught up with us, though. Collie took a second too long to ferret out a smell between two rubbish bins and *bam*, there was a woman

1

and her Dalmatian looking to bond with us. I wasn't antiso-cial, exactly, but dog walking had always been such a bliss-fully quiet endeavour for me and Collie — when she wasn't lost in a flower-bed or pond, that was — so whenever some-one tried to do the easy small-talk thing with us, it felt like an intrusion. *Which makes you sound antisocial* . . . I reminded myself.

'Yours is as bad as mine for smells,' the woman commented.

It didn't seem quite right, given that her dog was the pic-ture of absolute obedience — upright, alert, standing at her heel. And my dog was—

'Collie, come out, would you?' I tugged softly on her lead to encourage her along but whatever the smell was, it clearly had a greater influence than I could claim. 'She just gets distracted when it comes to . . . Well, everything.' I laughed. 'She'll come out and make friends in a second.'

I had to say it because the woman looked to be patiently waiting for it to happen. But the truth was, Collie had always been a bit weird about Dalmatians. She eyed them with a combination of suspicion and confusion, as though they were a code to be cracked. And when she did finally come out from between the bins, she gave the other dog *such* a wide berth that it looked a little like she thought the spots would explode, too.

'Oh, I—'

'Don't take it personally,' I interrupted the woman, because it sounded like taking it personally was exactly what she was about to do. 'There are just so many smells all at once.'

She laughed, then. 'Of course. We'll see you both soon, perhaps?'

'Perhaps,' I managed to say as Collie yanked me further along the path ahead of us.

When we got to a relatively quiet stretch, I reached down to unhook her from her lead — and that was arguably my first and biggest mistake. Collie, named fondly after the breed I expected to come home with, before I fell in love with her, was an obedient dog when she wanted to be, which feels like a kind way of saying she wasn't that obedient at all. She was what my mother would describe as "a dog with a mind of her own" — and while that may sound like a good thing, it was one of many throwaway remarks that my mother could make sound like an insult, especially when it came to Coll. Of course, while she was pounding her way across the field like a greyhound who had heard a starting pistol, I wasn't in much of a position to dispute the whole "dog with a mind of her own" theory. I was, however, in a stellar position to go bolting across the grass after her.

My Converse sank into patches of mud and the further I ran across the field, the more of a proverbial ice rink it became, too. *There's no way she's getting out of this without a bath.* I probably wouldn't be far behind her on that.

By the time I'd caught up with her, Collie was half the dog she'd been before. Instead of a fully formed beagle, she was now one of those novelty half-dogs that people wedge in their gardens to make it *look* like a dog is digging through their flower-beds. But in my case . . .

'Collie!'

Her head shot up and she had the audacity to turn around with an actual clump of soil — and what I soon saw was a dangle of roots — hanging from her mouth.

'Don't you *dare* move . . .' I edged closer to her, one tentative step at a time, until I was finally within lassoing distance. I threw the slip lead around her neck and tucked the handle end of it around one of my muddied shoes. I didn't have hands enough to wrangle my dog *and* replant a flower-bed, but I certainly couldn't leave it overturned and hollowed out either.

'Give me the plant, Coll.' I eased the roots and leaves out of her mouth slowly and, credit to my girl, she knew enough about my tone not to play-fight me on it. Though she did let out a little huff-whine when her mouth was empty enough. 'I know, I'm a rubbish dog dad for not letting you deface public property.' I rubbed softly at the slick spot between her eyes before turning my attention to the flower-bed.

3

I was not, nor have I ever been, a keen gardener. I was even more reluctant to try my pale-green fingers at it without tools, in the middle of winter. It was a toss-up between whether the cold or the wet of the soil would get to me first. It didn't matter, though, because it was the Green Fields dog park opening day, and I was not going to let my dog be *that* dog that tore the place apart. So with Collie fixed under my foot, I set about raking my way through the earth to re-bed the plants that hadn't *quite* come free of the ground, before digging a decent enough hole to push and shove and—

'Excuse me?'

Of course. I sighed. *Of course, someone has caught us in the act.*

'I know, right? Dogs, what can you do with them?' I answered without looking up. From the corner of my eye I could see a multicoloured pair of Converse about as stained as my own. I just had to hope that the wearer had enough of a sense of humour to leave me well enough alone while I finished digging a hole—

'No, excuse me?'

This time, she actually tapped me on the shoulder. A neat, two-pronged tap.

Arses.

'I know, I'm just trying to fix it.' *Lady, I'm doing my best.* But it wasn't *her* fault that *my* dog was a renegade.

Then there came a laugh. A bubble of a noise that did something to my stomach and though I still couldn't face the woman, the sound was enough to make me pause what I was doing.

'Excuse me,' she said again. 'But is this yours?'

And from my vantage point of having my hands in wet ground and my lower legs planted in mud, I looked up to see what may have been the most beautiful woman in the whole of the city, complete with wild chestnut hair and eyes that could stun a man. *Of course. And, oh, wait, there's more. Yes, yes, that* is *my dog's lead in that woman's hand.* I followed the lead down to where it was still looped around Collie's neck. Collie with *another* bunch of flowers tucked neatly between

4

her teeth. And like the idiot I am, I actually looked down at my foot to where Collie's lead had been, as though I could be in any way lucky enough for there to be *two* beagles who looked exactly the same and had the same penchant for ruining public gardens.

'I am so, so sorry.' I struggled upright, smearing my jeans with more mud, and slipping nearly arse over in the process. The woman — as though she hadn't done enough for me already — offered me her hand and I hesitated about taking it. 'I'm not exactly . . .' I didn't know how to finish the sentence, so just flashed my open hands at her instead.

She shrugged. 'It's only mud.' Then she smiled and moved her hand a little closer.

Style this out, Owen. Style this out as best as you can.

'I'm Owen,' I said, taking her hand in mine with an apologetic look. 'That mutt is Collie and she'll be going back to her cell shortly.'

The woman laughed again and handed over Collie's lead. 'I'm Nell. And that mutt,' she gestured over her shoulder, 'is Daisy.'

Nell's mutt was considerably chiller than mine. She was a bruiser of a bulldog who absolutely did not look like a Daisy. She did look like a quiet companion, though, one who had stayed sitting — despite not being on a lead — to admire the view over the hillside of the park, while her human mum returned my reprobate to me.

'How did you get such a calm one?' I pointed down to Collie, planted between our feet, flowers still hanging limply from her mouth. 'I just got one that causes damage.'

'Well, fortunately for you both—' Nell pulled up the sleeves of her coat and jumper — 'I am *excellent* at gardening.'

'Are you actually?' I leaped on the comment with more enthusiasm than I perhaps should have. And I couldn't decide whether it was the beautiful woman offering to help me or whether it was the offer for help and . . . Who am I kidding? It was definitely the beautiful woman offering to help me that had set my voice, embarrassingly, a good octave higher than it had been some five minutes ago. I coughed as though clearing my throat. 'It's a real mess and it's definitely not for you to . . .' I petered out as Nell held up a hand to stop me.

'How about I help you and yours with your gardening, and you buy me and mine a hot chocolate to warm us through afterwards?' She smiled and I couldn't help but notice the way the expression made her nose wrinkle up.

'That sounds like a really fair deal to me and mine. Let's try that.'

I didn't even have my wallet. But I would have happily stayed behind on pot-wash duty long enough to cover two hot chocolates, if that's what it took to drink one of them with Nell and Daisy.

SIX MONTHS LATER . . .

CHAPTER ONE: NELL

I leaned back and, while she wasn't looking, unbuttoned the top of my jeans. *Skinny fit for Sunday lunch — what was I thinking?* Now, able to comfortably exhale again, I scooped another whole roast potato into my mouth and mmm-ed around the crunch of its skin.

No one made roast potatoes like Nan. Fact. I have fond childhood memories of her making chips from scratch, too, the bubble of fat and the stink of oil soaking into the brick wallpaper of her kitchen. She always cooked chips with the windows open, the net curtains billowing in a breeze that made eggs and chips that bit more dramatic than they probably needed to be — but as a ten-year-old, I loved the theatrics of dinner at Nan's. She'd stopped making chips when Grandad died. There was obviously a link there, but I'd never worked out what it was.

These days she specialised in roasted, mashed or boiled potatoes and I had learned to love the Sunday dinners — that looked more like a carvery spread for a small army — that Nan built around them. She spooned another two potatoes onto my plate, followed by another awkwardly cut slice of beef. Her arthritis made wielding an electric knife akin to a tension-building scene in a horror film, but if I ever offered

8

to help, it ran with it the risk of dinner becoming an actual scene from a horror film. When it came to meat cuts, I took what I was given. Though I was about a mouthful of anything away from bursting free from my jeans, the seams splitting stitch by stitch like I was a throwback from a Roald Dahl cautionary tale about the dangers of greed.

'Nan, honestly—'

'Nonsense, finish your greens.'

The woman made a fair albeit brief argument. Thirty years old and broccoli was still sacrificed in favour of roast potatoes — or mashed, or—

'Are you thinking about a chap?'

My head snapped up. 'No, I was thinking about potatoes.'

'Eleanor. Good Lord.' She tutted, as though carbohydrates were something indecent, which was a style of thinking I was *really* trying to move away from. But I reasoned that as an eighty-six-year-old woman, there was a very real possibility that Nan was past the point of being a Diet Culture Dropout. So, instead of clambering onto my soapbox with my unbuttoned jeans and all, I scooped up another bite of mashed potato that was pockmarked with peas and hoped that would be green enough for everyone to be satisfied.

'Honestly, Nan, I'm done for.'

'There's apple pie in the fridge that needs to be heated through.'

'Okay, well, that's a different receptor altogether. How long will that take?'

Nan only chuckled, a throaty sound that scratched at something on its way out. Nan was also of the school of thought that cigarettes weren't bad for you. Whenever I played the cancer card, she laid down a hand that trumped it. Grandad had died from an undetected heart defect that had, apparently, been there his entire life, a small grenade in his chest cavity with anyone's guess when the pin might be pulled. Eight years ago was the answer. Then there was the King and Queen of the deck: Mum and Dad, dead on impact after a confrontation with an artic lorry and a tired driver. Nan didn't have to worry about cancer. The worst things in life had already happened to her and she'd ripped the seeds from the core of each, spat them out and grown something new.

'You go and put the telly on—'

'Nice try.' I stood and snatched her plate before she could grab it. 'You cook, I clean. They've always been the rules.'

Nan had been Mum since I was twelve — that's when the accident had happened. She and Grandad had raised me on fairness policies, with the equal distribution of labour in a household being one of them. When I — a smart-mouthed thirteen-year-old — pointed out the fact that Grandad did *nothing* around the house, Nan only said, 'Do as I say, not as I do.'

'Why don't you go and find us a nice bit of *True Crime*?' I suggested.

About six months ago, I'd taught Nan how to use Netflix, and it had at once been the best and worst thing I'd done in my life. When I'd got a text message late one evening asking whether I'd seen *Making a Murderer*, I'd known I'd created a monster.

I handed her the walking stick that she'd carelessly discarded halfway across the kitchen — in favour of being able to carry two plates at once. I saw the look on her face when she took it, the begrudging stare, but she didn't say anything. Instead, she struggled upright and took the aid before clicking her way out of the laminate-floored kitchen and onto the soft crush of the carpet that lined her hallway and living room.

The house was a mess of design schemes that had been, I assumed, stripped from every era Nan had lived through — of which there were many. The kitchen was the most modern of the bunch, with soft-close cupboards and a dishwasher that she still refused to strip the cellophane covering from, owing to the fact that 'God gave you two hands for a reason'.

* * *

I'd tackled Phase One of the clean-up, which was the washing-up itself. But then there came the mammoth task of Phase Two. Whenever Nan felt the burn of old age and needed a change of . . . something, she would rearrange. The sofa would somehow migrate to the opposite side of the living room, the bed to the opposite side of the bedroom. This week, it was the plates and the cutlery that had voyaged to cupboards and drawers otherwise occupied by takeaway menus and pans. *Lord knows where the pans are, then . . .*

I never queried how she managed it. I could only assume it was a sheer force of will that kept the woman going how she did. By the time I'd navigated my way around the newly unknown scape of the kitchen, and heated up the apple pie, I'd overheard the preview of as many as four documentaries, all of which promised the definitive story of one violent offender or another. I was serving up generous portions for the both of us by the time the living room fell quiet, which could only mean one of two things: *she's decided, or she's nodded off.* I looked in the fridge and found squirty cream, which I also took liberties with before carrying both plates in with me, half-expecting to see Nan slumped forward with her eyes clenched shut, sleeping as though in prayer. But instead . . .

'Ted Bundy or Jeffery Dahmer?'

I looked from one plate of apple pie to the other, then back to Nan.

'You're right,' she said. 'We'll go with Bundy.'

After a slice of apple pie and the first episode of a ten-episode series, Nan disappeared to make tea, despite my protests that I could do it. 'You did the pie, I'll do the tea,' she said — and there's that nightmarish equal distribution of labour again.

I thumbed my way around social media and, to my utter shame, glanced through my latest matches on Tinder. Although Bundy didn't exactly set the tone for romance . . . Besides which, all of them were recycled from weeks and months gone by anyway. It was a pixelated parade of *Here's what you could have won* formed from a line-up of the usual suspects: men in too-dark lighting, men gathered in a herd on a night out — thereby making themselves totally indistinguishable — and, it seemed, men who only wanted women to identify them according to the outline of their muscles. There were whole torsos listed and whenever I saw them I couldn't help but think, *is that all I'll be dating? The torso?* Like the man behind the profile was a creature befitting of an *After Hours Addams Family*.

Discouraged, again, I closed the app and went to check on Nan. As a standardised unit of measurement, we often classed things in terms of cups of tea — *I'll do that in a cup of tea. I haven't even had my second tea. I've had four teas in the time it's taken to fill in this form.* In a caffeine paradox, though, I thought it was taking Nan longer than a cup of tea to make our cups of tea. In the kitchen I found her sitting at the table, ignorant, it seemed, to the blow and boil and steam of the kettle behind her.

'Nell, just bloody wait.' She tutted and went back to looking at her own mobile in her palm.

I kissed the crown of her head as I walked behind her. 'The kettle boiled five minutes ago.'

'Did it?' She craned around as though I might have been having her on. 'Well . . .' She shrugged. 'I'll be buggered. Did you know Ted Bundy spent *ten* years on death row?' The words all knocked together as though they were part of the same thought, and Nan was at such an age now that when things like this happened, my knee-jerk response was to worry. But when I turned, kettle in one hand and mug in the other, I saw she was happily engrossed in her reading again. 'Forty shocking facts about Ted Bundy. Are you ready?'

'Honestly, Nan, I'm not sure that I—'

'Molested by his grandmother . . .' She muttered as much to herself as me. 'Over thirty women!'

'We're not going to need to watch that series.' I set a steaming cup and saucer — always a cup and saucer — on the table in front of her. 'You'll scare yourself if you read that lot.'

She cocked her eyebrow and made a sceptical face at the suggestion. 'Eleanor, the things I've seen . . .'

I blew steam level across the top of my mug.

'Mind you, a young lady drinking from a builder's mug still sends a shiver down me.'

I ignored the quiet criticism and only sipped my tea, waiting, but not quite ready, for the next Bundy fact.

'You're ever such a pretty girl, you know, Nellie?'

'Oh, Nan.' I set my drink down. 'Let's not start?'

'I'm not starting.' She held both hands in a defensive gesture and pretended to look shocked by the mere suggestion that she might be starting something — but I knew the tone. I recognised all too well the opener. I knew this could only be a prelude to — 'Wouldn't you rather be out with some young man rather than sitting with a wartime prune, though? And now, I won't be offended if you say yes.'

I laughed. 'You're an idiot sometimes, Nan.'

'Hey—' she tapped my forearm — 'manners.'

'Sorry.'

'Now.' She picked up without missing a beat. 'Is there no one? *No one*?'

'Look, I didn't want to make a thing of it until I knew anything for definite . . .'

Nan propped her elbows on the table, cradled her head in her palms and stared at me longingly — the human embodiment of the heart-eyed emoji.

'I *have* met someone, someone who I really think might be . . . I don't know, someone who's good for my life, I guess. And I don't want you to say anything until I've got to the end now, because some of this is going to be a surprise, but please know that I'm *really* happy with this decision, okay?'

She nodded with such enthusiasm that I worried she might sprain something — which I'd no doubt hear about tomorrow through a string of WhatsApp messages and/or an accidental video call.

'I have met someone. She's in her late teens, which I realise is young, and I suppose she is quite young. But, oh, she has so much character, *so* much character, you'll love her for that. She's quite into sport but between us both she isn't entirely built for it, and *I* love her for that . . .'

'Nell.'

'. . . I've actually known her a really long time now, practically since she was a newborn, which I guess is a bit weird, but, whatever, I don't mind people judging us for it. She really does make me incredibly happy, Nan, and I know it's not who you were expecting me to come home with but—'

'Nell!'

I choked up with a laugh that filled my cheeks and spluttered out. Her face was a picture of a serious reprimand, teetering on the edge of bursting, too. I recognised it from times when I'd come home late or chipped an ornament or flooded the kitchen with a bath that I'd left running while on the phone — all of which seemed like much more serious offences than idle horseplay on a Sunday afternoon.

'A day might come when you decide you need more in life than that bloody dog.'

On cue, Daisy grumbled from the corner of the room.

'Now you're waking up to chime in, I suppose?'

Daisy, my two-year-old, twenty-kilogram bundle of joy, came plodding over from her corner in the kitchen, where she'd spent much of our visit sound asleep. She'd lay on her side, her belly rotund and beached, and every now and then would let out those small, dog-dream whimpers that left me torn between waking her up — *it might be a nightmare . . .* — and letting her rest — *what if she's chasing cats through fields of barley . . .* Now, though, she shuffled as close to me as she could manage, dropped her bum and stared up at Nan, as though awaiting an apology or a retraction — or both, in the newspaper no less, nothing short of it would do.

'It's weird that she's slept like, basically the whole time we've been here, don't you think?' I reached down to pat Daisy's head.

Nan said nothing and the silence stretched out.

'I wonder if it's anything to do with all of the beef you fed her while you thought I wasn't looking?' I glanced at Nan over the rim of my mug — but she didn't even have the decency to look outraged. She only shrugged.

'That dog might be the closest thing I get to a grandchild. I'm entitled to spoil her.'

'Nan, *me*! *I'm* already your grandchild.'

But she waved that logic away like it was nothing but local folklore — interesting to hear maybe, but not to be trusted or believed. I laughed, then tipped the remains of my tea down my throat before moving to drop the mug in the sink.

'I'll leave that for you to do,' I said with another kiss on her crown. 'Anything you need before we go?'

'I'm an independent woman,' she replied, which I took to be a "No, thank you".

Nan leaned down to pet Daisy and coo into the wrinkles of her face. Never was a dog more beautiful, despite what every article on the internet might have to say about the best-looking dogs and their rankings — where bulldogs were often described as . . . niche? 'Who's a lovely girl then? Who's a lovely girl?'

Daisy's tail wagged and, subsequently, so did her bum. But on account of still sitting, it looked more like a side-to-side shuffle against the smooth floor.

'Come on, girl.' I encouraged her towards the door. 'You and I have got a fair bit of beef to work off on this walk home.' I looked back at Nan from the doorway and winked. 'Thank you for having us, and feeding us.'

'Any time, Nellie. See you next Sunday?'

'If not before. Love you, Nan.'

'Love you, girls!' she shouted after us.

I always counted myself lucky for having these Sundays, for being walking distance from a nan who still recognised my face, knew my name and how I liked my roasties cooked. And I wouldn't change her for the world. But — if only she'd go along with it — I wouldn't half feel better if instead of leaving her behind, I was leaving her behind with a dog. A rescue, maybe, an old girl in need of a home — not a puppy, or high-energy breed, but something that matched Nan's life down to the ground. Though it occurred to me that Nan probably had similar thoughts about me, albeit, with a man rather than just a dog, like there was anything *just* about my Daisy.

Only . . . Nagging at me during our wander home — thanks to Nan and her never-gentle probing questions — I thought, *maybe there is a man, mousy-haired and bright-eyed, maybe there is . . .*

CHAPTER TWO: OWEN

There was no need for a clock in my office. I was all too aware of the time it was by the disconcerting watercolour swim of my monitor, where the lines of the spreadsheet knew no bounds and the numbers collapsed together like a broken slinky. I blinked hard, rubbed at my eyes and searched through my top drawer for my reading glasses — prescribed specifically so this didn't happen. *But without the blurred vision,* I thought as I snapped open the case, *how will I know how far through the working day I am?*

I hadn't actually needed reading glasses at all until I took this job — or rather, until I took my last promotion. It was a strange and unwanted annual bonus that I now had to see my optician on a more regular basis, just so he could judgementally ask how long I was spending in front of a screen these days, and I could guiltily answer, 'Too long,' as though I was a teenager admitting to too much time in front of a PlayStation and pay-per-view television channels.

The reality being I was a financial advisor with an organisation that handled the portfolios of rich old white men, all of whom had so much money that it sort of didn't matter what we told them to do with it. And my reward for feeding that system? I put my reading glasses on, blinked hard again,

17

and when the numbers persisted in swimming out of formation I decided that tea might be a better route into saving the afternoon.

Though, of course, getting tea meant leaving my office. And leaving my office meant—

'Owen! P-p-p-owen.' Douglas, my senior — in age and experience but certainly not maturity — made guns from his fingers and played at shooting me with each plosive. 'How's the Norton advisory paperwork coming along? Anything you think we can throw their way before the week is out?'

No, I wanted to say. *Because you gave me the figures yesterday, and today is now Wednesday, and that maths means . . .* But instead I swallowed the smart-arse reply, rubbed at the back of my neck and said, 'I'm actually working on it now.' I gestured to the lifts. 'I was just going to nip downstairs and get a tea from the vendor, then I'll be back to it.'

'Great, I'll join you.' And he launched himself in the very same direction. 'I think the thing with the Norton is—' he punched the lift button like it had insulted his mother — 'they've got *so* much money hanging around since the stocks went bump on the last investment, that they don't know what to do with it anyway — Stevo! Good to see you, my man.' He broke up the formalities when another senior advisor stepped out of the opening lift — a man who didn't and likely never would know my name, never mind what I actually did at the firm. 'Where was I?'

'Norton, stocks—'

'Since that last little cock-up, that's the one. Since that, they're unsure of putting their money anywhere. So whatever we advise them, we need to make sure it's a sure bet. You see?'

It was, of course, information I'd already deduced — on account of being good at my job and all. But still, I nodded along with a meaningful expression as though Douglas was slipping me the key to the room where the company kept the golden geese. He carried on throughout the lift journey, down five flights that felt more like twenty-seven, before eventually drawing the monologue to a close with a compliment that caught me so off-guard I felt as though the man had soft-slapped me right there in the middle of the lobby.

'Anyway, I'm spoon-feeding you shit you already know. You're a good kid, you know what you're doing.'

And then he punched me playfully on the shoulder with a balled fist, as though literally punctuating the end of his sentence. I managed to mutter a thank you while inwardly thinking, *fucking hell, has it happened? Have I actually arrived as "one of Doug's boys"?*

There was an inner circle of junior workers at the firm who Doug mentored. It saved him doing actual work, and it meant that he could be the ringleader of a group of untrained puppies until one or more of them were either sacked or swallowed further into the company's clutches. When I took the promotion six months back, Doug had started to mentor me with good intentions — or rather, as close to good intentions as I thought the man could get. But when I refused to fudge the dates on a tax form that was two weeks late — 'Owen, don't be a square, just change the goddamn numbers' — suddenly the mentoring was dropped, and the account mysteriously disappeared from my system access. I hadn't said anything, because I remembered playground politics enough to know that you couldn't be a square *and* a grass. The sting of it still hadn't quite settled though. Between that and the fact that I'd always refused an offer of a lunchtime pint — in favour of a lunchtime visit home to boop Collie on the nose and let her out for an emergency wee — I'd never *quite* made Cool Kid status in the company. But now, maybe *now* we were finally getting somewhere, and Doug and I were working back to a place of male bonding where—

'So help me, I only come to this vendor because of the tits on this server. The coffee is so much better five minutes down the street.' He nudged me. 'Know what I'm saying?'

Nope, my mistake. I made an awkward and noncommittal noise. *Doug is still an arsehole, and I am not one of the boys.*

But I knew my place in the world well enough to pay for the man's coffee, and I tipped the vendor, too, as though my generosity might do something to assuage the guilt that Doug definitely didn't feel — or rather, assuage his misogyny the tiniest of bits instead.

'What about you, Owen? You with anyone these days?'

Oh, he wants small talk. With an inward groan I made another noncommittal noise and then said, 'Not really, no. I guess . . . Well, nothing, nothing that's really set in stone. Things are quite open . . .'

I had no idea what I was referring to, exactly, but Doug made a low whistle and I took that to mean I'd said something right.

'You dog.' Another nudge, his elbow bumping into my forearm and sending my tea spilling over the lid of its take-away cup, which was a peeve if ever there was one. 'Keeping things open. Christ, Owen, I didn't have you down as the type for that, but good for you, kiddo.'

I was trying to balance out the affection being thrust upon me by a man in a position of power — a precarious mixture of factors if ever there was one — with eye-widening shame running through me as I slowly realised what I'd said versus what Doug had heard. *Keeping things open?* I parroted back to myself. *Christ, who do you think you are?*

'If I'd kept things open with my ex-wife then the infidelity would probably have been less of a problem, know what I'm saying?' And then he chuckled, properly, heartily, red-faced chuckled. Meanwhile, I stood in front of him and wondered if there was a way, any way at all, to throw my hot tea over the smudge stain of a human standing in front of me, and somehow manage to pass it off as an accident. *Probably not.*

'Are you heading back up?' he asked, once his breathing had settled. 'Norton figures,' he added then, and tapped his watch.

'Yes, boss, heading back up.'

'Good talking to you, Owen. Thanks for the drink.'

'You too, Doug. Thanks for the company.'

He flashed a tight smile. 'Douglas.'

'Ah.' I nodded. 'Sorry, boss, of course. Douglas.'

Definitely not *one of Doug's boys . . .*

* * *

Like readying to call the doctors as soon as the phone line opens, or queuing outside of Truman's to get my first — and therefore best — flat white of a Saturday morning, I had my cursor hovering over *Shut down* at 4.59 p.m. As the time in the corner of my screen ticked over, I clicked the button and made for the door.

The office was a flurry of activity at that time of day, but I'd noticed people weren't in a rush to leave so much as they were in a rush to ask who was available for drinks? Antithetical though it was, people seemed to be rushing *not* to get home, as though they had nothing to rush back to.

But I did, and I used that as a balm to soothe the burn of the fact that none of the questions regarding social events were directed at me. I only got nods and the occasional wave from the opposite end of a hallway.

I took the stairs down to the building's car park. I ferreted out my Mini Cooper by sound alone — a cheerful click when I unlocked the doors. The place was a landscape of metal and I'd managed to lose the car more than once, much to the amusement of the security guard who had watched me doing laps. I climbed into the car, dropped my head back against the seat and took my first real breath of the day. I felt it all the way down to my gut. And though the intention was there for a follow-up breath, another deep one that moved through the diaphragm, my inhale was interrupted by the sudden hum of my phone ringing through the car's speakers.

'Please don't be work, please don't be work.' I slowly lifted my head to glance at the display, one eye closed as though I'd reverted to childhood and I was peeking at what could be nothing, but what could also be a monster. I laughed when I saw that my childlike trepidation had been right. I hit the button to accept the call. 'Hi, Mum.'

'Owen, are you well?'

For as long as I could remember, Mum had spoken to me with the same formality that had been used for staff. On more than one occasion I'd tried to remember how she might have spoken to me as a child, whether she leaned over my cot and cooed silly noises like an archetypal mother. But truth be told, I couldn't even wrap my head around her bowing to the inconvenience of having to give birth, never mind the inevitable nursing of a child that comes after it — and somehow, my mother had managed to do it as many as four times! Yet when my youngest sister had brought her newest offspring to the family home — while her husband had conveniently stayed at home with the other two brats — Mum had been so utterly flummoxed by the entire experience that all she'd managed to say to Hattie was a stunned, 'Well done,' as though she'd passed a GCSE exam with a semi-decent grade, rather than had a major hand in creating a life. Needless to say, my mother wasn't the maternal type. The fact that she'd called at all — rather than getting Dad to — was in itself a novelty. And I suddenly thought—

'Mum, is Dad okay?'

There was a brief pause. 'What a strange thing to ask, of course he is. Why?'

I forced a laugh. 'I just wanted to check. I'm well, thank you, and you're both well?' Faced off against her formality, I lapsed into my own and in frustration found I was dropping my head to knock once, twice, three times against my steering wheel as I waited for her answer.

'We're well, absolutely. Your father is at golf.'

So that explains that. 'How's Wini?'

Wini was our housekeeper — or rather, Mum and Dad's housekeeper. Though she'd had a key hand in raising Mum and Dad's brood as well, myself included. Wini spoke with the dulcet tones of someone who actually cared about the person she was speaking to, whoever they were, whatever the conversation. Even when Mum drunkenly barked orders at her or Dad grunted his own demands. In truth, the woman deserved much better than my parents. For some reason, though, she chose to stick around.

'She's fine,' she answered, and offered no more.

'Give me two seconds, Mum. I'm just trying to pull out of the car park at work.' I was attempting to join an offensively busy road that ran through the core of the financial district. At this time of day, it resembled a Tesla storage facility. I indicated and edged out a little, out a little and — 'Come on, one of you twats must want to give way.'

'Owen!'

Arses. 'Sorry, Mum, I — Thank you!' I stuck my hand up to the other driver, a kindred spirit who, from the state of his clapped-out Clio, also wasn't being paid what he was worth. There were a handful of us scattered throughout various companies, I was sure, and we could recognise each other through our downtrodden-ness — and the fact that we hadn't yet upgraded our cars to act as penis extensions.

'Okay, I'm on the road and all ears. What was it you called for, Mum?' I tried for persistent but polite. Now I was on the road, it wouldn't be long before I got home to the one small soul in the world who would always be eager to see me, no matter whether I'd been at work for the entire day or if I'd only been rooting around in the boot of the car for ten minutes. Either way, my homecoming welcome was akin to my having returned from a war-torn battlefield — a comparison that felt all too apt, given the sergeant major on the other end of the call.

'We're having a family dinner, this Sunday.'

Balls.

'I assume you'll come. Your sisters and brother will be coming, too, no partners, so you shouldn't feel too out of place.'

Shots fired. I held my breath, knowing all too well what the next thing would be.

'But your father and I have asked that it's adults only, so they're finding childcare for the day. It's only fair that . . . Well, you know.'

My shoulders drooped. 'You don't want me to bring Collie.'

23

'It's only fair, Owen.'

The last time I'd taken Collie with me to Mum and Dad's, she'd managed to tear her way through a blooming family of pink and white roses at the bottom of the garden. Once Mum's voice had lowered back to a discernible decibel, she'd managed to explain to me that they were award-winning roses. *Awarded what?* I'd wanted to ask and, *by whom?* Though of course, I'd known better. As had Collie, who'd only sat with her muddied snout and front legs, the archetypal dog from a cartoon, her beautiful beagle face hung in shame. She'd been obviously mortified — or play-acting at being so — so how Mum had managed to hold it against her was beyond me. But it was clear this was an extended punishment — for Coll and me both.

'Of course, whatever you want, Mum. Let me know if I can bring anything.'

'Only yourself,' she answered, and, far from affectionate, it felt more like a gentle reminder to *only* bring myself — and not that mud-covered, flower-eating, food-stealing dog of mine.

CHAPTER THREE: NELL

There were times when Green Fields Books was a tumble-weed breeding ground. Days, even, when I'm sure Daisy and I imagined customers, our heads snapping up in synchronicity to the sound of a ringing bell over the front door that turned out only to be an echo from the shop next door. On those days, I quietly panicked about Nan's investment in the place and whether I'd ever manage to pay it back. Though whenever I'd voiced those concerns to her, she'd rolled her eyes and reminded me that it was inheritance money.

'It can't be,' I'd answer. 'You're not dead.'

And she'd only wave the comment away like I was spreading old wives' gossip and nonsense. But the truth of it was that the shop wouldn't exist if it weren't for Nan. When the property first came up for sale, I was still slogging my guts out as an average-Joe bookseller at a reputable high-street retailer that needn't be named. Then the old bakery on the high street went bust and I visited Nan one Sunday afternoon with stars and hearts in my eyes, and the paperwork detailing the shop's particulars wedged into my bag.

'Wouldn't the property be *perfect for a bookshop*?' I mumbled around a mouth of mashed potato. There were the wide, double-fronted windows, the open-plan shop floor, the fact that it stretched back and back — I'd been in that bakery enough times to recall the exact layout of the place. I already knew where I'd put the shelves. But when I relayed it all to Nan she only shrugged.

'I'm old, I've no vision. But if you say it would be perfect, I'll trust that. Let's do it.'

'Oh, just like that?'

She shrugged again and said, 'What's a reason not to?'

'I can't afford it, to start with.' I was already paying out money on my own mortgage then, too, having finally moved out of Nan's and shakily stepped onto the property ladder, and a second mortgage on a bookshop that mightn't even take off was a risk that I couldn't — trying to be sensible — afford to take. Besides which, an equally sensible part of me knew there was more to owning a bookshop than just, well, owning the shop. There were the financial outlays to start with, there was the market research after that — or should that come *before*? I idly put together a list of things that my sensible brain would discourage. Meanwhile, the less-sensible part of me ran around in a field of daisies and made plans for life fulfilment in the form of a well-stocked fiction section.

'Put your cutlery down,' Nan said. 'Go upstairs into my bedroom. The wardrobe on your right, the free-standing one — if you look in the very bottom of that, there'll be a shoebox, red and white, or cream, I forget. Oh . . . maybe it's the blue shoebox.' Her face knitted into a show of concern while she tried to remember. 'In *a* shoebox,' she finally blurted out, 'there'll be something that can help.'

Fifteen minutes and five shoeboxes later, I came downstairs with what turned out to be a bundle of notes that levelled out just shy of £20,000.

'Nan, what in God's name . . .'

'There's more up there somewhere.' She spoke around a forkful of roast parsnip. 'I don't trust the banks . . .'

* * *

Nan had criticised the name of the place — 'It's not very inventive, Nell' — but other than that, every decision made had been my own. Besides which, when I'd explained the basics of SEO — 'Think about what people will google when they're looking for bookshops in the area' — Nan had backed down on even that, telling me instead what a clever duckling I was, with a look of genuine amazement on her face.

Quiet days nevertheless were worrying, and we did get those. Though not today. On this sunny afternoon the shop was so busy that I'd honestly entertained the idea of subbing out my lunchtime sandwich run for a deodorant one instead — but as it turned out, I didn't have the time for either! Daisy ate her bowl of dog food in the staffroom while I managed a cup of tea and a rice cake, and Eloise, my lunchtime lady, came and did her hour. Sorting through that day's delivery became squeezed in between sips of my drink and rabbit nibbles at my food, and before I'd even had the chance to so much as *think* the phrase "ham melt on wholemeal with no onion", Eloise was sticking her head into the stockroom to say goodbye.

'There are still customers out here, by the by, girls.'

By the end of the day I was ready for a shower and a lie down in a darkened room. I slipped on Daisy's lead, turned off the last of the lighting in the shop and locked and double-locked the door behind us. Then Daisy and I headed for home, playing pavement dodgems with the Friday afternoon crowds as we went. I tried to hold myself in an optimum position for letting some air finally reach my armpits, as though that in itself would be enough effort to carry away the waft of the day. It was a ten-minute walk home, though, and miracles must have been running short because by the time we'd made it through the crowds, it felt somehow like I'd done another round of dashing around the shop instead. When we got to our quiet street — safely tucked away from the bustle of city life, despite being in touching distance still — I breathed such a heavy sigh of relief that my waistband cut into my stomach.

'The sign of a good breath,' I said to Daisy as I took her lead off. She was well trained enough to plod the street's length home. 'What's the first point of action, babe?' I asked her, though I was already half occupied with planning possible outfits.

Meanwhile, Daisy's first port of call was her water bowl, where she lapped up a ridiculous amount in record time before collapsing onto the kitchen floor with her bloat. Summer had officially arrived with the hottest day of the year so far — and I wasn't sure it agreed with either of us. Daisy especially wasn't built for heat — literally, owing to her breed — which meant that we'd need to aim for the shady spots on our walks when we could manage it. I crouched down to rub the smooth-rough of her tummy and in typical fashion she lazily cocked one back leg, as though she were reluctantly doing me a favour in trying to make my job of a tummy touch that bit easier.

'You're such a giver, Daisy, aren't you?'

And she let out a hearty sigh as if to say, 'Yes, yes, I am.'

After a few more blissful seconds I checked the wall clock and saw that we were already running late. So I cut the belly rub short and left Daisy to rest, while I pounded up the stairs and straight into the bathroom. I peeled the day's layers off and left them in a heap on the bathroom floor for Future Nell to moan about, and had the quickest under-the-arms wash imaginable. 'Just like Grandad taught me.' I was still drying myself off when I went into the bedroom. The towel, much like the clothes before it, was also discarded, albeit on a different floor, and I considered writing a note to Future Nell to apologise for the mess. *You know how it is when you're rushing and panicking and getting ready to . . .* The thought died out. *What am I getting ready to do, exactly?*

I pulled a daisy-print dress from the wardrobe first, before forcing it back in — too on-the-nose. Then there came the light-blue floral print and the black polka-dot and the sunflower skirt and, and, and . . .

'Why does everything I own make me look like a flower?' I huffed and dropped a pair of leaf-print trousers onto the floor too. There were skirts, shirts and dresses galore and I felt like a spoiled girl from a children's story having looked at them all with crushing disappointment, as though I were hard done by for only having *this many* clothes. There was a blue cotton dress shoved at the far end of my wardrobe that caught my eye, soft to touch and flowy. It paired well with the weather and, if I was lucky, it might even let in a breeze.

I slipped the dress on over my head and looked down. It was cut short at the knee, which meant if I did a fairy-tale twirl at any point during the afternoon it would kick out neatly around me. I imagined myself in *The Sound of Music*, arms outspread and flowers all around, as though Green Fields dog park had suddenly morphed into a Swiss landscape. *Is that film set in Switzerland?* I shook the thought away. *Not important right now.*

Dodging all the clothes dotted over the floor, I made it to the full-length mirror on the other side of the room to inspect myself. *This is as good as it's going to get.* My hair was still held together by a precarious amount of bobby pins — *that I'll no doubt be rooting out for days* — and the make-up that promised to last thirty hours — *what do they think women do for thirty hours straight?* — had in fact failed to last a whole day working in the shop. But when I smiled, I thought, maybe, just maybe, *I don't look* that *bad.* 'Do I, Daisy?' I asked, when I spotted her reflection in the mirror. She stood in the doorway behind me, *very* disinterested in my embarrassing human problems.

'Come on, then,' I said, turning. 'Let's aim for the shady side of the street.'

Daisy galloped from the room like an excited piglet, her back legs not quite able to keep up with her front, though she still managed to make it downstairs before me. She was sitting pretty at the front door — her bum on the floor already, such was the house rule — desperate for the drawer to be opened and the lead to be pulled out and the poo—

'Bollocks.' Daisy's head tilted and I gestured at the dress. 'No pockets.'

I scrunched up the bags into the smallest cluster I could manage and — ignoring the inner monologue of mortification that was running in my nan's voice — I pulled my dress forward and shoved them firmly into the left cup of my bra. I'd have to keep my keys in my free hand. Every bra has its limits.

'Needs must, Daisy, needs must.'

And she whined, like she knew just what I meant.

* * *

Green Fields dog park was Daisy's answer to the Holy Lands. The fields were somehow both limitless and securely fenced, making life that bit easier for even the nerviest of owners who would otherwise shudder at the prospect of letting their dog off the lead. Once we were through the gates, it was a free-for-all of four-legged antics with dogs gambolling over each other, owners talking, and sun shining. But true to form, even when she was off the lead, Daisy stayed close by.

On this side of the park, we picked up the tarmac path that ran from one side of the open space to the other, where Daisy could stop periodically to literally smell the roses, and I could crouch awkwardly to take her picture for the shop's Instagram account. It was shameless marketing but — 'Needs must, Daisy, needs must,' I said, squatting level with her and hoping my thighs would hold long enough to capture her with her nose buried in a bouquet of pink petals.

'She's a beauty,' a voice I didn't recognise said from somewhere behind me.

In turning, and attempting to glance up, I pushed my thighs a manoeuvre too far and found myself flat on my arse, the heat of the tarmac quickly spreading through my dress.

'Oh, shit, I'm so sorry.'

The man offered out a hand and in a disgusting meet-cute I looked up at him, one arm shielding my eyes from the early evening sun as I did. I swallowed hard. *You're . . .* I didn't even know how to finish the thought. He looked

30

as though he'd slipped from the front page of a *GQ* sports special. The man had a chiselled jawline and hair that would make anyone envious. *Seriously*, I wondered, *does he blow-dry that himself?* I was dangerously close to being open-gobbed, as well as flat on my arse, so I moved to take the man's hand and awkwardly pushed and pulled myself into a standing position. By this point, Daisy had sat down, as though sensing the embarrassing scene due to unfold and having decided to make herself comfortable for it. *So much for female solidarity.* I brushed the loose grit from the back of my dress while the man apologised again.

'Honestly—' I managed an awkward laugh — 'I don't think you should feel too guilty for what is very obviously clumsiness on my part.'

He managed a smile then, too, and held out his hand for a second time. 'I'm Ben, Benjamin. Well, my friends call me Benji.'

'I'm Nell and this piglet is Daisy.' I gestured behind me. 'I think you were in the middle of saying how beautiful she is? Which is basically her favourite thing in the world, so, go right ahead and carry on.'

'She's a real sweetheart. How old is she?' He moved to scratch at her head and Daisy upturned her face towards him.

'She's two, a baby still.'

'Have you had her from a pup?'

'Thirteen weeks. I can't really remember what life was like before her.'

'Well.' He turned his attention back to me. 'I hear that dogs are often coming along and filling up heart space for people like that.'

'Oh, that's a truth and a half.' I laughed along. 'Where's your dog?' I looked around for signs of a conventionally beautiful spaniel with crimped ears and bright eyes.

But Benji hesitated before answering. 'I actually don't have a dog . . . Is that weird?'

Yes. 'No?' I said instead. 'So, what, do you just come here to admire the pretty things running around?'

31

'Pretty much. I love dogs, I just don't have a life that facilitates one. I work a lot; it wouldn't be fair.'

'What do you do?' Daisy had fitted so seamlessly into life at the bookshop, it was beyond my imagination to think of an alternative life where that couldn't be the case. Though I was aware that most people had grown-up jobs, too, rather than their childhood dream jobs.

'I'm a doctor.' *Of course you are. You probably even rescue kittens from trees in your free time.* 'I work up at the children's hospital, the other side of town?' I nodded along. 'So this is a nice walk actually, just to stretch my legs at the end of it all. Especially this time of day. Plus—' he gestured first to Daisy then me — 'I get to meet great people and their dogs.'

I smiled. 'I know exactly what you mean.' Taking the comment as a cue, Daisy stood up and started to plod her way along the path again without so much as a backwards glance in my direction. 'It was really nice meeting you, Benji, but I'm being summoned. And I'm actually meeting a . . .' *How to finish that sentence . . . friend? Or, my Owen? Well, not* my *Owen, but . . .* 'Well, *we're* meeting friends, I should say.'

He nodded and his smile downturned into something that looked like disappointment. 'Maybe I'll bump into you both again, then?'

'Maybe!' I shouted back.

Of course, it was completely possible to bump into someone at Green Fields dog park more than once — imagine six months' worth of more than once, in fact . . .

CHAPTER FOUR: OWEN

Nothing in the world is quite as magical as waking up to the sight of a beautiful woman with her head on the pillow beside you — but instead, I had a beagle who had, apparently, been watching me sleep. I huffed a laugh and reached out a hand to ruffle her ear, and Collie grumbled a soft, happy sound. I never used to be one of those dog owners who didn't let the dog go everywhere, anywhere. When I'd first got Collie, there'd been stricter house rules — or rather, my ex-girlfriend had had stricter rules. But when it had become just the two of us, Collie had had an access all areas — something she took absolute advantage of when it came to my having a wee first thing in the morning and when it came to sharing my bed.

I closed my eyes again, hoping for another five minutes. But seconds later I felt the cold and damp press of another's nose hard against my own. I went cross-eyed when I opened my eyes again and found Collie's snout waiting. She huffed, a hard snort of a sound that sent spittle flying out of her mouth and over my face.

'Collie!'

She launched the attack, climbing over me with an enthusiasm that was too high on any scale for this time on a Sunday morning. Weekends used to be for lying in, for resting. Nowadays, they were for socialising while watching the world wake up. They were for seeing Daisy — and Nell. But then, every day was for that now.

A wistful sigh fell out. 'Right, you crazy mutt, let's smash the day.' She bounded off the bed, landing on the floor with a sack-of-potatoes thud. The bedroom door opened with a horrible creak as she pushed her way out and I used those blissful seconds of quiet to shut my eyes for a beat longer. Unfortunately, today was also the day of Dinner with the Family — a prospect so deathly terrifying that it warranted capitalisation. It could be used as the title of a horror film and everyone would know, *just* from the title, the indecencies that were about to unfold in ninety minutes. All of which I had to bear without my dog.

I rubbed hard at my eyes before opening them again and turning to double-check the time: 5.30 a.m. On. A. Sunday. I threw myself out of bed before I could tumble too far into grumbling. Given the dinner that awaited me that afternoon, this quiet morning and luscious walk was going to be the thing that saved the day. And I managed a smile when I sat up and saw Collie waiting bright-eyed in the doorway.

'That's the part that saves every day, isn't it?'

And Collie whined, like she knew just what I meant.

* * *

I heard Daisy and Nell before I saw them. My back was turned while I bent over to pick up Collie's business — a creature of habit, she'd got it into her head that she could only possibly poo on the morning walk and only ever when we were out, as though she were offended by the prospect of shitting in her own back garden — but there came a thundering grunt from somewhere in the distance, a sweating and huffing sound that was soon followed by a—

'Daisy! Daisy, you get back here!'

I hurried to pick up the last of Collie's deposit — though as one dog parent to another, Nell was hardly likely to be surprised — and get the bag knotted. By the time I'd managed that, Nell had come skidding to an abrupt stop in front of me, narrowly missing a fall. She'd been wrong-footed by a patch of mud that Collie had torn up only seconds before in a misguided attempt to wipe her paws — or rather, dirty them even further, whether she realised it or not. It had only been days, but summer sunshine had fast turned into summer showers, and the dog park was worse for wear because of it. Now, Nell was staring down at her poor, poor choice of footwear — pumps that may have been light grey to begin with, but they definitely weren't now — leaving me with nothing but dead air and unease. *What the hell do I say? What the hell do I—*

But the panic was broken by the maniacal laughter that burst out of Nell just seconds later. She giggled and giggled until her cheeks were bursting pink blossoms. She wiped a tear from the corner of her eye — somehow managing to leave behind a speck of dirt that I didn't know whether to point out, but somehow I felt like it would ruin the moment if I did.

Still, Nell was easily the most beautiful thing in the dog park. *Which probably isn't the compliment I think it is*, I cautioned myself before my lips could part wide enough for the words to sneak out. *How about, 'You're the most beautiful woman in the world'? Perfect. Why don't you tell her?*

Why don't you *tell her?*

I didn't know who the many voices were or which various parts of my brain were responsible for them — but it didn't feel right to leave them talking for any longer without saying a single word to the woman who was actually in front of me. I *desperately* wanted to have a handkerchief or some other such stately, gentlemanly gesture to offer her, to wipe her pumps clean. But I only had a bottle of antibacterial handwash wedged in the back pocket of my jeans and I didn't know whether that would do.

'This wasn't quite the entrance I was going for,' Nell said. 'I was hoping for something a little less . . .'

'Muddy?'

'Dramatic.' She laughed and started to brush at the mud clinging to her footwear. 'Serves me right for dressing for the weather I want, not the weather we have. Wasn't it blistering summer when we were here with them on Friday? Did it rain *that* much while I wasn't looking?'

I sniggered. 'But it's a British summer. How many sunny days do you expect?'

Nell was wearing a black dress with no pattern at all, which was wildly out of character for her. Instead, it was neat and clean and cut just above the knee, and it looked like something one of the women at work might wear — or rather, be encouraged to wear by one of the dickheads at work. Nell looked beautiful whatever she wore but the dress was . . . different. And I wondered . . . *Is she trying to . . .*

'My hands are a mess.'

'Oh!' I reached out and pulled back with the antibac bottle as though I was part of a quick-draw. 'Never without it.'

She smirked. 'That's very health conscious of you.'

'I think it's a hangover from the pandemic.'

'Ah.' She squirted a blob onto one hand, then passed the bottle back to me. 'That makes sense. Besides which, I've just had to beg it from your back pocket so I can clean my gunky hands, so I'm in no position to judge you. Thank you.' She looked at me square in the face then, her eyes locked on mine, and a really long second ticked by. I wondered whether there might actually be a problem with time, the look seemed to last such an unfathomably long second and I . . . *I could kiss her right now. I could lean in and I could kiss her. Or I could lean across and terrify her with the sight of my face lunging towards hers and then everything would be ruined because she'd think* Where are the kids?' She looked around in search of the dogs.

Collie was mud-covered and only visible from her backside, which was sticking into the air in an unladylike fashion while she ferreted about under a rose bush. Meanwhile, Daisy — lovely, bullish, chilled-as-a-Sunday-morning Daisy — was lying next to the same rose bush, but, instead of sharing in Collie's investigations, looked to be completely enamoured of a butterfly that kept floating, flying and landing again on a cluster of petals within sniffing distance. Nell and I held a beat of quiet while we watched Daisy rest her nose to the petals' edges but not stray any further, as though to avoid disturbing the small creature finding its way.

'Collie would eat that.'

Nell made a noise. 'I don't know that it's compassion, necessarily, that prevents her from eating it, so much as . . . fussiness, I suppose.'

'Ah, you see, Collie doesn't have any of that either.'

Nell let out a little snort of a laugh, a sound that I loved two-fold. First, the knowledge that I'd said something worthy of a laugh, which I have to confess was deeply reassuring in most situations, but certainly when I was with Nell. Secondly, just the sound. The small catch of amusement that got caught somewhere between nose and mouth, and somehow sounded . . . *Beautiful*. I sighed.

'Rough day already?' she asked.

Then *I* snorted. 'Perfect day so far, will be a rough day by, I'd guess, mid-afternoon.'

'You're seeing your family,' she said and I made a show of groaning. The family dinners were happening on a semi-regular basis now. There was no occasion for them, beyond my mother feeling a twinge of a need to torture her offspring for a few hours at a time. 'Come on, let's walk. They'll both follow when they're hungry.' Nell steered us towards the pathway and away from any hidden patches of mud — once bitten and all that — and then asked, 'Are you taking Collie with you?'

'Nope.'

'And you're not very happy about that.'

'Nope.'

'And will you be discussing this in multi-syllables at any point?'

I let out a louder laugh then, and immediately felt embarrassed by the awkwardness of the sound. 'It's just *hard* seeing your nearest and dearest when they tell you *all* the things you're not doing that they think you should be, you know?' Turning my words into a question was stupid. In one of our earliest conversations, Nell told me what had happened to her own parents, and I'd quietly vowed never to moan about mine to her after that. But somehow on days like today she just sensed the need.

'Do you think they'd be happier if you had actual kids, rather than, you know, the . . .'

Perfectly timed, Collie came tearing up the field space alongside us, shortly followed by Daisy who looked slightly less happy to be on the move.

'But to have actual kids I'd need to have an actual partner and . . .' I shrugged and upturned my hands. *And I'm too chicken to ask you on an actual date.* 'Besides, I'm not even sure whether I'd want kids.'

'No?'

'Well, do you?'

Another laugh, though this one slightly more nervous. 'That was a break-neck turn. But no, I don't think I do. I've always said Daisy is enough and I really think she is. Nan has been an amazing mum but I just don't think I've actually got the . . . I don't know, the mum-ness?' She seemed to put some thought into the phrasing before she carried on. 'Yeah, the mum-ness, I guess. I don't have that in me.'

I opted for a neutral answer. 'Some people don't.'

'Did you not get the memo? *All* women do.' Her tone sounded as sarcastic as it was bored. 'Anyway, back to you, Owen. Kids or no kids?'

'I don't know.' I shrugged. 'I don't think I've got the mum-ness in me either.'

'You're a dope.'

Yes, but your dope, I wanted to say but didn't because alongside being a dope I was also a chicken.

'Did it ever occur to you,' she asked in a tone that somehow made me edgy, 'that maybe your mum just secretly enjoys spending time with you, and having you all together and . . .' I don't know what face I made but she petered out when she saw it. 'It's *really* that bad?'

'I'm being dramatic.' I lied. I wasn't being dramatic in the slightest. But Nell and I were too early in our relationship — *relationship?* — for me to dump quite so much bile on her, *quite* so early in the morning as well. Besides which, knowing how close she was to her own family, I was low-key concerned that having such a wavering bond with my own might be a strike against me.

We both looked ahead for a while then, without saying anything more, and instead we walked and watched the dogs tumble over each other in the distance. They were a regular made-for-television movie when you got them together like this and, Nell aside, it had become one of my favourite things to see Collie and Daisy together over the last six months.

'They love each other a lot, don't they?' Nell said eventually. 'Like, they just have a spark.'

'Some people do,' I said, then immediately corrected myself. 'Dogs, obviously I meant dogs.' I turned in time to catch the smile on Nell's profile.

'Some people do, too.'

It was the perfect moment for a smooth suggestion. *Let's do coffee, let's get breakfast. I'll cancel with my family and the four of us can run away to a life by the sea. Say anything, Owen!* 'Don't suppose you've got free time to help me fake my death in the next six hours or so, have you? I can pay you fairly for your share of the work.' The sheer relief when Nell laughed at the suggestion was the best of tonics.

'Come on, let's talk about something else, see if we can take your mind off family.'

'Okay.' I took the bait. 'What does your Sunday look like?'

'Oh, big plans!' she answered, using a similar sarcastic tone to earlier. 'Daisy and I are going to go home and have a light breakfast, and read. Then we're going to go to the shop to see the state that Past Nell left things in, and make sure everything is right for kicking off a fresh working week tomorrow. Then I'm going to Nan's.'

'Of course, Sunday lunch?'

'And Ted Bundy.'

I clicked my fingers. 'Mustn't forget Ted. The ideal dinner guest if ever there was one.'

'At least it's not Ed Gein.'

'Or Dahmer.'

'It was nearly Dahmer!'

Another laugh erupted out of me. 'Of course it was nearly Dahmer. So help me God, your nan.'

'She's a case, isn't she?'

'She's bloody brilliant is what she is.' I hadn't even met the woman but so help me, I was as fond of her as I was of her granddaughter. *Which is both a whopping understatement and entirely untrue . . .* 'So, who would your ideal Sunday-lunch guest be?'

'Ooh, new ground.' Nell rubbed her hands together. 'We haven't covered this small talk yet. Dead or alive?'

'Dealer's choice.'

'Oscar Wilde,' she answered too quickly.

'Do you want to take a second to think about that?'

She laughed and touched her face, nervously maybe, though she left behind more mud in the process and given that I'd left it *so* long without mentioning the first smudge, it didn't feel right to comment on the second.

'*Dorian Gray* was the book that made me love reading. I swallowed all of his plays after that, like, one a day easily for a while until I realised how quickly I was going to run out of them. Plus I have so many questions about life *and* writing, and he strikes me as the type who would dish the dirt on other writers from the same period, I think?'

I tried for convincing enthusiasm. 'Oh, absolutely, yeah, I totally agree.' And it fell on its arse.

'You don't know anything about Oscar Wilde, do you?'

'Not a jot,' I admitted, and Nell softly, playfully, punched my upper arm, before calling me a dope for the second time. 'You know, a guy could get a complex with all of this dope talk. I think I'd like a nicer nickname.'

'You're right, you're right.' She held up her hands as though to concede. 'What do they call you at work?'

Oi. P-p-p-owen. Steve. 'I think I'd like a unique nickname, one that only you use.' Which felt like the biggest gesture I had presented to this woman to date. A small pebble held between my beak and dropped gently at her feet like a prized offering. I imagined her taking it and holding it tight in her pocket, working her fingers over it until the edges were smooth — which was exactly how Nell made me feel, coincidentally. Soft, well-handled, pocketed.

'I'll have a think, for when I next see you.'

I checked my watch. 'How have we lapped this place so quickly?'

'We always do! I think it's the morning walks? It's just us and . . .' She gestured and I turned in time to watch Daisy thwack her paw against Collie's face, as though keeping her grime and grub at a safe distance. 'When it's us and them, time goes a bit quicker and the walk somehow isn't quite so long.' She smiled, a tight-lipped flash of . . . something. 'This is where we hop off anyway.' Nell pointed in the opposite direction to where Collie and I needed to be. *We can walk further*, I wanted to say. *We can get breakfast or at the very least tea, and somewhere for you to wash your face.* I tried for a steady breath. *Maybe not the last part. But we can definitely get tea.*

'I'll see you tomorrow?' Nell asked.

I nodded. 'We'll be here. Five thirty p.m. on the dot.'

'We'll be here, ten minutes late like always.' She laughed and then narrowed her lips to form an O. A short, sharp whistle came out and on cue Daisy came hurtling in our direction. 'Good luck for today,' Nell said before she turned.

'You too. Don't get lured in by Bundy.'

'Hey.' Nell was a few metres along the path already by the time she turned. 'You didn't tell me your ideal dinner guest.'

I shrugged and threw my arms to mimic an "I don't know" gesture. But of course, it was the easiest question anyone had asked me all week.

You.

CHAPTER FIVE: NELL

Felicity Williams-Graham and I had been mortal enemies since Year Six. Yet, somehow, here I was, on a Wednesday evening, hosting her baby shower in my bookshop. I was one of those people who had managed to keep in touch with some of the girls I'd gone to school with, despite my best efforts to escape them. Though when I'd opened the shop — and one by one at different random points in time they'd come in and realised that little Nellie was the owner of the place — suddenly the ties that I'd managed to loosen pulled taut again. And thanks to the godforsaken terrain of social media, those ties had since wrapped around me in a cat's cradle and, while I looked out across the expanse of flowery women filling my shop to the brim, I thought, *Please, let today be the day those ties hang me.*

Eleanor — "The Other Eleanor" as she'd been known in school, even though everyone had known me as Nellie by then — had asked me whether I'd mind donating the book-shop for the night and I had *desperately* wanted to explain to her that that was not how donations worked.

I'd rolled my eyes when Eleanor had mentioned Felicity's name and she'd sighed. 'Nell, sooner or later you have to let things go.'

I bit back on asking her whether she'd let go of the time that James Graham had told everyone that she was an easy lay as soon as we'd reached high school. But for so many reasons — not least the fact that James had since managed to marry and impregnate Felicity — I decided against the snideness and said, 'Of course, I'd love to host everyone for the evening. Daisy and I would be delighted.'

Eleanor tilted her head. 'Do you really think a dog is suited to a baby shower though?'

Now, on the night of the blessed event, Daisy was sitting alongside me with bright pink meshing wrapped around her collar and a neat headband made of flowers that looked as though it might pop off any second — but I thought if I could keep her still enough we'd probably be fine, which seemed to be something swinging in my favour given that a) keeping still was one of Daisy's favourite things in the world and b) she seemed so stunned by the bird noises periodically rising from the gaggle in front of us that I thought she wasn't likely to go much further than her current resting spot behind the counter anyway.

Felicity hadn't spoken to me since she got there. Instead, Abi Ruther had led her by the hand to her seat and she hadn't moved from that spot since. The mother-to-be was wearing a light-blue, loose-fitting chiffon dress that made her look every bit the Madonna and I wondered whether that's what she'd intended. *Or maybe she just wants to be comfortable and you should stop being such a cow?* I rolled my eyes at my own scepticism. People changed all the time, I reminded myself, and there was no reason to think that Felicity mightn't be a better person now than she'd been at school. After a parents' evening one night, she'd started a rumour that my nan was *really* my mum and that I had in fact got the oldest mum in the world because Nan was verging on ninety-five — which she wasn't now, so she definitely hadn't been then — and that I must have been a test-tube baby because there was no way that someone as old as Nan could conceive naturally *and* there was no way someone would want to have sex with her anyway and . . . On and on it had gone until one day, at the end of breaktime, I'd stood on a desk in the centre of a classroom and shouted, 'My mum's dead you stupid cow!'

I hadn't been reprimanded at school. At home, Nan had been less than impressed. And last week when I'd told her about the baby shower, she'd said it was my chance to make amends, but I wasn't altogether sure that I was the one who needed to be mending anything, even now. Still, the more I thought about it now, the more I stewed, and that wasn't going to help anyone. I slipped away quietly into the storeroom at the back to drink two hefty mouthfuls from a can of fruit cider that I'd chilled for the occasion — and hidden, on the assumption that I may well be the only one in need of a drink.

'You too, huh?'

I snapped around at the voice in the doorway: Sarah Briggs. From what I knew — which wasn't much — she'd been a good enough egg in school. When she pulled a small whisky flask from the baby handbag balanced on her arm, I knew that whatever Sarah had been in school, she had absolutely blossomed into being my kind of people now.

I laughed. 'Hitting the hard stuff?'

'Oh, it's white wine. The hip flask was a present from my dad.' She waved away the comment with, 'Don't ask. I think he'd always hoped for a blue baby shower rather than a bright pink one if you catch my drift.'

'Shouldn't you be out there with the madding crowd?'

'Please.' She took another mouthful. 'I didn't get along with Flick when we were in school, never mind now. I think she only invited me so she could brag about being pregnant before me.' *Maybe so, but you're close enough to use her nickname still.* 'Which is fine, by the way, I'm not drinking out of bitterness. I'm drinking because I'm still the right side of thirty-five. That's *my* cut-off.'

'I see.' I set my can down and made for the door to try to signal the end of our talk. 'Oh, I think the guest of honour is about to make a toast.'

Felicity was struggling into an upright position. She held a champagne flute filled with apple juice. Soft applause sounded before she started to speak and I tried to remember the last time someone applauded me for getting upright from a chair. *Honestly, if this is the sort of treatment people get when they're pregnant* . . . But I cut the thought off before it could form. There was no sense in getting pregnant for gentle praise, which wasn't at all a fair counterweight to the baggage you were left with afterwards. Then, as though sensing that train of thought, Daisy soft-bumped her nose against my right leg and I crouched to be level with her as Felicity started speaking.

'Honestly, I'm just so, *so* touched that so many of you, especially so many faces that I haven't seen for so long, would come here specifically to celebrate me—' she laughed and cupped the bottom of her bump — 'to celebrate us.' And everyone laughed along with her. That's about the point at which I switched off. That was, until I was lassoed back into the room by, 'And of course, a huge thank you to Nell for putting a roof over our heads for the evening. It's so, so appreciated.'

'You're welcome.' I half stood and gave everyone a wave before lowering to Daisy's view of the room again. Down here was quite enough of a vantage point, just about enough of a safe distance.

* * *

The baby shower lasted approximately four years. By the time people were filtering out of the room, I had images of poor Sarah grabbing any man she could find on her journey home, having realised her five-year buffer zone for having children had been entirely taken up by celebrating the offspring of a woman she claimed not to like. *First-world problems*, I thought as I threw another empty can of something non-alcoholic into my recycling bin. I was doing a sweep of the room. Despite being a gaggle of seemingly prim women, they looked to have *no* concept of good manners and had

45

instead opted to leave behind their gutted papers and their wrappings, anticipating, I assumed, the hired help would clear up after them.

'Hi, that would be me,' I muttered, thinking I was well out of earshot of the few partygoers left lingering in the doorway. But then I spotted something — someone — in my peripheral vision and I realised help was closer to hand than I'd known. An exhausted Felicity was handing over three crushed cans for the open mouth of the bin.

'Bunch of bloody animals, aren't they?' Her tone was more familiar than I would have expected it to be, and there was a slight awkwardness to the way she held herself, too, though I wondered whether that was more to do with the baby bump, strapped to her midriff like a beach ball. And the thought of that sent a sharp pang of sympathy coursing through me, like a nerve that had been finger-plucked. 'I wanted to catch you, actually, once everyone had gone, just to say thank you.'

Ah, so that'll explain the awkwardness.

'There's no need.' I smiled. 'You already did.'

She shook her head. 'Not just for letting us use the bookshop, which is bloody beautiful, by the way. How long have you been here?'

'Around eighteen months now, I think? Daisy was . . .' I flashed back to images of a rotund puppy snowballing around the empty space. 'She must have only been a few months when I got the licences approved, so I guess around eighteen months now, yeah.' I took a good look around the space and pulled in a hefty breath, even though the air was full of perfume. 'It sort of feels like we've always been here, to be honest.'

'You always wanted a bookshop.'

My head snapped around and I found that I couldn't help but stare at her.

'I remember you talking about it once at school.'

'I talked *a lot* at school. I'm surprised you remember.' I went back to cleaning up then. I didn't want to invite further small talk, further walks down memory lane. From my limited experiences of the place, it was riddled with rattlesnakes that hummed through the grass and the tarmac of the road was too hot to touch — though of course you weren't allowed shoes down memory lane either, so you had a perfect rendition of walking over hot coals specifically to get to a memory that you had probably a) at least in part fabricated and/or b) definitely sort of wish you hadn't even bothered remembering once you'd got there.

'Oh, I remember a lot from school.'

Bollocks. I could tell from the tone where it was going but before I had chance enough to rebuff her, she continued.

'I'm really sorry, for everything I said about your nan.'

I sighed, set my recycling bin down and looked over at her. Felicity had turned into a truly beautiful woman. *Her kind always do*, I thought with embarrassing spite — and, seeing her now, a hundred years after "the incident", I realised that I really didn't know *anything* about the woman she'd become — other than she clearly no longer thought it appropriate to tease someone about their maternal lineage, especially without knowing the full scope of context surrounding their guardianship situation. And while that seemed like a *very* specific type of growth for a person to go through, it was growth all the same.

'It really doesn't matter, Felicity, it was—'

'Childish and pathetic?'

I snorted a laugh. 'I was going to say it was a long time ago but sure, it was also childish.' I shrugged. 'But then, you were a child, so it makes sense.'

'You're very kind, Nell, you know?'

'Eh, I always was.' I turned and flopped down on a chair. The shop was empty by then, the last birds having flown the nest and left behind their litter. 'I just don't know how much we value kindness at that age versus how much we value it at this age. I think we grow into it.'

Felicity struggled to lower herself down onto the wooden stool next to me. 'How's life been? How is your nan, is she . . .'

I understood the hesitation. When a person reaches a certain age there's always a loaded ellipsis after *any* question

47

relating to their health — or, more generally, their life. Nan had reached that age around five years ago and, to start with, it had wounded me. A constant reminder that at some point, she wouldn't still live in the spaces of an ellipsis, but instead, at some point, she'd . . . Now, I was used to the hesitant tone that people used though. The softly-softly footsteps that might potentially lead them into a land of head tilts and sad grimaces. Felicity's relief was writ large when I said that Nan was doing well — better than well, since she'd discovered Netflix and a passion for true crime documentaries.

Felicity let out a little high-pitched laugh. 'She always was a bit quirky though, wasn't she? If you don't mind me saying?' She set a hand on my forearm and took on an apologetic tone, as though genuinely worried that having stitched the seams of past mistakes, she might have just gone ahead and walked right into another. I shook my head and laughed.

'I think Nan's quirkiness will be the last thing to go.'

'And what else has happened? You have the shop, you have . . .' Daisy had plodded over to us by then and curled up in a curved lump in front of my feet. 'This little one.'

I let out another snort. 'I don't know that anyone has ever called Daisy the little one, but, yes, I have her. She's my life companion. My little,' I lingered over my phrasing, 'well, maybe my not-so-little shadow.'

'That's no bad thing.'

'You'll know soon enough.' I gestured to her stomach but took great care not to touch it, as though there was a red-line laser barrier around the space because *why the fuck do so many people think it's actually okay to go touching someone's stomach like that?* 'You're due soon, right?'

She groaned and tilted her head towards the ceiling.

'Two weeks' time.'

I expelled a sharp huff. 'James ready for it?' From what I remembered of James from school, he wasn't exactly the paternal kind — but then, Felicity hadn't exactly been the doting, motherly type either. I wondered when they'd both changed: in synchronicity, or did one of them grow up then the other?

48

'I don't know that anyone is ever ready for it.' She righted herself then and looked back at me. 'That's what they tell me, anyway.'

'In which case it must be true. They never lie.'

'What about you?' She tapped my arm softly as though we were friends and I wondered whether in a butterfly's wing-beat that's what had happened here. 'We've covered work and family. Anyone special in your life?'

It used to be my least favourite question. A tentative prod from an outsider to assess how well life was *really* going. The emotional equivalent of lifting my back leg to check for lameness, or holding my proverbials and asking me to cough. But more and more lately, whenever Nan or customers or old enemies/new friends asked this question, the answer was a quiet but knee-jerk one, a folded flutter of paper that darted around my chest and used the rungs of my ribcage as a perch, though it wasn't the simple yes or no that people were expecting to be written on the answer sheet. Instead, it was only a name. Instead, somehow, it was only ever Owen.

CHAPTER SIX: OWEN

The recipe was one that I had strategically chosen, not for my level of interest in the dish, as such, but rather for my level of belief in my cooking abilities. The BBC webpage gave it a single chef's hat ranking for ease and I wagered that that was about where Collie and I lived. Not that Collie was actively helping me prepare this meal for two that was, according to the tagline that sold it to readers, perfect for an occasion like Valentine's Day. *Which also sort of seals the deal,* I admitted begrudgingly as I turned the oven to gas mark seven. I brushed my hands in a half-clap gesture and then stood with my palms pressed against my hips, admiring the oven as though that alone was the meal. I was halfway to congratulating myself on completing step one of the recipe when I realised that step one was in fact deconstructed into six — *six!* — constituent parts.

'So it's actually steps one through to seven that I'm look-ing at, Collie, that's what they're telling me here.' And she cocked her head to one side and set free a small, high sound, as though she too were bloody outraged by the discovery. 'Christ, as if the twenty minutes prep already wasn't enough,' I added, looking at the four hundred and thirty grams of potatoes that I'd gone to great lengths to cut into even (give or take) one-and-a-half-centimetre slices. As instructed. I huffed and filled a large pan of water for the stove before adding the potatoes.

I wasn't a cook, by any stretch of the imagination. But every now and then I got caught up with the idealised notion that cooking mightn't be a bad skill to master — or rather, cooking mightn't be a bad skill to master for when I actually had someone to cook for. Collie's disgust at the sight of me shredding cabbage made me think that perhaps she wasn't the target audience for smoky steak with Cajun potatoes and homemade slaw – cabbage wasn't exactly her favourite, but she'd been known to tuck into green beans before now. Then I wondered whether Nell would eat it. We'd talked about food a handful of times. I knew she liked pizza and pasta — together, sometimes, but separately, too. I knew she hated cauliflower — which I'd found out through a hilarious story involving her also hilarious nan — and that she loved broccoli, preferably soaked in some kind of cheese sauce. But also that broccoli would never win out against roast potatoes. And all of those things I knew made me wonder exactly what the hell I thought I was trying to pull off in making Cajun potatoes when I should so blatantly be practising how to make pizza dough from scratch, which would no doubt be much more impressive.

I opened the oven to check on the potatoes and "tossed" them — which was a technical cooking term that I had to pause and google. I viewed my Facebook notifications while I was on my phone, too, and momentarily fell down the black hole of what friends and fake friends were doing.

My friends were mostly men in their early thirties who were either at home looking after families or at the gym/a football match/the pub, basking in the fact that they didn't have to look after families. My fake friends were people I went to school with who I hadn't kept in touch with, but somehow we'd kept in touch through the connective tissue of social media that allowed us all an insight into each other's lives. And the arsehole part of me decided then that, depending on the results, I would definitely upload a picture of tonight's meal — complete with a glass of red wine.

I took another swig from the glass alongside me. *Assuming there's any left by the time dinner is served.*

It was when I saw Lisa's name floating around my timeline that I back-clicked from the app and crossed to Collie, now lying in the doorway of the kitchen looking every bit the malnourished and uncared-for dog.

'Any sadder and you'll be the face of RSPCA,' I said, crouching down to scratch at her head. 'How could she leave you behind, you lovely girl?' It was telling that on all the occasions I'd wondered this very same thing, it had never crossed my mind to ask how Lisa could so easily leave me behind, too. I huff-laughed. 'That, I completely understand. But you?'

It had been my suggestion to get a dog. Lisa and I had been together for three years, living together for one. Neither of us wanted kids but *everyone* kept asking whether that, or marriage, was next for us. So I suggested a third option: 'What if we get a pet?'

Lisa was lukewarm about the idea to begin with, but then she got sucked into idly scrolling through puppy pictures on Instagram and that soon changed her mind. Her disappointment when I suggested we start with a rescue centre was observable, though she went along with it anyway — or rather, she seemed to go along with it, and actually back-pocketed the entire experience for the arguments that would come further down the line of our relationship.

I found the details of a local shelter and we arranged to visit on one of their open days.

'Is there a breed you're more or less interested in?' I asked on the drive there and she shrugged, said not really and asked what it was that I wanted. 'I've always wanted a border collie,' I said, indicating into the centre's car park. My grandfather had one when I was growing up. He owned acres and acres, and she would lap the perimeter, respond to commands and stand by his side like a model. I yanked the handbrake up and thought of our own humble back garden, my nine-to-five and Lisa's freelance-work-from-home life. We were hardly country folk. Lisa would be there during the day but, faced off with the entrance of the rescue centre, I was beginning to second-guess whether we were built for a collie. 'I mean, I don't know how often they're turned out or . . . I don't know, I guess dogs wind up in rescue centres for more reasons than that. But I don't know whether they'll have . . . I don't know, we'll have to see whether there are collies, or whether there's something else that we like, or click with.'

Lisa migrated towards a pen of puppies and I watched her from a distance. I knew she didn't want children, we'd talked about it at length, but something about the dog expedition seemed to have awakened this need in her to nurture something from the ground up. I overheard her talking to one of the centre workers who explained the puppies were the litter of a bitch who'd been left pregnant on their doorstep. While Lisa cooed and aww'ed over the babies, I wondered where the mother was now. Whether we might be able to take her home with us instead. I was on my second lap of the room when I realised that a pen that looked empty actually wasn't. Only, the dog who occupied the space was origami-folded so small behind her basket and bedding that you had to squint and focus *really* hard to see she was there at all.

'Ah, this one is a little nervy.' A worker drew up alongside me, having noted my interest. 'We're not really sure what happened to her.'

'What do you mean?'

The man shrugged. 'There's literally no way of knowing. One of our teams got called to a dog whining late into the hours. We found this one chained up in a derelict house, no signs of life, owners, nothing.' He shrugged again. 'But at least she's safe now, right?'

'Right . . .'

After the worker disappeared, Lisa took his place. 'She isn't a border collie.'

'She isn't, no.' We both watched quietly until the dog slowly appeared from behind her bed and though she didn't quite close the distance to us, she did sit and watch, and, soon after, she stopped shaking, too. I don't know how long we watched her before I turned to Lisa and said, 'But I think I'm in love with her.'

The centre arranged a home visit for three days later. Collie moved in with us four days after that. Now, I scratched at her head again and said, 'And the rest, as they say, is history.'

Of course, alongside that there was the additional history of how Lisa, six months into us having Collie, decided it was time to leave — without Coll, which was somehow a harder pill to swallow than the thought of her leaving me. Sure, she hadn't been as keen to bring Collie home as I was, although she'd flashed her winning smile at the woman who interviewed us for the adoption. But through all their time together, where Lisa was the one at home every day, they'd only grown closer as the months went on — I'd thought. *Besides, who the hell wouldn't want custody of you?* I was looking into those big, bright eyes — so clearly hungry for steak . . .

Something hissed from the oven. 'Those bloody potatoes.' I turned the heat down but left them to crisp. They'd be more brown-crisp than golden-crisp, despite what the recipe called for. I opened the fridge and pulled out the steak. Like a Pavlovian response, Collie's head shot up. 'Ah, so this'll be the part of the meal that you're interested in?'

Collie tilted her head and let out another high noise. Then she watched me with love and adoration while I oiled the steak, and then went hunting through the kitchen cupboards for a griddle-pan substitute.

'Because I am not Gino—' I slammed one door and opened a drawer instead — 'and this is not the sort of thing I have lying around, Coll.'

To add to the commotion of not knowing my way around my own kitchen, my mobile's ringtone started to hum in the background, meaning I lost sight of the recipe explaining what I even needed the pan for.

'All right, mate?' I answered.

'How you doing, bud — you about for a drink?'

Luke and I had been friends for about three years now. He started at the same firm on the same day as me and we instantly bonded over our new-boy status. Though he'd left before his probationary even timed out.

I looked from the raw steak sitting on my sideboard, to the starving dog sitting in my kitchen doorway. 'I'm right in the middle of making dinner.'

'Got company?' he asked in a tone that sounded offensively jovial.

'Is it Nell?' came Alan's voice in the background.

'Of course it's not Nell.'

'How do you know it's not Nell?' I butted in.

'Because,' Luke answered in a teasing schoolboy voice, 'I'd like to think that if you finally got Nell across your threshold that you wouldn't answer the phone to me if I happened to call you at random.'

Arses. But he had a point. 'Mate, I'd always answer. What if it were some kind of emergency?'

'No offence, Owen, but I'm not sure you'd be my first phone call in an emergency.' There was a brief pause. 'In fact, none of the lads would.'

I stood with the thought for a second. 'Probably wise.'

'So that's a hard no to a drink?'

I looked at Collie again. 'Hard no, I'm afraid. But I'll see you on Saturday?' I put my non-stick frying pan — *that I am grown up enough to own* — over the heat and watched for the magic indicators to turn red, showing the heat moving through the metal. 'We grabbing lunch first?'

'Lunch then cocktails,' Luke answered. 'Apparently we're a group of women in our late teens. Tell Collie we said hello.'

'And Nell!' Alan added in the background — to which I passed along a polite "sod off" before saying a more cordial goodbye to Luke.

I lowered the steak into the hot pan, enjoying that satisfying zing as the meat hit the heat. And as though practising a summoning spell, Collie no longer lingered in the doorway but instead managed to drag her starving body to sit directly in front of my legs, between me and the oven unit. She stared up to where the meat cooked, as though bracing for it to jump free of the pan and land directly in her mouth.

'Nice try.'

After two minutes on one side and three on the other, I lifted the meat and set it down on a chopping board to cool. Then I freed the potatoes from the oven where they had most definitely turned brown rather than golden, but I reasoned they were relatively close on a cooking colour spectrum. I served two spoonfuls onto a nearby plate.

Collie followed me around the kitchen by her nose. I speared a potato with my fork and held it down for her to sniff. As a dog, there wasn't much that Collie actually turned her nose from, but she wasn't intrigued enough to try the sample offered so I threw it into my mouth instead. *Not bad, Owen, not bad,* I thought, biting through the hardened skin.

'Now . . .' I took a sharpened knife over to where the meat lay cooling. 'The real test.'

I cut the slab of steak into neat and relatively even strips before serving up half the portion onto my own plate. By then, Collie had gone as far as to paw the back of my left leg with the same fury that she used when trying to escape into the garden for a wee.

'All right, all right.' I scraped the other half of the sliced steak into her bowl. I set it down on her food mat, next to the dining table, while she danced around the space. 'Bon appétit.' I leaned back against the kitchen counter to watch her appreciate my handiwork. But Collie barely made it through two mouthfuls before she started to nose-roll the edge of the bowl.

'Are you for real?'

Her head snapped around. If she'd had the anatomical capacity, I think she would have shrugged.

Dejected by my own dog, I brought my plate over to the dining table and sat down to start eating my own serving. I was hardly two mouthfuls in — and *incredibly* impressed with myself — when Collie came to sit between my legs and stare up at me from the gap between my body and the table.

'Get lost, you've got your own.'

She made a disappointed whine then, engineered to stir guilt. I pushed back from the table and peered down at her.

'Daisy's mum could be eating this, you know?'

Collie tilted her head as if to say, *No, she couldn't, because you won't ask her out.*

CHAPTER SEVEN: NELL

To my utter and absolute shame, when I saw Owen trek up over the lip of the hillside with Collie trotting beside him — his top button undone and tie blowing gently in the wind — I thought, *I'll bet this is just how Lizzy Bennet felt*. Though I was certain that Owen was already better than Darcy on account of always being lovely and kind and funny and — *get a grip of yourself, they're nearly here*. I managed to stifle one last wistful sigh before the distance was closed.

Despite the sunshine — which usually meant every seat with a view across Green Fields had been bagged by dog-walkers — I'd managed to get a bench overlooking the city. Daisy shared in my admiration of the view — of the city, that was, not of Owen — and stared straight ahead from her lolling position underneath the bench. Which could only mean she hadn't spotted her playmate yet. Even though I'd waved at Owen and Collie when I'd first seen them, by the time they were settling down next to us I was trying for polite but aloof.

'You're early,' he said.

'It happens.'

Daisy came to life when she saw Collie, dipping her head under the bench, bum in the air to garner a look at her. The two dogs soon emerged and toppled into an excited greeting where one looked to be rolling over the other, and the other over the other until their tops and tails were indistinguishable. They weren't exactly equally matched by size, but somehow the pair knew how far each could push the other when it came to these excited outbursts. 'I wish I was ever as excited about anything as those two are about each other.'

Owen didn't say anything for what felt like a really long time and when I turned to look across at him, I thought I caught a . . . look, a flavoursome one that made my heart feel like I'd swallowed too much popping candy. *Or read too many books.* I autocorrected romance for cynicism, such was my default.

'I think there are some things I'm that excited about.' He turned to face me then. 'Cooking, maybe. I made this mean dinner the other night for me and Collie.'

And I smiled and nodded while Owen regaled me with details: something, something, potatoes, something, something, homemade slaw. It happened in slow motion. Like a soft dawn rising and displaying a room in the perfect mood lighting, I watched as he became that little bit more lovely. Christ only knows what face I must have made throughout the whole story though, because before Owen even came to the end he broke off and laughed nervously.

'What?' he said.

'What?' I snapped out of my reverie. 'Was I dribbling?'

His second laugh was an easier one, a more relaxed sound, and I thought, *Thank God, I think I saved it.*

'I don't know,' he continued. 'You were giving me . . . I don't know, just a look.'

'Don't think me rude.' I started to buy myself a second longer to polish the lie. 'It's been such a bonkers day at work that I didn't manage to get lunch and the further you got into that story the more you started to look like a talking cartoon steak.'

'Round bone sirloin?'

'Just like in *Tom and Jerry*.'

Owen laughed until his cheeks were pink and my tummy was skipping and . . . 'Do you want to get food?' he asked and all laughter stopped. *Is this it? Is it finally happening?* I was stunned silent and Owen either misread the reaction *or* he read the reaction entirely right and didn't want me to get the wrong idea. But either way he stuttered out, 'F-from the vendor? Just because of what you'd said about food, about being busy.' He smiled. 'We've got a walk ahead yet and I don't want you passing out on us.'

Well, that was a short-lived excitement. I turned to check on the girls who were taking it in turns to wade through a mound of brilliant green leaves that a poor groundskeeper must have spent considerable time sweeping together earlier in the day. Daisy slowly moved through the rustle, a strong swimmer doing laps of a pool. Meanwhile, Collie floundered as though any moment now the pool floor might give way and she'd be left in the wild ocean. God knows what she thought was underneath the leaves.

'I'll be fine.' I stood then. 'Shall we?'

* * *

Once I'd recovered from the shock of Owen not asking me on a date — though why it was a shock at all when it hadn't happened every day for nearly seven months now — we lapsed into our usual talk. I let my mouth run on automatic while I told him about my day in the shop — the colourful blend of kind customers versus frustrated ones, the latter of whom were always surprised that you didn't have *exactly* what they wanted in stock, as though for your entire retail life you'd only been waiting for them to come along and ask for . . . whatever it was they were hoping to spend their upcoming Saturdays reading.

'Doesn't it drive you nuts?' Owen said as he handed over cash to an ice-cream seller. He passed the single cone back to me and smiled. 'I know you said you're fine without eating but honestly, I'd feel better if you had something — even if it is rubbish,' he added with a laugh. He turned to collect his change and quickly backpedalled in the face of the salesman. 'Not that *your* ice cream is rubbish, or any ice cream for that matter, I only meant . . . well, it's not a meal, is it? Or a meal replacement? Does that make sense?' Owen looked to me for help and I nodded.

'I'm sure the man knows what you mean. Thanks ever so much—' I gestured with my cone — 'delicious.'

And the ice cream itself really was. Though Owen had caused such a swell of heat in my lower abdomen, moving up through my stomach and settling in my chest, that I worried when I opened my mouth for another lick of the vanilla soft scoop that the ice cream would collapse back to liquid instead.

'Sorry,' Owen said then, when we picked up our pace. 'You were telling me about retail. It doesn't drive you nuts?'

'Oh, it does. But what else is there?'

He laughed. 'I mean, plenty?'

'Well, until someone's going to pay me to write extravagant surrealist plays, for a niche local theatre house stashed away somewhere—' I shrugged — 'I'm going to have to take my second-best and biggest life dream and stick to being a bookseller. Although this is much better than *actually* being a bookseller, because when you're selling someone else's stock you can't really refuse to serve someone for being rude. Which you can in your own shop.' I licked a dribble of vanilla that escaped down my cone. 'Not that I do, incidentally. It's just nice to have the option.'

Owen clamped his mouth around his own ice cream — a Solero, impeccable choice — and bit off another chunk, which I had some strong feelings about. 'There's a lot to unpack in that one small paragraph you gave me there.'

I grinned. 'Where do you want to start?'

'Okay.' He thought for a second. 'Surrealist plays?'

'I'm not actually fussy.' I ran a finger along the bottom edge of my ice cream and held it down for Daisy, who lapped at it like she'd never known the joy of sugar before. 'I would happily get famous from writing anything, bar a kiss-and-tell memoir, which I think is where I'd draw the line.'

Owen caught my eye as I stood tall again. 'So anyone who kisses you is relatively safe from newspaper headlines and scandal?'

I shrugged. 'Relatively.' I wanted to wink. I so *desperately* wanted to be the person who was cool enough to pull off a wink. But alas, instead I only tried to hold the eye contact for as long as possible while grappling with two deep-seated fears: *do I let my ice cream melt down my hand or do I lick it in time to save any spillage but run the risk of something accidentally phallic happening here?*

'You're dribbling.' Owen nodded at the cone. 'Well, not you, but . . .' He nodded again.

It saved me from decision-making, at least, though if he could have said something, *anything* other than "you're dribbling" that would have been good, too. I turned to carry on with our walk while working my way down the ice cream. 'What about you? Was your childhood dream to be a financial advisor?'

The largest laugh I'd ever heard erupted from him. People actually stopped to look. Owen wound up with Solero on the end of his nose and that moment quickly moved up the chart as one of our finest in Green Fields to date. Even Collie stopped to check he was okay.

'Oh God,' he said when he spotted my expression. 'That was a serious question.' He laughed again and wiped his nose. 'No, no, it was not my dream. I somehow decided, or maybe someone else decided . . . I don't know, I somehow decided that I'd take Business Studies at university and Dad encouraged me towards a lot of the finance modules, because I had a head for numbers. After that there was talk of accountancy, which I flirted with for approximately three minutes, but I still bounced between a lot of finance roles before winding up where I am now.'

'So what did Little Owen want to be?'

He went quiet for what felt like a really long time. 'Lollipop man.'

'It's a real shame that didn't work.'

'I think I would have excelled.'

'I agree.' I took a cursory look around for the dogs who had disappeared somewhere behind us and saw that Collie was terrorising a small Yorkshire terrier while Daisy was shifting from paw to paw, as though not quite sure how to wrangle her friend. 'Daisy, come on!' I tried to take the initiative in the situation and when Owen spotted what his own wild girl was doing, he shouted for her to come back, too. But as soon as Daisy started her pony gallop towards me, the Yorkie launched itself after her.

The small dog yapped and yapped in a high-pitched tirade and Daisy, despite having a size and stature that could squash the dog with a well-timed sit, looked truly terrified. No matter what people thought of her breed, Daisy had always been a lover, not a fighter — and sometimes she couldn't even muster the energy for that level of enthusiasm. I tried to reassure her the closer she came to us, but the more the Yorkie barked the more Daisy looked to pick up speed. Collie came to an abrupt stop alongside Owen as though even she was flummoxed by the show of it all. Meanwhile, I launched after Daisy who coasted right past us. Even her pony pace was too much for me to catch up with her. 'Daisy, baby, come on, you're okay.'

Suddenly, just as quick as the yipping Yorkie had started, it stopped. Daisy did, too, and we both turned to see whether the owner had finally wrangled it back onto a lead. Instead it was Owen holding the small critter by its collar, his body bent at an awkward angle so he could half walk and half pull the dog back to a woman who still hadn't even closed the distance to catch her howling rat.

I felt a stream of rage course through me.

'Come on, baby,' I said again when Daisy was closer and I crouched down to run my hands over her face and kiss her nose. 'It's okay, I promise.' Collie appeared, nudging her head beneath my arm to get a look at her friend's face and the two dogs bumped heads before setting off together at a trot.

'Funny breed, that,' the woman said as she walked past me, Owen trailing behind her. Her dog was on its lead now but still pulling towards mine.

'I've heard the same about Yorkies,' Owen shouted ahead. The woman's head snapped around at speed. I couldn't see the look that passed between them, but the snide cow didn't say anything else then. Instead she wandered off in the opposite direction, and Owen slow-jogged back to me.

Then, he did something so entirely unexpected that I nearly felt — *nearly* — like the breath had been snatched clean out of my lungs. He wrapped an arm around my shoulders and gave me a gentle squeeze. He held me there while he asked, 'Are you okay?'

I managed a nod. The real answer was trapped in my throat somewhere and, to my shame, it wasn't the shock of Daisy being chased by a Yorkie that had done it — it was the physical contact with Owen, something more than a soft arm punch or an accidental hand knock.

'I swear, those small breeds are the worst for it sometimes.' He unleashed me, but I still felt that the distance between us had lessened in comparison to what it normally was. Owen presented an impromptu Ted Talk then about small breeds and other dog owners and, and, and—

'You could have been a vet,' I said and we both laughed. 'Honestly, what you did there was really kind — I appreciate it. And Daisy does.' I looked around to find her basking in a patch of sun. 'She might not show it, but she definitely does.' I fumbled with her lead then, as though indicating the end of the walk was nigh. This was often — always — my least favourite part of any day. 'I better go and lead up my terrifying beast.'

'Mine too.' He nodded to Collie, busy digging up a flower-bed. 'Are you sure you're okay?'

'Absolutely. Daisy isn't built for speed, but neither am I,' I said jokingly. 'So it's always a horror when she does a runner. But she genuinely only ever does it when she's being chased.' Owen walked with me in Daisy's general direction and Collie managed to lap us, arriving next to my girl while Owen and I were still a few metres away. 'I've really enjoyed this.'

'Being chased by wild animals?'

I reasoned that was an appropriate time for an arm punch, so I knocked him gently with my fist. 'No, this. The walk, the ice cream, the fact that I don't need a coat.' I'd worn one of my favourite sunflower-print dresses — and I hoped Owen had taken note, though, of course, there was no bloody way of knowing. 'It's been a nice one, wild hounds aside.'

Owen was a syllable into his answer when I put an arm out to stop him. He had turned to talk to me, so he hadn't spotted the girls yet. But I saw them, sharing what was seconds ago Daisy's own patch of sun, but it now housed both dozing bodies quite comfortably. Daisy had moved from her original position and Collie slotted in neatly around her. Looking at them both from this angle gave them the appearance of two linked commas — a couple of neat pauses, right there on the hillside. And on a whim, I folded my ankles and lowered myself into a cross-legged position on the grass, too, taking great care to make sure my dress a) flared around me with a touch of the theatrics to it and b) didn't hike up at an awkward angle thereby showing my knickers in the process.

Owen laughed. 'What are you doing?'

'Wouldn't it be a shame to disturb them?'

He looked at the girls, their post-walk, puppy-like breaths that somehow looked to be timed around each other. He didn't need to answer.

'Besides which—' I patted the ground in front of me — 'we haven't even scratched the surface of this whole Lollipop man thing . . .'

CHAPTER EIGHT: OWEN

I mightn't have made it into the official boys' club at work, but outside of work I had a steady set of friends. We belonged to the social group of thirty-something men who hadn't settled down but also weren't messing around like they were twenty-something. I never really knew what that made us in terms of our acknowledged category — or rather, I knew exactly what it made us, but none of us were yet willing to admit how unlucky in love we'd been to date. Instead we spoke like singledom was a choice, even though none of us were exactly making the most of it.

The lads and I tried to get together at least once a month and we usually packed in good intentions about a grown-up lunch date and a catch-up. It invariably collapsed into too many pints with one of us — usually Zee — suggesting that we get a bag of chips apiece while on our way to another, less crowded, watering hole.

On this particular Saturday, we were all two pints ahead of Zee by the time he arrived — something you could tell from the way he eye-rolled when he thumped down in his seat at the table. The rest of us had been in the Mad Hatter since 12.00 p.m., which was, we thought, a *just about* acceptable time to start daytime drinking. This was usually where we started, because it was quiet until at least early afternoon and we knew that we could tick our "having a sensible catch-up" box before the conversation inevitably collapsed into more drunken and idle chatter about nothing at all.

'What did I miss?' Zee sipped his pint and looked around the table.

Alan counted off topics with his fingers as he spoke. 'Luke still doesn't know what he wants to do with his life, I still know but don't like what I'm doing with mine, Kai and Sam have wrangled themselves a double date with two best friends, *aaaaand* . . .'

Zee snapped his fingers. 'And Owen still hasn't asked out the dog walker girl.'

'Got it in one!' Kai chimed in.

'Mate.' Zee clapped me on the shoulder. 'What's going on?'

'Can't we talk about their double date first?' I gestured to the testosterone twins sitting opposite me. Part of the reason why Kai and Sam — identical twins and all-round tricksters — were still single was that they refused to date outside of being a pair, which I'd always thought was the tiniest bit odd. But then I'd been dating/not dating a woman I was crazy about for seven months now and still couldn't bring myself to ask her out without canine supervision, so what position was I in to critique anyone else's approach to romance?

Kai shrugged. 'I mean, we *can* talk about it, but it's only going to delay the inevitable.'

'Janine and Susan are two women that Kai met at Zumba class. He got talking to them and mentioned me, obviously, and he thought they both seemed like stand-up women so he suggested a drink, with both of them, and me, obviously, and now we've arranged to see them next weekend for a light lunch and a few cocktails because apparently we live in an episode of *Sex and the City*.' Sam underscored the final comment by taking two especially large swigs from his pint, as though reasserting his masculinity via a drink choice. 'Did I miss anything?'

Kai shook his head. 'Sounds like everything to me.'

'Your turn,' Alan said. 'When are you asking her out?'

It wasn't through a lack of inclination or interest — or even a lack of trying! There were at least three or four days a week when Nell and I would be walking the girls and I would think, *I could ask now, I could suggest dinner now, I could ask whether she prefers tea or coffee now.* And somehow, whenever I opened my mouth to actually voice the words, I typically asked inane questions about work, sometimes questions about her nan, then questions about the shop. Between brain and mouth, all manner of things bumped the queue ahead of asking Nell if she'd like to spend time with me, which, logically, she *must* have liked spending time with me already, otherwise she'd simply walk Daisy at a different hour. Yet, despite that logic, despite it . . .

'You're overthinking the whole thing.' Luke gestured the shape of a large circle as though really underscoring the height and breadth of my overthinking. 'She obviously likes you, man.'

'Then why hasn't she asked?' I asked — finally giving voice to a thought that had crossed my mind more than once. Nell was a bold and forward-thinking woman. She wasn't the type of person to think that a man *should* make the first move, I was sure of it. 'Maybe that's a sign?'

'A sign that she's big into books and the classics have brainwashed her into believing that Rochester will come knocking one day, even though he was an arsehole,' Alan said, his face angled at his phone as he spoke, which meant he missed the raised eyebrows and looks of shock around the table. Every now and then, Alan reminded us without reminding us that despite his half-wit approach to things, he was actually *really* bloody clever. When no one answered he looked up and glanced from one of us to the next before sighing. '*Jane Eyre*, you fucking heathens.'

Luke sipped his drink and made an appreciative noise. 'I'm not sure it's the literary reference we're struggling with, exactly.'

'It's my crystal insight?' Alan shrugged in a "what can I say" sort of gesture.

'No, it's the fact that we always tank in the literature round at the pub quiz,' Luke answered.

'I'm not good under pressure!' Alan shot back.

'Back to Romeo over there, though. If she's spent her entire life bingeing on books about men riding up on horseback, maybe, *maybe*, she just wants one who'll ask her out for a coffee. It's not like you need to rent a stallion and ride through the high street to her.'

'Though that would also be cool,' Zee added.

'Are you friends with her on Facebook?' Kai already had his phone out, tapping away. 'Nell . . . what's her surname?'

'I don't know.'

'You don't know?' Sam butted in.

'I said what I said, mate. I don't know.' I took too large a swig from my lager then, and it came back in a splutter over the table. 'I know that her favourite colour is lilac, her favourite flowers are sunflowers, she lost her parents when she was young and she dotes on her nan. Her dog is her most prized *everything* and she owns a bookshop.' I held a finger up and added, 'Which was her childhood dream job, I recently discovered.'

There was a long silence where I caught a couple of glances between them all, before Sam said, 'But you don't know her surname?'

'No.' I took another sip and this time *really* concentrated on swallowing so as not to ruin my stiff-upper-lip pose. 'I do not know her surname.'

'Put in "Green Fields Books",' Zee suggested. 'That's the name of the shop, right?'

I was taken aback. 'How do you even know that?'

'Mate,' Alan said through the beginnings of a laugh. 'Do you have *any* idea how much you talk about this woman?'

'Got her!' Kai shouted and the group moved round to crowd him and steal a look at his phone. Meanwhile, I propped my elbows on the table and cradled my forehead in my damp palms, wondering whether it was the alcohol or the early stirrings of some panic that was causing the sweat on me. I kept quiet while they narrated various book promotions, posts from visitors, five-star reviews, which didn't surprise me in the slightest because I would always give Nell a five-star review. More stars, if they were available.

'Oh my God.' Luke sounded stunned.

'Is that her?'

'Jesus, she is *adorable*.'

'Look at that face.'

'What?' Their tension-building had caught my interest good and proper, and I was out of my seat then, too, crossing to stand behind Kai and get a look at his screen. 'What have you found? Is it—'

My sentence snapped clean off when I saw that what they'd actually found was a picture of Daisy. She was prettily dressed in a pink, floral headband that looked precariously balanced on her ears and, instead of a collar with a conventional tag, she was wearing a sign that said *Summer Sale*. To add to that, Daisy wasn't just sitting in the shop like any common mutt. She was sitting on a throne — or rather, a wobbly-looking seat — made of books, and I could imagine how Nell would have assembled it brick by proverbial brick, and probably even tested it herself before letting her girl perch there. I could imagine a hundred versions of this photo that Nell would have had to choose between, with various outtakes that would no doubt show Daisy scratching or fidgeting with her collar, or one of her other tics — such it was that I knew the dog by her likely behaviours, as much as I now knew the tics of her owner, too. But there was still so much I didn't know. I sighed and Kai bent his head back to look up at me.

I laughed. 'This is just . . . this is so Nell.'

'Why don't you go to the shop?' Zee asked plainly, making it sound like the simplest suggestion in the world.

Everyone filtered back to their own seats, apart from Sam who was collecting up our empties from the table. 'Everyone having the same?'

I tried to tally up the number of times I'd thought of going to Nell's bookshop. It was probably around the same number of times I'd thought of suggesting a date.

'You could go at the end of the workday?' Kai said, then rushed to add, 'But not today, because you'll be pissed.'

I hesitated, knowing already the reaction I was going to get. 'That's when we walk the dogs.'

There was a chorus of "Oh, boy" and "Jesus wept", and Alan even went as far as to say, 'For goodness' sake.'

'What?' I shrugged. 'We have a system. The *dogs* have a system.'

'So we can bump the dogs up the list of reasons why Owen isn't asking out the dog walker,' Kai told Sam who had come back carrying a tray loaded with lagers.

'Oh, cool, I'll update the spreadsheet.'

'What else is on this list?' I asked, grabbing my drink. 'And who's the one updating the spreadsheet?'

'See.' Luke gestured with his pint, thereby spilling some of it in the centre of the table. 'You're far too fucking interested at the mention of a spreadsheet, my friend. There's more to life than quantifying data sets.'

'Hear, hear!' Sam moved his drink into the centre for a group clink. We all obliged and everyone was deliciously quiet while we supped our pints and made our thankful noises.

'I'm just . . .'

'You're nervous,' Zee said, his tone a little softer round the edges now, 'I get it. These pricks get it, too, don't you? They might talk a good talk, but none of them are exactly settled or beating women off with sticks.'

Luke frowned and opened his mouth as though he were about to dispute the comment. Before any words could inch out, his face relaxed and instead he shrugged and said, 'The man might have a point.'

'Set yourself a deadline,' Sam said, and Alan slow-clapped the idea.

'Bloody brilliant — he's on to something.'

'Seriously.' Sam carried on. 'Mate, you *love* a good deadline for things. So set yourself a deadline to ask her out, and then you *know* you'll get it done by then.'

'And if you're in any doubt,' Kai added, playing the odds from the outset like the smart man he was, 'set up an insurance policy.'

The boys all murmured in agreement so I was sure it was a good idea. The trouble was, I had no bloody idea what Kai was actually talking about. 'I'm going to need more of an explanation. That means nothing to me.'

'You know . . .' Luke paused to wipe his mouth of lager foam. 'You know in an action film.' Which meant that I probably didn't know anything at all about what he was going to say, but I made an encouraging noise all the same. 'When you find out at the start that this bomb is going off at X time on Y date, and the heroes know that that's the amount of time they've got to fix the world before the bad guy fucks shit up.'

No one said anything for what felt like an uncomfortable stretch of time.

'So you're saying . . .' I started without knowing rightly where my own sentence was going to end. 'You're saying I need a bomb?'

'A proverbial bomb?' Sam double-checked.

Luke rolled his eyes. 'Yes, dumbass, a proverbial bomb. I'm not suggesting he rolls a stick of dynamite down the high street one Saturday afternoon.'

'For what it's worth, I'm very glad you fact-checked where he was going with that analogy.' Sam and I shared a laugh that the others soon joined in with. 'So I need something, like a romantic gesture, that'll happen whether I ask Nell out or not. And that romantic gesture needs to happen, at some point, after a self-imposed deadline, by which time I need to have asked her out on a date, or this gesture is triggered, thereby taking my readiness out of the equation and kind of, effectively, confessing my feelings for Nell no matter how shit-scared I might still feel about it all.'

The group weighed up my assessment of the situation and then Alan, the self-elected spokesperson, said, 'Yes, that seems to be what we're, as a collective, proposing that you do.'

I nodded, took another measured sip of my pint, then nodded again. 'Well, this all sounds very romantic, lads, thanks for the help . . .'

CHAPTER NINE: NELL

It had been a genuinely lovely day at the bookshop, rounded off with a genuinely lovely walk. Owen had had a rough day at the office — something to do with numbers, something to do with his utter arsehole of a boss asking him to fudge them again, or at least that was my basic and layperson under-standing of the situation — but watching Collie dive-bomb into the Green Fields dog park stream, closely followed by a tentative and surprisingly delicate Daisy, who only went as far as dipping a paw in the water, seemed to have turned things around for him. He was smiling by the time we were edging closer to our parting point at least — the spot on the park's map where Owen went one way to his half of the city and I went back to mine, like fairy-tale characters banished from the light of the other's lands. Seconds before we got to that point though, Owen asked what my plans were for the evening and my stomach did a nice version of a somersault — not an uncomfortable spin, but a dolphin twirl in warm water. It crossed my mind that this might be the segue . . .

'I myself have got an online games night to look forward to.'

Though of course, it wasn't. Owen was playing some-thing to do with war, something to do with battle, with friends from his university days. That's the only way they made time for each other now, so he said, though truthfully I found it endearing that they made time for each other at all after all these years. *How many people* actually *keep in touch when they say they will?* I wondered as I slipped Daisy's lead on.

'I've got a dinner date,' I answered, and, really, it was uncharacteristically cruel of me to phrase it that way. I hadn't been out to cause trouble — but I had been looking for a reaction and I was a grown woman who should have known better than to try it. Still, I thought I saw an eye twitch from Owen, the slightest nerve-ending response of disappointment at the prospect of there being . . . a someone. 'My best friend moved out to Chicago . . . wow, I guess around two years ago now. She's a photographer out there, living the big cliché.' I giggled and Owen smiled in answer, his face notably more relaxed now. 'Anyway, at least once a month we have a dinner date together to catch up on things. It can be hard keeping up with each other day-to-day now, with the time difference and all.'

Owen checked his watch and did some fast maths. 'Dinner date for you and a lunch date for her?'

'Exactly.'

'That's nice,' he said. 'That's really nice.'

I shrugged. 'Same time tomorrow?'

'We've got to stop meeting like this,' he answered but from his tone I couldn't tell whether it was a line or a genuine sentiment — and my face must have echoed the confusion. 'I'm kidding, obviously. Just kidding,' he said, his hands flapping as he spoke. 'Wow, memo to self, do not try to be funny.'

'It's been a long day,' I said, lying. 'I was slow on the uptake.'

'We didn't even get to your day! Balls, I was so busy—'

And then, I did the bravest thing that I think I have ever done — second only to the whole jumping-on-the-school-table-and-shouting-at-Felicity-at-the-top-of-my-lungs thing that is, which had been admittedly an act fuelled more by pure rage than it had been bravery. I reached out and squeezed Owen's upper arm. 'I like hearing about your day.'

A long, quiet moment passed between us. 'Thank you, Nell, that's . . . thank you.'

'I'll see you tomorrow, Owen.' I crouched to be level with Collie, her face upturned as though she was already prepped for me. 'I'll see you tomorrow, you gorgeous girl. Ah, yes, I will. Yes, I will.' I scratched at the rough spot of fur beneath her chin, and her back leg thumped at the ground. When I stood I saw Owen poised to say something, his mouth slightly open like a poorly crafted statue of someone thinking. 'Everything okay?'

He opened his mouth wider then, which only made the expression even more strange to look at. But with an abruptness he snapped his mouth closed, gave a single, sharp nod and said, 'Yep, all good. We'll see you tomorrow.'

Owen turned and rushed to walk away with Collie close at hand, leaving Daisy and I dumbstruck on our side of the path. But no sooner had he turned, he came hurrying back and lowered into his own crouch. 'I'll see you tomorrow too, you lovely creature.'

Then he was gone, again. Even Collie looked thrown by the whole thing — and that was saying something.

* * *

Lucia and I had quickly become best friends after falling for the same man on our university course. We'd been innocent and naive first-year students, who'd soon realised that we'd not been each other's only competition. In fact, there had been an *entire* cohort of men and women alike who had promptly fallen arse over heels for Dr Don Rule, the English literature lecturer, who'd seemed to like absolutely no one, thereby making him inexplicably more attractive — most significantly to his first-year undergraduates. Lucia and I had discovered our shared appreciation for the man when, at the beginning of a lecture on *Hamlet*, he'd walked into the lecture

76

hall and we'd both made *exactly* the same admiring sound as each other. Sitting side by side when it happened, we'd promptly fallen over ourselves with laughter that Dr Rule evidently had not approved of — and he'd made that disapproval clear to everyone else in the room.

'*Hamlet* is no laughing matter, ladies,' he'd said. In unison we apologised and from that moment, we synced.

Lucia didn't keep the same interest in literature as me — having fallen for an arts and media lecturer in her second year instead, not that that went anywhere — but even that difference bonded us in the end. We spent long and tortured hours discussing our respective crafts and interests over noodles and fruit cider, and nothing much changed into our adult-adult years either — not to be confused with our we-thought-we-were-adults years, also known as the university years. There were whole chunks of our lives that we deconstructed in this way, marking out set points that we wanted to arrive at by the time real adulthood rolled around. In the end, that was what made Lucia leave.

'What if I don't get this chance again?' she said, holding her phone out to me so I could see the job offer from a media agency in New York. She played the "What if I don't get this chance again?" track so many times that I began to wonder whether she was taking life advice from Nan. Ironically, the New York thing hadn't worked out, but Chicago — oh, Chicago became Lucia's one true love.

These days we did everything we could to make sure we still saw each other. This usually came in the form of a Zoom catch-up. But when the video call from Lucia started to ring at the exact moment that the pizza-delivery man rang the front doorbell, it was a close call as to which got my attention first.

'Don't go anywhere,' I answered the call, 'I'll be right with you.' I was already off-screen, running from my living room to the hallway to the door — 'Thanks so much!' — and then back again. 'Christ,' I panted as I settled down. 'I am so not . . . *so* not a runner.'

Lucia laughed. 'Did you get pizza, too?' She waved a slice at the camera. 'Cheers.' She moved as though to clink the melted cheese and mushrooms into the screen and then tucked a solid half a slice in her mouth instead. Even when chewing an inordinate amount of food, Lucia was still one of the most beautiful women I'd ever known — in all senses. She had natural corkscrew curls that framed her face in a way that was somehow both wild and completely tailored. The make-up she wore was understated, but there was a distinct kohl outline around each eye — complete with eyelid flicks — that I knew, from too many years of watching her do it, must have taken a good fifteen minutes to get just right. There was a ghost of red lipstick on her mouth, too, washed away from a morning of slamming coffees like they were tequila shots — an educated guess — and, now, shovelling down pizza.

'Tell me,' she said, her mouth still part-busy with dough. 'How's Nan?'

I fumbled with my own pizza box and picked a pepper from the first slice I saw. 'She's good! We're still doing Sunday dinner and we're still talking every day. No health hiccups. She's still flirting shamelessly with the man who runs the corner shop at the end of her road.' I pulled a whole slice free then. 'How's everyone your end?'

Lucia's parents lived in separate countries — and that was just how everyone liked it. 'Eh, Mum is okay. Another financial scare on the horizon but she's coping. The business will tick over with time, I think. Dad is basking in the beauty of a midlife crisis.'

'Didn't he *just have* a midlife crisis?'

'Right. But apparently that was a trial run.'

'I see.' I bit off another mouthful and spoke around it. 'So what flavour is this crisis?'

'This is a spicy, I'm-dating-someone-younger-than-my-daughter cliché with that added bonus of . . .' She paused for dramatic effect. 'It being one of my friends.'

I winced. 'Who?'

'Shanice,' Lucia answered with obvious distaste.

'*Shanice*!'

'Right? I never liked her anyway.'

We collapsed into the rhythm of a familiar catch-up after that, taking it in turns to talk about life while the other scoffed another slice of pizza as though we were running some kind of eating relay race between us. Though given that Lucia was squeezing this talk into her lunch break, relaying was a valid approach to make sure that we got everything in.

'Anyway,' she eventually said with so much purpose that I already knew where she was going next. 'I have two questions for you and then I've got to shoot.' I wiped my greasy fingers on a nearby serviette and gave her my full attention. 'What are you doing in December?'

'What, like, the *whole* of December?'

'Mmhmm.' She nodded. 'The whole of it.'

'I don't have an itinerary but I like to think that I'll be fighting customers off while they prepare their Christmas stockings for people, having decided that books really are the perfect present, and then Nan and I will be eating too much on a semi-regular basis in preparation for Christmas Day . . . when we'll also eat too much.' It was like stretching before exercise and it was a yearly ritual that our Sunday dinners got progressively bigger the closer it got to Christmas proper. In our family, Christmas Day was the London Marathon of meals — and despite being five slices of pizza down, my stomach joy-rumbled at the thought. 'Why, what are you doing?'

Lucia made a show of thinking before she shrugged and said, 'I'm not sure, really. I thought I might help my best friend in her bookshop while she fights off customers—'

I disintegrated into howls of excitement, my hands flapping as though they were now moving independently from the rest of my body. 'You're coming home?'

'I'm coming home, baby! I've been offered some work in London and normally I wouldn't be arsed but I thought, if it's not a pain for you to have me there . . .'

'Are you mad? Of course it isn't!'

'Perfect. Well, that's Christmas sorted.' She bit off a mouthful of crust. 'Now, ready for my second question?'

I rolled my eyes. 'No, he still hasn't asked.'

'Jesus H Christ, Nellie, what are you playing at?'

'What am *I* playing at?'

'That's what I said. Why aren't you asking him?'

'Because what if he says no?' I was painfully aware that our pitches were rising higher with every question we asked, like birds communicating danger in the wild. 'And why do I have to be the one to ask?'

'Why does he?'

'Why wouldn't he?'

'Why wouldn't *you*?'

I pressed my fingers to my forehead. 'We're a question apiece away from becoming characters in a Lewis Carroll novel. I haven't asked because I'm nervous he'll say no, and I know—' I held my hands up in a defensive gesture, pre-empting her rebuttal. 'I know he could be thinking exactly the same. But it's been dragging on for so long now that I can't help but think that if he really wanted to ask, like, if there was *really* something there, he would have asked. So maybe . . . I mean, maybe I've just imagined the whole spark thing. That could also be a possibility?'

Lucia raised an eyebrow. 'And you don't think that maybe, if he wasn't interested in you, he might have missed one, just *one*, dog walk at least, by now?'

I groaned. Of course, logically, Lucia was right. There was every possibility that Owen was waiting for me to ask, while I was busy waiting for him to. Besides which, I also knew there was every possibility that Owen not asking was nerves, or him being respectful, or him having his worries, or, or, or . . . the list went on. Meanwhile, I was harbouring my own nerves, doubting my own attractiveness, and a million other things, not to mention the fact that my long-term dating experience was limited to a six-month stint with a man who'd turned out to be a monumental arsehole — and a married one at that — which was *five* years ago. Though it felt generous to call it a relationship really, given that I'd spent the majority of our time together believing empty promises. After I'd found out about his wife — because *of course* he hadn't volunteered that information on his own — I'd blindly clung on to every lie and cliché like a flailing climber on a cliff-edge: 'The marriage was over long before I met you . . . She doesn't understand me like you do.' And after months of this, he did exactly as promised: he left his wife. For someone else. For someone who wasn't me. I spent a long time after that wondering whether the single life mightn't just be better, or at least, less painful.

'Baby, look.' Lucia was back to loving best friend. 'I have to go, but listen to me, okay? You are literally the most beautiful person I know. You and Daisy are a dream team of all things good, and any man would be *blessed*, I tell you, to have you both. If you like him—' She held up her hand as though she was expecting a snap back from that. 'If you like him, which I know you do, please, *please* consider giving yourself a chance at this? You have a home, you have a dog, you have a business. Don't you deserve . . . you know?'

'The sex?' I filled in the blank to try to break how serious the talk had become, but Lucia squinted her judgement at me in a way that suggested the comment perhaps hadn't landed well. 'The happiness.'

'The happiness. Baby, you deserve that.'

I sighed and ran a hand through my hair. 'I'll think about it. Is that a fair deal?'

'I sense it's as good a deal as I'm going to get,' she said with a questioning tone and I murmured in agreement. 'In which case, I'll take it. We'll talk soon?'

'We'll talk soon.'

'Love you, babe, love you, Daisy.'

I held Daisy up to the camera and paw-waved goodbye. 'We love you, Lucia!' When the call disconnected, we both collapsed back into the sofa. Daisy lay curled on my belly, mimicking the position of being in utero, and I stroked her back while I re-ran through Lucia's speech on things. 'Maybe she's right, Daisy, maybe we do deserve the happiness. What do you think?'

As though in response, Daisy looked up at me with her wrinkled and thoughtful face. I wondered what answer she'd give me if she could talk me through this experience, too. But then I spotted her side-eyeing the rest of the pizza, and realised at that moment that Daisy's mind was on her own happiness.

CHAPTER TEN: OWEN

I took Luke's advice and planted a bomb — or rather, I planted a delivery, for the end of the working week. Whether I asked Nell out on a date or not, there would be an embarrassing bouquet of peonies — her second-favourite flower, she'd told me once, owing to the fact that she could never keep sunflowers alive for very long, and I'd banked the information for Just In Case use — delivered to the bookshop on Friday afternoon, complete with a card that said: *Reader, will you go on a date with me? Owen*, which I personally thought was very bloody clever. And given that it was now Thursday lunchtime and I was yet to do anything in the way of asking Nell out, I'd come around to thinking that Luke's plan hadn't exactly been the worst in the world — not that I was prepared to admit it to him, obviously. Because I'd never live that down.

I closed one spreadsheet and opened another. I locked my laptop screen and grabbed my jacket from the back of my chair. The lunchtime rush and shove would have passed at the deli down the road and I was burning through so much nervous energy — about the flowers, the note, that night's impending dog walk — there was no way that I could get through the rest of the afternoon without a tuna-and-cheese sub in me. And maybe a cookie. Alongside the dopamine hit of going home and getting cuddle-attacked by Collie for a quarter of an hour, too. I hit the button for the lift and bounced on my heels as I waited.

'Owen!' The thump on the back of my shoulder was so forceful that I had to resist the urge to put out a hand to steady myself against the wall. Instead, I turned to meet the assailant and found Oliver, part-time middle management, full-time tit. 'How does it feel to be the man of the hour?'

I frowned. 'I'm sorry?'

'Oh, bugger-nuts, Doug hasn't caught you yet?' He looked around as though checking whether Douglas was in earshot before he pressed on. 'Don't tell him I've told you — he'll want to deliver the news himself, I'm sure — but the advice you passed along to Credence Co? About the investment opportunities coming up in Leeds?'

I tried to flick through the many spreadsheets clogging up my laptop's hard drive to land on the right one. Credence Co were a charity organisation who had been given a substantial grant earlier in the year, and we'd been working with them on a pro bono basis since. 'It looks good to be seen doing charity work,' Douglas had said when he'd landed the case file on my desk. I'd put together a package outlining investment opportunities in a cluster of arts-based companies on the rise in Leeds, given that Credence were looking to endorse the healing power of creativity, though they had a more sophisticated — less wishy-washy — strapline for what they were doing. And now it seemed that not only had they taken the idea, but . . .

'They ploughed money into the Leeds groups?'

'They did, planted little penny seeds—' he wiggled his fingers in a sowing motion — 'and pounds have shot up everywhere. The Hernan quarter has blown up with popularity, over-bloody-night, if you can believe it. If I didn't know better—' he nudged his shoulder to mine — 'I'd wager you had an inside tip on how favourably people were looking on that creative codswallop.'

Or I actually know what I'm talking about. The Hernan quarter already had properties allocated to several key businesses from the wider area. It didn't take a genius to see that someone was already putting money into the arts up north — and money breeds money. But still, I felt something like pride at hearing the advice had paid off. Rather than fallen on its arse.

'And Doug, Douglas — he's happy about it?'

'Positively brimming. But hey—' another thump on the shoulder — 'you didn't hear it from me? Well done, sport.'

If he hadn't sounded so patronising, I might have been pleased with the congratulatory note. Still, I gladly took his praise. I pocketed it into each empty space of my suit, in fact, until I was bursting enough with the stuff to have what Alan would have referred to as Big Dick Energy — which was a crass and hideous phrase that I normally wouldn't subscribe to, but given that there was a huge neon timer over my head for asking Nell out, on that evening's dog walk, I reasoned that a good dose of BDE might actually do me some favours.

Alas, when I strolled out of the lift on the ground floor and bumped straight into Douglas — carrying what, from the state of his shirt, I guessed was a full cup of coffee — the energy abated somewhat.

'Shit, fuck.' I made to catch the coffee cup as it fell, as if there was any point. 'Douglas, I'm so sorry.'

He only chuckled. A good and hearty sound like grandparents at a dinner table. 'I don't know that I've ever heard a curse word leave your mouth before, Owen, and the one time it does it's for a coffee.'

I stood and shakily held the empty mug out to him. 'I'm sorry, boss, I should have been—'

'Nothing of it. Are you heading out?'

Please don't come with me. Please don't come with me. 'I was just going to grab a sandwich to eat while I work. Those spreadsheets have got too many empty cells for my liking.'

'You're a good kid, Owen.' He reached around me to call for the lift. 'Tell you what, on your travels you grab me a large latte with about twenty-six sugars, or thereabouts

— you're the numbers guy.' He laughed at his own guess-work and I couldn't help but take note of the implication that *I* was the numbers guy and *he* wasn't, though that may have been the ego in me doing the thinking. 'Bring your sandwich and my latte up to my office and we'll have a little chat, eh? I've got some stuff I want to run by you. You've got no meetings for this afternoon?' He stepped into the lift and, when I shook my head in answer, he pointed his finger at me and fired like a gun. 'Keep it that way.'

I resisted the urge to play at being shot. The childlike dork that lived rent-free inside my brain thought it would just be *hilarious* to grab at my chest and buckle at the knees and let my tongue loll to one side — an act that, in reality, was only amusing to Collie, who would promptly come over to search for my fake wound, and then we'd go back to whatever we'd been playing with before the not-so-fatal blow was delivered.

Nell had never seen that act, and at the memory of it I wondered whether a future memory would be her rolling her eyes at us both, Daisy joining in, even. *You're making some mighty fine assumptions about those flowers.* I snapped out of the future memory. It was then that I realised that Douglas had long ago stepped into the lift, the doors had closed and the relevant pulleys had been, well, pulled — and I was about to greet, with loved-up eyes and a dopey smile — whoever was going to step out from somewhere further up the building. I made a beeline for the deli and decided that I would definitely treat myself to a cookie while I was there — a pat on the head for me, from me — but I'd pocket it until after the talk with Douglas, when I could celebrate quietly on my own.

Until I can celebrate with the girls. I felt my eyes flood with small hearts.

* * *

In the time it took for me to get my sandwich and get Douglas's latte, Douglas's office had been invaded — by none other than Oliver, who was exhibiting such a level of comfort that I felt desperately uncomfortable on seeing him. He was sitting in one of the visitor chairs, on the socially acceptable side of the desk at least, but with his feet propped up on the other visitor chair, showing *far* too much familiarity with the space *and* blocking me from sitting down anywhere. I thought when he saw me walk in he might offer to move but, no, no, the boxers-stain kept his feet exactly where they were and only flashed me a Christmas-bonus smile instead.

'Ah, my coffee!' Douglas held a hand out. 'Owen is the one responsible for this mess.' He gestured to his shirt. 'When we literally ran into each other.' Then there came that same chuckle as before, though it no longer had the grandparent comfort to it and instead it crept up my back. 'Well, *he* ran into *me* actually.' Oliver tut-tutted and laughed along with our superior, and he still didn't move his feet.

'I didn't know how many sugars to get,' I said, handing over the drink. Then I dug about in my pocket to retrieve the seven sachets of white sugar that I'd brought up to go with it. I offloaded them onto Douglas's desk and then stepped back to linger by the visitor chairs.

'Oliver tells me that he already told you the good news?' Douglas said, lifting the lid on his coffee. *Funny*, I thought, *because Oliver told me not to tell you that*. Douglas ripped across the top of all seven sachets at once. 'So that's cocked up the big surprise.' Oliver flashed his palms in a weak jazz-hands gesture. 'Seriously, Owen, good work,' Douglas continued and then an awkward silence fell over the three of us while Douglas upended the sugar into his cup and swished it around, in place of going to get a spoon. It seemed to take him a minute to realise I was even still there. 'I'm sorry, Owen, something's come up with a case we're working on anyway, so my afternoon just got booked right up.'

Again, Oliver made that same weak gesture. 'When the boss is needed, the boss is needed.'

'Yeah, yeah.' Douglas waved the comment away. 'Go and put your feet up for the afternoon. Save some random documents, give yourself an easy one. We'll catch up soon.'

'Yes, boss.' I gave a mock salute that I instantly hated myself for. 'Oliver, pleasure as always.' Then I left before the swine could say something charming and unwelcome in return.

Over the course of the afternoon, I put my "Away" status on my Teams and ignored two phone calls from my youngest sister — for Hattie to call at this time of day I knew without answering that it must be drama, and I had far too much nervous energy to hear the latest unfolding between her and, if I had to place money on it, our mother. No fewer than twenty-eight emails filtered through in the space of time it took me to watch three episodes of *Schitt's Creek* on my laptop, and by then I was so buoyed by David and Patrick's romance that all I could think about was the potential of my own. I decided, then, that tonight would be the night to ask Nell for drinks, or coffee — or rather, *anything* that didn't involve walking dogs and parting ways for our respective sides of the city at the end of it all. I went as far as writing a script — *Nell, we've known each other for a while now . . .* — which I hoped to God I wouldn't need. Failing that, if I did need it, I hoped Nell at least might find it endearing rather than utterly embarrassing and hopeless. It could go either way, but it was better to be prepared.

By the time I had drafted and redrafted my writing, I had, somehow, very nearly made myself late to go and collect Collie from home. For the first time since working at the firm I finally understood how people managed to keep themselves busy by doing nothing, and wondered how many times on the average day a Netflix login must be pinged out from our building.

On the hurried journey home I listened to Hattie's voicemail — 'You'll never guess what the cow has had to say about my baby this time . . .' — but I deliberately didn't read the WhatsApp she'd sent me, for fear of being given away by a read report. I was running on a cookie energy high with chocolate-drop optimism and I didn't know how long it might last. I couldn't waste any of it on my family. *You're a terrible person.* I pulled into the traffic of the main street out of town.

Terrible, but fair. I indicated to change lanes, pressed my foot down harder on an amber light and, for shame, even refused to give way to someone who was already wedged across a lane of traffic, too. When I pulled up at home, I found that I was so physically pumped from the drive and from the upcoming spilling of feeling — *don't back out, Owen, don't back out* — that I literally felt out of breath and I wondered whether I needed a shower before setting off to leave again. I smiled then, and felt my chest start to settle. *Like Collie would* ever *wait for you to have a shower before a walk.*

Beagles were notorious for separation anxiety but, whether it was through her rough start in life or some deep and sure understanding that I would always come back to her, it wasn't a hurdle that we'd had to jump at all when we first brought her home. I did it in small amounts to start with, having booked annual leave for the very purpose of doing practice runs. In the years since, she had become accustomed to me disappearing in the morning and reappearing at lunchtimes for an emergency wee, a treat, and a cuddle, providing one simple rule was adhered to: there was always a walk at the end of it. Even on the days when I was working from home — and Collie was keeping me company through my spreadsheets, my emails, and my camera-off meetings — there was *always* the end-of-the-day walk. And thanks to the assistance of a friendly neighbour — Kevin, who came complete with his own dog, Bruno — I happened to know there were mid-morning and mid-afternoon walks for Collie, too. Kevin had agreed to pop in on Collie periodically when we first moved here after the big break-up with Lisa. I'd said no at first, insisting that doggy daycare would work out just fine. But then the thought of leaving Collie with her home comforts won out instead — and the baby-cams I'd installed at various points around the house gave me peace of mind, too, as did the knowledge that Kevin was only ever a couple of hours away from checking on her.

I struggled free of the car and paced to the front door with my key in hand. From these years of experience, I was braced for the body-slam impact of her the minute the door opened but . . .

'Coll?' I shouted into the hallway as I closed up the entryway behind me. 'Collie?' There was a rumble of worry in my stomach. *What on earth is she doing that she's too distracted for a walk?*

I shrugged off my jacket and threw it on one of the hooks on the wall. 'Collie!' I whistled. 'Walk time, girl. Come on.'

And then I heard it. That soft and tired whimper, that harbinger of . . . something.

CHAPTER ELEVEN: NELL

I made my tea with two sugars — which would have been fine, if I took sugar. I let my porridge boil over in the microwave. Daisy had honey loops for breakfast instead of her usual bowl of dried food. And I started the day in odd shoes that I only noticed when we were already halfway to the shop. It was a toss-up between walking home, changing, and making myself late, or powering through the day wearing one black-and-white Converse pump and one white with a sunflower print. In Nan's voice I heard, 'It's probably bad luck to change them,' so Daisy and I pressed on in the hope that everyone I happened to serve that day might be as distracted as I was.

As it happened, I wound up being late to open the shop anyway on account of three schoolboys who insisted on walking abreast on the pavement, even though the little sods should surely have already been in a classroom by that time of day. After Daisy and I *finally* managed to struggle round them — dropping ourselves into the road to overtake — we arrived at the front door a solid ten minutes later than normal and I tried, tried, tried not to let my anxious brain believe the blatant lie that we had probably missed a day's worth of customers by then.

After struggling with the key in the lock — on account of it being the wrong key for the first three attempts — I went immediately to the backroom where I flicked the lights on for the store and flicked the kettle on for me.

The first cup of tea of the day — which would ordinarily have been the best, such are the laws of tea-making — had ended up being poured down the drain in the kitchen at home. It had been a rich brown with small crystals of sugar still sitting on the surface. Nan would have bloody loved it — she's not been allowed sugar in a brew since the diabetes diagnosis, something that she bemoans on a regular basis.

Daisy soon plodded into the room while I attempted a second cup of the brew. She dropped her rump onto the floor and stared up at me with sad yet adoring eyes.

'I know, baby.' I let myself slide down the makeshift kitchen counter until I was crouched in front of her. No matter what people might have to say about dogs, they always had an innate ability to sense when something wasn't quite right — and that morning, Daisy knew.

Owen and Collie had never missed a dog walk. Or at least, they hadn't missed a dog walk in the entire time we'd known them. We'd hung around the dog park for an extra hour, too, in case work had run over, or Owen was caught in traffic, or, or, or a hundred other things that might have made them late, but there was no sign. 'There's going to be an explanation,' I told her in my softest voice. 'There'll be an explanation and I'll bet it'll be something silly and funny and . . . very Owen-like.' I realised then that I was reassuring myself as much as I was her, though I wasn't sure either of us felt especially convinced by the effort.

'Come on, let's make . . .' I petered out when the sound of the shop bell caught my ear. Daisy's head cocked at the noise, too. 'First one of the day.'

I stood and brushed myself down, shaking loose my shoulders for good measure, then stepped back into the open space of the shop floor to find . . .

'Nan?'

'Nellie!'

'What are . . . Why are you here?'

Nan came to a stop at the counter, somewhere she'd be able to lean. I took note of the fact that she didn't have her walking stick with her.

'Well, what a bloody greeting. No wonder the place is dead if that's how everyone gets their hello.'

I laughed, crossed the space to her and pulled her into a tight hug. 'I only greet people I *really* like like that, so if anything you should feel special.'

When I pulled away from her, she narrowed her eyes at me and let a beat of silence pass between us. She knew something was wrong. In a similar way to Daisy, Nan also had the innate ability of sensing when there was some kind of a disturbance in the Force. 'Do you want to tell me now, or over a cuppa?'

'How about you answer my question first?'

Nan only shrugged. 'I couldn't sleep with these blasted leg pains. I thought a walk might do the trick and really, where else was I going to walk? You don't mind?' Her tone sounded more sincere then, as though she might actually be worried that I didn't want her there, and my heart sank a little. Short of Owen walking in — or Lucia — Nan was about the only person I *did* feel like seeing that morning.

'Don't be daft. I've literally just boiled the kettle.'

She set a hand on my arm. 'I'll make it, Nellie. You sit.'

It was my turn to narrow my stare then. 'There's no sugar in the kitchen, if you're thinking of slipping two in while I'm not noticing.'

'In that case—' she hobbled around to what would normally be my side of the counter — 'you can make it. Got any biscuits?' She struggled onto my stool that lived behind the till space.

'I feel like it's counterproductive to say no to sugar and then give you a custard cream anyway.'

'Nellie, you aren't half a . . .' She was shifting from one side to the other on the stool. 'Bugger me, do you sit on this thing all day?'

93

I leaned forward to kiss the side of her temple. 'No, I'm usually rushing around the shop.'

'Right answer!' she said with a smile. 'Now, I'll take a tea with no sugar and two custard creams on the side, as you were the one to bring them up.'

I rolled my eyes as I turned away from her but really, I couldn't deprive her of everything — nor would I especially want to. *Imagine getting to that age and having to* still *monitor everything you bloody eat.* I had to hope that when I got to Nan's age, the sugar and fat contents of anything would be the *least* of my concerns.

While the kettle boiled again I shook four biscuits onto a plate, then brewed up for us both. I knew us well enough to know that taking the whole packet out would be a recipe for disaster. But, as though she'd counted the clink-clink of biscuit on porcelain, Daisy sat in the doorway with her head cocked to one side. I wouldn't normally deny a girl a biscuit. Unfortunately, Daisy wasn't a girl. She was a bulldog with a waistline that could do some damage to her health long term. Which felt like a good enough reason to say no — even if she mightn't agree with me . . .

'I love you whatever your size, baby,' I told her, 'but it's still a hard no.'

In answer, she huffed, turned, and wandered out to where Nan waited. I followed with a mug in each hand and the plate balanced on my arm. Nan winced when she saw the *Go away, I'm reading* mug I was serving her drink in, but it was the best I could do.

'Be grateful I'm not throwing a teabag into your mouth and asking you to gargle with warm water,' I said, joking, as I put her drink on the counter in front of her.

'It might be preferable.'

Nan took a biscuit straight away and, ever-prepared, she pulled a dog biscuit out of her pocket to feed to Daisy at the same time. My delicate girl took the biscuit softly, as though she was dealing with a child made of glass, rather than an old bird made of something much tougher. I was proud of how she was with Nan. Daisy wasn't exactly the smallest of dogs, but no one could ever criticise her for being careless. She padded away with such purpose, her treat folded into her mouth, seeming to take great care in not cracking the biscuit until she was settled in one of her three beds dotted around the shop. When she was curled up neatly to eat, Nan giggled — a schoolgirl sound that I loved to hear from her. Then she took her own biscuit and dunked.

'Come on, let's be having it, Eleanor.'

I knew she meant business.

'Owen didn't turn up for the dog walk yesterday.'

'I see.' She chewed slowly and I couldn't work out whether she was thinking it all over, or waiting for something more. 'First one he's missed?'

I nodded, then threw my hands in the air in a defeated gesture. 'And of course, I can't even check whether he's okay because—'

'Because you never asked the fella out.'

'Because I never asked the fella out.'

From her expression it was a clear certainty that she was thinking. She squinted her eyes and looked off into space, her chewing slowed and every second or two she let out a small, contemplative noise. Meanwhile, I detached the top biscuit of my custard cream.

'You told me you weren't that fussed about him.'

'I lied,' I answered plainly, biting into the free piece of biscuit.

Nan shrugged and made a "sure, that figures" sort of expression.

'I didn't want to make it into a thing, because it wasn't a thing. We were only seeing each other because we were walking the dogs, and that isn't dating, so it wouldn't have been right to call it anything, least of all a thing, but—'

'It was a thing.' She interrupted my ramble. 'I mean, dear girl, it's *very* clearly a thing.'

I dropped the remains of my deconstructed biscuit back onto the plate and wiped crumbs onto my jeans. 'So, what do I do now?'

Nan searched about under the counter, lifting up one item then another. I half managed to ask what it was she was searching for before she held a finger up to pause me mid-sentence. I sank back to my side of the till. When the search was over, she'd retrieved a rough notebook that I only ever doodled in, and a pencil. Nan didn't believe in writing in pen —far too permanent, she always said.

'To start with, we're going to write a list . . .'

* * *

Nan and I spent two hours, three cups of tea, and twelve custard creams — *so much for her bloody sugar intake* — making a list of pros and cons to pursuing Owen. By the end of it, I had two equally balanced columns that did nothing at all in terms of helping me make a decision, to which Nan said, 'Well, at least now you know you're not ready to make a decision.' It was a level of wisdom I hadn't, but perhaps should have, expected from her. She told me to sit with the lists, see whether he turned up, and what he had to say for himself when he did.

'There might be a perfectly sensible and reasonable explanation,' she said on her way to the kitchen again. I realised then that we were talking about Owen in grey terms already, as though he'd done something dreadfully wrong by not walking his dog.

But I suppose the fact that I'm bothered he didn't walk his dog might mean that I'm more bothered about him altogether than I realised, I thought as I doodled around the list columns, writing love hearts one side and broken ones the other. I thought of calling Lucia but the time difference would probably make it an unwelcome call, even by best friend standards. And frankly, there was no one else in the world who knew mine and Owen's obscure situation well enough to give me any advice on how to proceed. Not least because, despite what Nan and I might have scribbled on the lists, there really were only two options: write him off   it was nice while it lasted — or, I continued to worry. I didn't have a phone number or an address, I didn't even know where his office was, short of ringing every single firm of financial advisors in the city and asking whether an Owen worked there — an Owen was all I could give them, of course, on account of not knowing his last name.

'That would be a step too far, wouldn't it?' I asked Nan as she joined me on the shop floor again. She only raised an eyebrow in response. 'Yep, noted, definitely too much.'

The ring of the bell over the door interrupted our flow of scheming and I looked up to see a customer I recognised — but not from the shop. He looked out of place here, wandering around and thumbing at spines as though he were looking for something but didn't know where to start in finding it. Nan clocked my observations of him then, and misread them entirely as interest, intrigue, attraction.

'I think I know him,' I whispered.

'Even better!' She slapped my arm, nudging me out from behind the counter and in the direction of the handsome stranger who I recognised as . . .

'Benji, right?'

He looked startled to have been recognised but then his expression slackened, a smile taking over. 'Oh my God, you're . . .'

Please remember me otherwise it's weird that I remembered you.

'Nell. I'm trying to remember . . . Daisy!' He snapped his fingers. 'I couldn't place her.'

'That's new.' I laughed. 'Usually it's the other way around. I'm sure she won't be too put out though.' I gestured to where Daisy lay, belly up in her second bed of the day in the Classics section of the shop.

He looked around. 'You two work here?'

'Well, I work here, she's just eye candy for customers.'

'I can see that much on her part.'

'It's my shop, actually,' I hurried to add, though I wasn't sure why I felt the need to tell him. 'Can I help you with anything?'

He shrugged and his smile widened. 'Yes, please. I'm looking for kids' books. *Any* kids books.'

'Work or pleasure?' I had a half-memory of Benji telling me he worked in children's medicine and I hoped I was right.

'Work, definitely. The wards are *dire* in terms of their reading materials and it takes so long to get approval for anything round there, I thought I may as well use my day off wisely and—'

'Buy books for sick children?'

His smile thinned. 'Sad, isn't it?'

No, it's the stuff of romance novels, I wanted to say but didn't. Instead I reassured Benji that it was a genuine act of kindness. And how often did those happen these days?

I gave him a walking tour of the shop, leading all the way up to a small children's section at the back. There had never been a high demand for these books among my own customers, but there was certainly something for him to choose from. 'Give me a shout if I can help?' I smiled too enthusiastically. *Thank God you're not a dentist.*

Nan had watched the whole exchange unfold. She smirked. 'Still thinking about the dog walker?'

My smile still fixed in place, I watched Benji move around the space before I sighed like a storybook heroine and sadly answered, 'Yes.'

CHAPTER TWELVE: NELL

On account of being alive in the twenty-first century, I wasn't exactly unfamiliar with the concept of ghosting. Though dating apps weren't my go-to method of meeting people, I'd certainly given Tinder a college try once or twice, resulting in embarrassingly failed attempts at human connection. Nevertheless, I'd been fairly new to the online dating life when Lucia had explained to me what ghosting was — disappearing on someone without a trace. Disappearing on a dating app, I could understand. It was rude, make no mistake, but I could understand. Giving someone your phone number and then ghosting them? Ruder still, but at a stretch, I could even understand that one. Walking your dog with someone *every* day without fail for over seven full months, not showing up one day, sending them flowers the next, and *then* not showing up for days after that. *Is that even ghosting?*

I played "he loves me, he loves me not" with the ridiculous bouquet of peonies that had taken over my kitchen table. I had three different sets of data in front of me: the pros list, the cons list and the card that Owen had sent with the flowers. There was a fourth data set in the form of Benji's business card, which he'd boldly given me after he'd bought a bag full of books to take back to the hospital with him. I had made lots of hesitant noises before Nan had kicked me under the counter — 'Gosh, sorry, these old-age spasms' — and I'd graciously accepted the offering of his phone number. It had been stashed in my kitchen drawer ever since. As though the man himself were standing in front of me every time I glanced at it, I found I couldn't even look the business card in the eye. I'd taken that data out of the equation entirely.

I let my head fall and felt my forehead press against the cool veneer of the table. 'How much must we love Owen for me to be using terms like data set and equations?' I felt as though, mentally, he had rubbed off on me. And I'm sure Daisy looked at me with an expression of disappointment at my drastic change in lexicon, too. 'Don't worry,' I said to her reassuringly. 'I'm sure I'll be back to ditzy, daft Nell any second now.' I thumbed Owen's card — *Reader* . . . — I heard the notation in his voice and sighed. 'My mistake, I'm not sure ditzy, daft Nell ever left.'

Daisy came to me and softly tapped at my calf with her front paw. She looked forlorn and frustrated. I'd interrupted her walk schedule entirely over the last couple of days and it was starting to show. After the flower delivery, we'd stuck to our usual walks on Friday and Saturday — still no Owen — and from sheer spite I'd vowed to go a full hour later on Sunday morning. We would still have been in time to catch Owen and Collie towards the end of their normal walk — if they'd been there. Then today, after leaving work I'd encouraged Daisy straight home where she'd admittedly run upstairs and waited for me to perform my usual ritual of ten outfit changes, after a sweaty day in the shop, before leaving for the park. Neither thing had happened.

Instead, I was sitting at the kitchen table, still wearing the same T-shirt that I'd had on all day coupled with mom jeans that still bore a wide rip in them from when Daisy was a puppy and playing had got out of hand. I fingered the ragged hole in the left knee of the fabric and remembered fondly the flashback of running round Nan's kitchen with Daisy one

Sunday, only to feel her clamp at my knee, get skin, and hold on for dear life, too.

'Ah, good times.' I reached down to pat her head. 'Walk?' She noticeably perked up. The only effort I could bring myself to make was tying my hair back. I knotted it into a ponytail, checked that I wasn't leaving the house with panda eyes, and put on Daisy's lead.

He can't bloody stop us from walking. But while I ferreted out poo bags from the stand by the front door, I started to wonder where, *anywhere* else we could go, to save a trip to Green Fields dog park.

* * *

On Tuesday we visited the countryside centre on the outskirts of town. On Wednesday we commandeered the local running track and walked their winding pathways. On Thursday we walked through the city bustle and absolutely did not look for Owen on our travels. By Friday, I felt like Daisy and I were living in a dog walker's remix of a Craig David song. Propped up against the shop counter, I thought of all the ways I could take her back to Green Fields without running into Owen: I could shut the shop for a lunch hour and we could go then. I could shut the shop early. We could go home for a while, wait until Owen might have hypothetically finished his walk with Collie and *then* we could go on our walk in peace. And soon after listing these many options, I realised how utterly bloody ridiculous it was to be entertaining any single one of them — not least the ones that were likely to leave me out of pocket.

'Come on, let's wipe everything down and get gone.'

It crossed my mind to call Benji — 'Fancy a walk in the park?' — but I really didn't want to be *that* girl, no matter how let down and/or confused I felt by Owen. I was still oscillating between worry and rage, and when I hit the peak of either emotion I remembered what Nan and I discussed on our List Making Day. I reminded myself that my options for dealing with both sets of feelings were fairly limited any-way. More often than not when the anger ebbed to concern, I considered trying to track Owen down on social media as a way of finding out whether something had happened — which was to say, I absolutely tried to track Owen down on social media to find out whether . . . But it was a bunch of conventionally attractive men in a city-sized haystack. It didn't matter how many pages I scrolled through, I still couldn't find the Owen I was looking for. Nor could I find him in the headlines of local papers and, yes, I had tried to more than once. But there was a distinct lack of tragedies involving conventionally attractive financial advisors — not that I thought that was how it would be reported, exactly, but I thought his job might at least get a mention. *And maybe they'd include a picture.*

I turned off the lights in every book nook, double-checked the kettle was turned off and made for the door with Daisy close at heel. I'd *just* put my palm on the handle when the shop phone started to ring. *5.10 p.m. on a Friday.* I weighed up the possibility of this being an important call. *Would Owen call the shop?* I hated, hated, hated how I'd classified that. But still, there was a lingering doubt big enough to make me cross to the age-old handset and answer.

'Good evening, Green Fields Books, how may I . . . No, no . . . No, I'm afraid we don't have that in stock . . .' I had no idea whether we had the book in stock or not. But it just so happened that by then I was all too willing to miss out on an £8.99 sale for the sake of taking my dog to her favourite park, and I needed to do it before worry and guesswork got the better of me and I backed out.

'Come on, we're going to be brave.' Daisy pulled me out of the shop with a determination that she hardly ever used, but one that I felt especially grateful for in that moment. We bolted the latches on the door and set off in the direction of the park. My stomach immediately let out such a violent and sad growl that Daisy stopped and turned around. 'Don't mind me,' I said, and she didn't as she proceeded to carry on.

'I'm just busy crapping my pants,' I continued in a lowered voice, but it just so happened to be in the moment we walked past a busy bus stop and I'm sure at least two people looked up at me from their phones.

Thankfully, the world was actually quite beautiful that afternoon. It was one of those delicious early evenings with a miraculous amount of heat in them and I felt the prickle of my skin five minutes in — the signal that freckles were answering the low sun's call. When I was a child I'd hated the summer months, when it became impossible for me to leave the house without ghostly amounts of suncream on. As I'd gotten older — and as Daisy had taught me the joy in long walks — I'd come to appreciate the warmth that only comes from actual sun exposure. The way our human husk, hardened from a day of labour, began to soften and shed, leaving us with shoulder rolling and deep breathing. I made a conscious effort, as we walked, to inhale for three and exhale for three, and in the seconds when I held my breath I reminded myself every time of the joy that was hidden in these moments. *Whether bloody Owen was at the bloody dog park or not.*

The park was already packed when we arrived and we'd hardly tumbled through the gates before Daisy was batting off the attention of smaller, barkier dogs. It was something she seemed to bring out in them. And while they yapped and their owners cooed at them — or sometimes snapped at them to be quiet — Daisy only carried on with her merry plod, looking one side then the other as she went. It crossed my mind that she was looking for Collie but I tried to set that to one side because, frankly, the thought was too heartbreaking. Daisy had never bonded with another dog the way she had with Collie and, if Owen had decided suddenly to finish things with me — *I say, like anything had even really started with us* — then I couldn't outrun the reality that that meant Daisy had lost a friend, too.

'No more men with dogs,' I said quietly to myself, before shaking the threat away. 'What am I talking about

— *only* men with dogs.' I followed Daisy onto the walking trail that was notably quieter than the stretch of grass as we first came in, and both of us lulled into a comfortable pace.

As though suddenly fitted with a strange sort of homing beacon, I found that *every* man who was walking a dog that afternoon caught my attention. *Is there a word for that?* There probably wasn't, but I couldn't help but wonder as I nursed this hypersensitivity to tall men and their Staffordshire bull terriers; shorter men and their Great Danes; men the same height as me and their . . . *Is that a chihuahua?*

Throughout the entire walk we didn't see a single beagle and part of me was glad. I was worried twofold that a) Daisy might spot it in the distance and go bounding in the other dog's direction, only to find that it wasn't Collie after all, and b) that I might fall hopelessly in love with the owner, no matter who they were or what their relationship status happened to be, owing to the fact that they owned a dog breed I now loved and adored. Collie had been the first beagle to come into my life and I honestly felt as though I'd fallen for her as hard as I'd fallen for Owen.

Such was tradition when Daisy and I happened to be alone at the park, we found a bench to perch on. It overlooked the city and I let out a hearty sigh as soon as my backside touched the seat, thinking how Owen was out there somewhere in that big wide space.

That also happened to be the moment that I decided I would unleash Owen — or try to unleash myself from him maybe.

Daisy flopped down in front of me, angled so that she, too, could appreciate the view, and she stretched her back legs out far behind her in that way that made me laugh, and made her look about two inches taller than she actually was when upright. Of course I missed Owen from the scene — but I was reminded in the moments, too, that Daisy and I had actually been just fine before we'd met Owen and Collie.

'And we'll be just fine after,' I said as I leaned forward to scratch at the top of her head.

I would throw away Benji's business card when I got home, too. Nan would be beside herself with disappointment — 'Nell, he's a doctor!' But he didn't have a dog and, frankly, even if he did have a dog, he'd come strolling into our lives at exactly the wrong time.

I dropped down from the bench and sat on the hard earth next to Daisy. I ran my hand along the rough of her back and finished with an ear tickle that made her grumble softly with delight, and a laugh escaped me. *A good view and the bestest of dogs. What more could a woman in her thirties need?* I was sure Nan would have a firm and no doubt unsavoury answer to the question.

But for now, it felt like Daisy and I had just enough.

CHAPTER THIRTEEN: NELL

The date was ringed in red on my calendar even though it didn't need to be. Like Christmas or the time of the month when my period should arrive, there were certain dates for which my brain was hard-wired. The workday had been spent on autopilot with a coat-hanger smile fixed in place and my best telephone voice, which I only usually reserved for consultations with my doctor. But those fixtures had got me through the day without any explosive outbursts. Outbursts that, historically, have ranged from screaming in someone's face all the way through to sobbing at the checkout in Tesco because for the only time in my life, I had cash at a counter that only accepted cards.

So having clawed my way through to 4.45 p.m., at which time I decided to start wiping down the shop's kitchen and neatening the shelves, I thought I deserved a hearty pat on the back for having not unhinged my jaws at any point and swallowed a customer whole — especially that pillock who had come in asking where the specialist travel books were, and then complained that the book he wanted was out of stock. I offered to order it, I took his name and I took his grumbles throughout — and I managed to bite my tongue, too. A second pat on the back earned.

At the end of it all, Daisy and I went for a shorter walk than usual to make sure we could get to Nan's on time. Though after stopping to buy a ridiculous amount of cream cakes — that would no doubt be surplus to demands, owing to Nan having likely made her own — we wound up being ten minutes late all the same. We rounded the corner into her road and we were a mere eight strides away when I spotted . . .

'Bollocks.'

Aunt Eileen and Uncle Myles's car sat bang outside Nan's front door. She hadn't told me they were coming — probably owing to the fact that I wouldn't have come if I'd known, which would be Nan's weak defence when questioned about her decision-making later. Eileen was Mum's sister, so Myles was only my uncle by marriage, a fact that he'd become very vocal about after Mum and Dad died, just in case anyone had thought he'd been personally under any family obligations to take me in. They'd both begun looking at me like I'd been a Dickensian orphan and, in the years since, I wasn't sure that had really stopped. Which was probably why I opted to spend as little time with them as possible. That, and the fact they harboured a not-so-secret theory that had Dad been a better driver, then Mum might still be alive. That was a problematic hypothesis if ever there was one, not least because the car was stationary when the lorry smashed into them.

I swallowed back the sting of that — *you can never unhear, unsee such things* — and called Daisy to one side when we were just three houses away. She looked up at me with wide eyes that looked watery already, and I wondered whether she, too, was near to tears over the thought of spending a night with relatives we hated.

I sucked in a greedy breath and blew out slowly, my hand on my stomach to feel my body move as I did so. 'We've got this, Daisy. We've absolutely got this.'

By the time we'd walked the last handful of strides I felt as though my legs were ready to buckle beneath me. *We haven't got this at all.* I pressed down hard on the bell, followed by two short rings afterwards. Nan hated answering the door to people — lest there were salespeople waiting to throw leaflets at her like wedding-day confetti — so we had our own code for when it was me and Daisy waiting on the other side of the door. I heard the click-click of her walking stick coming along the hallway.

When the door opened, I was waiting with folded arms and a cocked eyebrow.

'Good,' Nan said. 'You spotted their car.'

'You're a sneaky old woman.'

She clipped me with her stick as I walked past her. 'Less of the old. They're your family.'

'Oh, please.' I turned round and spoke in a sharp whisper. 'You hate Myles.'

Nan weighed up the statement with a head tilt, one side, then the other. 'That's a fair argument, Nell, but he is married to my daughter.'

'Yeah, and you're not keen on her either,' I muttered as I trod the length of the hallway. There came another clip with the cane, delivered playfully but I still scrunched up my face in discomfort.

At the end of the hallway I found Eileen and Myles already at the kitchen table, which was neatly laid with Nan's best china. She always made an effort on the anniversary of Mum and Dad's deaths. Eileen was the first to stand and launch herself in my direction with open arms that implied a hug, and I braced for impact like you might on seeing a driver come up too fast behind you — which was a terribly timed comparison. But instead of a hug, she grabbed me by my shoulders and kept me at arm's length.

'Eleanor.'

'It's still Nell.' I smiled. 'How are you doing, Aunt Eileen?' I tried to force her arms to bend, to inflict close contact on her that I knew she'd hate for fear I followed her and Myles home at the end of the night and lingered outside their front door, chanting, 'Please, sir, can I have some more?'

But her elbows were locked — there was no getting closer to the woman.

She rubbed up and down along my upper arms as though warming me. 'Good, good, my darling. How are you?'

'Getting by.' I craned around her to get a look at her husband. When Myles saw me looking his way, he stood, too. 'Uncle Myles, pleasure as always.'

'Nell, always good to see you, kiddo.'

Eileen still held me, a human shield for them both. It wasn't until I gestured with the carrier bag I was holding and said, 'I'd better get these in the fridge,' — that she finally let me go.

'What did you bring?' Nan asked as she scooted back to her steaming stove.

'Cream cakes. I thought—'

'Oh, El . . . Nell, you shouldn't have. We've brought a homemade white chocolate cheesecake for everyone to share. The place we get them from is just stunning, isn't it, Myles?'

'Stunning, yes,' he mumbled.

I laboured over their idea of "homemade" but decided not to say anything. 'That's okay, Daisy and I can always take them home and eat them one after the other in front of the television later on.'

Eileen laughed nervously, as though she wasn't sure whether I was being serious or not. I was.

'Do you want a drink, Nell?'

'I'll grab one, thanks, Nan. Do you want one?' I saw her side-eye me. 'Does anyone want one, actually, while I'm at the fridge?'

'Sparkling water, please,' Eileen said as she sat back down at the table, joined by Myles — who also wanted sparkling water.

'I'm not sure . . .'

'It's okay, Nell.' Nan caught my hesitation. 'They brought their own.'

She and I swapped a knowing look and I managed a smile then. 'Of course. Will you want any ice with that?'

'As it comes, thanks, my darling.'

'How's the little bookshop coming along, Nell?' Myles asked and I practically felt the pat on the head that came along with the question. When I turned around with a drink in each hand, I saw him giving Daisy a little pat-pat on the head as though he'd never stroked a dog before in his life.

'It's doing well, thanks, Uncle Myles. I've got a good—'

'Mum, do you have much to do with the place?' Eileen interrupted me. It was a festering wound in the family that Nan had given me money towards setting the shop up. Eileen thought that, with Mum gone, all of Nan's money would go directly to her when she passed away. *Morbid cow.* So once she found out that my "inheritance money" had come to me already, there had been hot words passed between her and Nan. I told Eileen it was an investment, to try to apply aloe vera to the wound. But all that had actually done was to force this recycled line of questioning, asked over and again whenever we were all together — and I wagered she likely asked something similar when I wasn't around to defend myself either.

'Oh, I'm there every other day, aren't I, Nell?' I looked up in time to catch Nan's wink. 'Get yourselves settled, anyway. This food is nearly ready.'

Nan served a feast of roast chicken with *all* the trimmings. There were as many as four different types of potatoes — *so it must be a special occasion* — including dauphinoise, which had been Mum's favourite. I helped her to manhandle the various serving dishes to the table while her guests sat there and did nothing at all, bar continue their chatter about the bookshop and launch various questions in my direction that Nan helped me to field. I politely batted them back, asking about their own jobs — Myles was an insurance salesman and Eileen a teacher — and their daily lives. I absorbed a solid two per cent of the information that they shared.

Nan winked at me from across the table while Myles regaled us with a recent hiccup at the office. I knew that she knew I was making an effort — which was really all that counted.

Nan served up a plate of chicken for Daisy that was placed in the corner of the kitchen while we all tucked into our own portions. But true to form, once Daisy had finished her meal she saw fit to offer assistance around the table, in case any of us needed help with ours. Of course, this was largely mine and Nan's fault. During the average meal, neither of us were shy about "accidentally" dropping one thing or another on the floor and ushering Daisy over to sweep up. We'd set a precedent. And even now, while Eileen was frowning over the behaviour, I noticed Nan cough into her hand and not-so-subtly send a piece of chicken breast flying out of her palm and onto the floor where Daisy waited.

'Do you really think that's right?' Eileen said, cutting across her husband who had been in the middle of another dead-boring work story.

'I'm sorry?' Nan answered, playing ignorant.

But Eileen turned on me instead. 'If that dog of yours can't behave while we're eating, should she even be here at all?'

I set my cutlery down. 'You think she's misbehaving?' *I'll show you misbehaving . . .*

'Well, look at how it's sniffing around for scraps.'

'She.'

'Okay, look at how *she* is sniffing around for scraps. Honestly, Nell, I would have thought you'd taught her better than that, and I'm surprised you're standing for it either, Mum.'

Nan rolled her eyes, rested her elbow on the table and cradled her forehead. It was an anticipatory move, of course, because she knew that a snap like this from Eileen would lead to . . .

'Aunt Eileen, you are absolutely right.' I was up and out of my seat. 'Daisy, come on, we shouldn't be here.'

Eileen laughed, a smug, sanctimonious teacher laugh. 'Eleanor—'

'Eileen.' I tried to borrow from her patronising tone. 'That dog so happens to be the best thing in my life on any given day.' Daisy fixed her stare on Eileen then, whether through her own smugness or just from general support, it was impossible to say — but I'm sure I saw her attempt a dog's answer to an eyebrow raise. 'Her, and Nan, are about all that get me through these godforsaken anniversaries. And if Daisy isn't welcome at this meal, then frankly, I think it's best we both go.'

'Nell . . .'

'Honestly, Nan, it's fine.'

'Let her go.' Eileen waved a hand. 'If she wants to act like a child.'

'I do, and I don't need permission for it.' I tucked my seat back under the table and walked around to Nan's side. 'Nan, I'll call you later. Thank you. What we *both* had of dinner was lovely.' I kissed her forehead. 'I love you.'

'Nell.' She made a grab for my arm. 'You really don't need to . . .'

I nodded. 'Oh, but I do. Eileen, Myles, always a pleasure. Come on, Daisy, we're going to buy a bucket of KFC and eat it off the kitchen floor. Bye, everyone.'

'Love you, girls!' Nan shouted after us in her usual way and I was sure I heard her giggling ever so slightly on our way out.

* * *

Nan called me the following morning and asked if I wanted a do-over of the an anniversary meal, just the two of us. 'I promise I won't invite any other family members,' she said and I laughed. There were no more *to* invite, unless she was planning to bring along my grandparents from Dad's side — which would never happen, on account of her relationship with them being about as good as my relationship with Eileen. Grandpa and Grandma, on Dad's side, had whittled down their anniversary phone calls over the years, but they always sent a letter and in return I'd send a card, complete with pictures of Daisy. Those were our niceties done until

Christmastime. And I *longed* for that to be the extent of my relationship with Eileen and Myles from now on, too.

'You're going to try to get me to make up with them at some point, aren't you?'

There was a long pause down the phone line. 'No?'

'Ha, nice try. I can't imagine I'm their favourite person at the moment, after yesterday's outburst.'

'Well, I can't imagine I'm their favourite person either. Shall we get jackets? We could get a small T-shirt made for Daisy, too.'

'I love you, Nan.'

'If you love someone, have dinner with them.'

I laughed. 'Tomorrow night?'

'Perfect. Chicken?'

'Nan, you're such a—' The bell jangled from the front of the shop. 'Two seconds, Nan, there's a customer.' I trod my way from the Classics to the contemporary romances and prepared to fix my happy seller face in place. 'Morning! Welcome to Green Fields. If there's anything you . . .'

And there he was, his shoulders scrunched up and his hands buried in his pockets, looking every bit the caught schoolboy who'd come to apologise for bad behaviour.

'Nan, I have to go.'

'Is everything—'

'Owen is here.'

'Take no nonsense, Nellie!'

There was no nonsense to take, I realised then. I only needed to take a long look at him and suddenly, it all made sense. It was Collie. Of course, it had been Collie.

CHAPTER FOURTEEN: OWEN

I just looked at her and I knew she knew. If there had been any doubt in Nell's mind, then the way in which I folded onto the floor to greet Daisy before sobbing uncontrollably was a surefire way to seal the certainty — and perhaps lose myself even more points than I'd no doubt lost in the last ten days.

I'd thought so many times of going to the park to meet them both, to explain, but also the thought of, *Christ, all those dogs running around* . . . it was enough to break a grown man's heart. But then the way in which Daisy had balanced her legs on mine to crane an inch or two closer to me wasn't doing my heart any favours either. She flopped the dead weight of her head at an awkward angle, somehow part balanced on my thighs and part pressed into my stomach, and once there she let out a sincere and sad sigh that was so deep I felt it move through us both at once. I had my head pressed down close to her and I was all too aware that I was dripping tears onto her wrinkled head and while I *desperately* wanted to care, I also didn't have it in me.

Nell probably hates you by now anyway, I thought, not for the first time in the last week. The fact that she hadn't thrown me out of the shop the second I'd walked in seemed promising

— or rather, another marker of her all-round compassion and kindness if nothing else.

Then, as though she'd been privy to this run-on sentence of sad theorisations, I heard something like a huff, something like a laugh from Nell's side of the shop floor. I looked up in time to see her arms drop in a semi-defeated gesture.

'I don't even know how you take your tea.'

I managed a wan smile even though I was uncomfortably aware that tears and snot still flowed. But after a week of telling myself to "man up" while staring through photo albums of Collie and slowly packing away her things, I'd come to the conclusion that anyone who wanted to be in proximity to me for the foreseeable was just going to have to suck it up and accept the waterworks. I reached into my front pocket to free a packet of tissues — I was bulk-buying by then — and was hit with a muscle memory of poo bags, treats and, more than once, the squeaky innards from a toy. They'd all made appearances in my pockets over the years, but now . . . I forced out slow breath while I unfolded a fresh tissue, and hoped my voice would hold long enough to answer Nell.

'Do you have sugar?'

'Oh, my nan is going to love you.' No sooner had she said it, her eyes widened. I half expected her to slap her palms across her mouth as though she was part of a children's sitcom that called for over-acting. 'Not that you're going to meet my nan. Not that . . . I mean, you're not *not* going to meet my nan . . . Buggering hell. How many sugars?'

Any shadow of doubt that had lingered over my decision to come here fell away then. 'Two.'

Nell nodded and turned away, I assumed towards the kitchen. But she'd hardly managed two steps before she turned again. 'Do you mind a builder's mug?'

How else would you serve it? 'Ah, no?'

'Okay, okay, that's . . . okay.'

And with that she was gone, the next sign of life being the sharp whistle of a kettle from a far-off back room. Meanwhile, Daisy and I stayed fixed to the spot, holding each other in grief and gratitude — the saddest set of shared feelings.

* * *

Nell introduced me to Eloise as her "dog walker friend", and the fact that I took umbrage with that probably spoke volumes. It was painful twofold: firstly, because I still so desperately wanted to be more than all of the above and secondly, because I was no longer a dog walker. Though as I trod around the shop with Daisy at my heel, it felt remarkably like being a dog walker again and I could have cried with the delight of it — but crying in front of Nell for a fourth time probably wouldn't go down too well, no matter what she'd said about the first three outbursts.

She'd told me that Eloise was her lunchtime lady who covered the shop while Nell grabbed a rushed sandwich in the backroom, but she could ask her to cover for a little while longer today. 'You really don't need to,' I'd said, though I felt overcome with something warm and tingly at Nell's answer.

'Of course I do.'

Now, Daisy and I both turned at Nell's voice. 'I'm going to leave Daisy here, if that's okay?'

We soon saw she was talking to Eloise, who nodded along like a woman who would have agreed to anything. She struck me as the type of older lady who had seen so much in her time that little would fazed her now, and I wondered whether that's who Nell would grow into.

Daisy trotted over to the opposite side of the shop as though following a set of instructions that hadn't been given, and I tried to imagine Collie *ever* doing something quite so obedient.

'Ready?' Nell asked as she straightened the collar on her denim jacket. I'd never seen her in workwear before. I'd never even stopped to imagine what her workwear might be, having assumed that when she said she rolled straight from the shop to the dog park, there hadn't been a clothing-change pit stop between. But looking at her now, I couldn't help but wonder. The *Ssh, I'm reading* T-shirt suited her down to the ground, though, and the way she'd tucked it into jeans gave her something of the 1990s Cool Kid. Either way, she was every bit as beautiful as every other time I'd seen her. And for the first time since losing Coll, I felt the balm of something — *the balm of Nell?* — soothe an ache that had been spreading through me. *Was it romantic to compare a woman to Tiger Balm?*, I wondered as I followed her out of the shop and back onto the main street. *No, no, it isn't, don't say that.*

Shall I compare thee to an aloe vera rub?
Thou art more lovely and—

'Are you thinking about Collie?'

My head snapped up. 'No, I wasn't, actually,' My admission came with a heady mixture of relief and guilt. 'Which is about the first time in a week I've managed not to.'

'I can't believe it, Owen, it's just so . . .'

'I know.'

And I really did know. Collie had been fine, or seemed fine, when I'd left for work in the morning. Kevin had checked on her part way through the morning, too. He said she'd seemed quiet, but not worryingly so. I hadn't been able to spot her on the baby-cams, despite my best sleuthing, but I'd thought that only meant she was in the spare room, or my office even! There were unavoidable blind spots in the house. But then somewhere along the line the beagle had got the better of her. She'd eaten something that she shouldn't have done and everything started to . . . twist. I forced out a long breath then but I was winded when Nell stopped walking suddenly, grabbed me by the arm and pulled me into a hug. Despite the beginner's tension — I hadn't exactly been prepped for so much contact — I found that I relaxed into it, my arms wrapped so tightly around her that I was sure I heard the soft crack of vertebrae.

'I'm sorry, but it sounded like you really needed it.'

Her words hit the spot between my neck and shoulder, and I'm sure I felt my own spine straighten out a touch at

117

the heat. 'Thank you, Nell.' I eased out of the hug then and managed to hold eye contact with her without wanting to cry. 'Thank you.'

'Any time. The deli place is just up here?' She pointed. 'Have you managed to eat?'

'Bits.' I'd somehow managed to string two frozen pizzas out across a period of six days having only cooked one quarter at a time, because that's about all my stomach could handle in a single go. Whenever I tried to eat I only imagined the shark-at-tack glide of Collie's eyes, appearing slowly from the other side of the dining table, or over the top of my slobby I'm-eating-in-the-living-room tray. The dog had been an absolute dustbin. I would never ever not blame myself, because I should have been more careful. But even the vet admitted that dogs could pick up anything on their travels — on walks, but just as easily around the house — and he suspected that's what Collie had done, especially after I mentioned the excessive flower-bed investiga-tions she liked to conduct. More tests would have clarified what the blockage was specifically, but I couldn't stand the thought of her being there, of them . . . She'd passed by the time I'd got her to the vets, somehow peaceful, blanketed on the backseat of the car. Even though I knew the vets would have been gen-tle with her still, I couldn't quite bring myself to let them go looking around. My breath caught in my throat again then, and I was thankful Nell was too busy to notice, holding open the door to the deli for a party that was leaving — none of whom said thank you.

'Ignorant arses,' I said — forgetting whose company I was in.

Nell groaned ahead of me. 'Agreed.'

I registered that we had that in common. Though Nell and I weren't exactly strangers, I was minute by minute becoming painfully aware of the divorce from where we were then, to where we were, now. With no dogs to chase after, no muddy hills to slide down, and no clear parameters between my half of the city and hers — what if she ended up thinking I was a total tit?

'What are you having?' I pulled my phone out in a quick-draw move to pay.

'Oh, honestly, let me?'

'It would really make me feel better if I bought you a sandwich and a coffee, and maybe even cake.'

Nell narrowed her eyes. It was a low blow, playing the *it would make me feel better* card, but I had to hope she might let me get away with it. 'Don't even think about playing that a second time.' Though there was something jovial in her tone, I could tell that she meant it, too. She turned around to peruse the board. 'The special sounds good?'

I scanned the blackboard script and spotted it: *Roasted vegetable panini with side salad and slaw.* 'Are you invested?'

'I think I am.'

'We'll take two of those, please? I'll take a Coke Zero, too. And for the lady?'

She smiled and I thought I saw a flicker of a blush. 'Tea, please, splash of milk, no sugar.'

I tapped my phone to the card-reader and thanked the waitress. With the promise of incoming food, we shuffled around those already eating and found ourselves a window seat. It wasn't a proper table, but one of those space-saving tabletops that runs the length of the window, with stools punctuated along the way. It wasn't exactly the romantic, candlelit dinner that I'd imagined with our eyes locking over an open but entirely safe flame. Having said that, it did at least give us both somewhere to look if we soon decided that we couldn't stand the sight of the other — which was still a very real concern.

I corrected myself. *You're concerned she'll feel that towards you.* I'd already assumed that I could never feel that way towards Nell — and I couldn't even blame the dizzy lows of grief for making me latch on to her like that, because I'd felt it all along.

'I really thought you'd just gone,' she said, looking out the window, and I felt a twist of guilt so severe that I wasn't sure I'd manage the sandwich.

'I wanted to come and see you both . . . in the park, but—'

'Oh my goodness.' She cut across me. 'Don't even. I wouldn't have been able to stand the sight of the place either. I *completely* understand, now I know.' She looked at me, abandoning the safe view of the window. 'I'm just glad you came to the shop, you know? Like . . .' She hesitated a second or two before saying, 'Just *really* glad.'

I dropped my head and rubbed at the back of my neck. The skin there was nervous-hot and I was self-conscious of the prospect that there would be a childish red flush moving up my neck to my face by now. 'I didn't even have your number, and I could have called the shop, but . . . I don't know . . .' I laughed then, but it came out as a nervous noise. 'I figured just randomly turning up on your doorstep would be easier, apparently.'

Nell held her hand out to me then, palm up, and I faltered before placing my hand in hers. There was an embarrassing heat spreading through my whole body and I thought there was no way I wasn't red all the way up to my gills now. And the heat only worsened when Nell spluttered a laugh.

'Your phone?'

'Oh. Of course.' I reached into my back pocket to pull it free and then unlock it before handing it over. Everything in me shuddered at once with touched-for-the-first-time nerves and I tried foolishly hard to steady the feeling, only to realise seconds into my masterplan that I was in fact just holding my breath, which would no doubt make me look like even *more* of a weirdo if Nell happened to notice.

'I saved it as Nell and Daisy,' she said, handing it back over to me. 'And there's a flower emoji. I hope that's okay.'

'That's perfect.'

'Hot sandwiches coming through, my lovelies.' The waitress leaned over us to set a tray with our food and drinks down on the tabletop. I found I was craning round her as she unloaded everything, inherently unwilling to give up any seconds that might be spent looking at Nell. 'Anything else I can get for either of you?'

'I think we're all good, thanks very much.' Nell lifted the lid on her teapot to check the brewing status of the tea, before swishing it about with her teaspoon. 'Okay, just so I know where we're at . . .' There was another gut churn that I worried might be severe enough to be audible but if it was, Nell was too polite to comment on it. 'Do you want to talk about . . . everything, or do you want to avoid everything?'

I had spent the last week on bereavement leave from work oscillating between these very two points. So far I'd managed to lie with my head in Collie's bed and bawl my eyes out, and take six bags of clothes to my local shelter donation point (most of which I'd probably wind up re-buying somewhere down the line). I'd rearranged the living room furniture and I'd stripped the wallpaper in my spare bedroom, which served no other purpose than housing my crap that I hadn't found space for anywhere else in my home. Though it was now all piled on the upstairs landing, waiting for me to decide how to redecorate the walls that, in their ragged and stripped state, were a physical representation of exactly how I felt. Then of course, there'd been crying in the kitchen, crying in the garden and crying in the bathtub, too. And all of that ugly grieving meant there was only one way that I could possibly answer Nell's very kind and gentle question.

'I don't know.'

'That's okay.' She bit off a chunk of sandwich and spoke around it, and on anyone else it would have been disgusting enough for me to want to get up and leave the table. Somehow, on her, it was just lovely. 'How about we start talking about other stuff, and if you find you want to talk about it, that's okay, and if other stuff is enough of a conversation starter, then we can just stick with that?' She took another bite and covered her mouth as she chewed.

I picked a shred of onion out from the edge of my toasted bread and laboured over putting it into my mouth, as though I'd never felt the texture or known the taste of the thing before. 'That sounds like a good approach.'

'Cool, let's start with something easy?'

'Even better.'

'What's your ideal first date with a woman?'

Oh, this is so not easy . . .

CHAPTER FIFTEEN: NELL

Owen's favourite cake was lemon drizzle. His favourite sandwich filling was tuna mayo with red onion and cheese, preferably heated through so the cheese would melt a little, but he wasn't going to throw a wobbly if there wasn't a sandwich press on hand for the job. He also preferred wholemeal bread complete with seeds because he thought the texture was more interesting than plain old white bread. He loved Jelly Belly beans and could, by his own admission or boast (I couldn't tell which), eat an entire sharing bag without batting an eyelid. He enjoyed all sorts of cheese crackers indiscriminately but he hated having them *with* cheese, on account of it being "too awkward to keep everything together". He liked skin-on fries and hearty meaty pizzas, and garlic bread *with* melted cheese and a thin layer of mayonnaise over the top if it was available.

Over one single coffee non-date, I had become a walking, talking encyclopaedia of all things Owen. And it wasn't just food. I knew his middle name was Max — his dad had wanted Marx, apparently owing to his deep-rooted passion for German economists, but his mother had put her foot down — and that his favourite colour was navy blue and that his favourite song was "Iris" by the Goo Goo Dolls even though it made him cry — the latter part of that fact being something that I had since been sworn to secrecy on.

It turned out that my not-so-subtle first-date question hadn't been as endearingly cheeky as I'd hoped it would be. No sooner had I asked, tears pricked Owen's eyes again, and I found that I was apologising profusely while throwing napkins at him. It transpired that his perfect first date would be a dog walk followed by a picnic. *The same as mine.* But I hadn't said that because it didn't seem like the time. I'd banked *all* of his favourite foods, though, which was something we talked about endlessly. If one date became two dates, or five dates, or — *marriage!* I dropped my head against the shop counter and knocked, knocked, knocked some sense into myself. *Don't be that girl, Nell, don't be that romcom girl who plans marriage* before *a first date.* All the same, though, if one date became more, then I wanted to have a hit list of food for when he was ready, so I could be picnic-prepared.

To no one's surprise, while Owen and I had *a lot* of empty spaces where new knowledge might fit, there was an awful lot we knew about each other already, too. So while I quizzed him on food and the minute details of colour choices, middle names and music, I was also asking whether he'd managed to escape dinner with his family over the last week, how his nieces and nephews were, whether his dick boss had been understanding about him needing time off. There was a strange dislocation happening between dog-walk dating and . . . whatever was happening in the deli shop that lunchtime. And I wondered whether that would continue, if we started to unpack more about each other. Or whether we'd soon find that without the dog walks, there wasn't anything of interest to unpack at all.

'You mightn't like me when I'm not plodding around a green space with Daisy,' I said jokingly when we arrived back at the shop that day, before I launched into an afternoon of daydreaming and mispricing books.

Owen shrugged and said, 'Or I might like you more.'

I'd dined out on that line for days. I thought if I looked hard enough through the romantic comedy section of the shop that I'd likely find it printed somewhere already.

123

'You look like a smitten woman,' a customer remarked on their approach to the counter. I don't know what face I made but she laughed. 'Nothing to be embarrassed about either. Young love?'

I rang up her three detective novels and gave her a complimentary bookmark. 'Something like that. That'll be £27.97, thank you.'

'Make the most of it, my girl,' she said as she ferreted through what sounded like boundless amounts of loose change in her purse. 'You never know when The One is going to roll around.'

I looked under the counter to where Daisy was sleeping and smiled. I had a pretty good idea of when that had happened. 'Thanks ever so much.' I handed over her change with what I knew must look like a gooey sort of smile.

But . . . *maybe Owen could be The Two.*

* * *

Daisy was in her kitchen bed, blissfully distracted by the new toy I'd given her. *Nothing to do with guilt, nope, nothing to do with it* . . . I hated leaving her alone for any period of time, but also felt sure that given the extra fuss I rained down on her whenever it happened, that she probably didn't mind that much at all — not least because it didn't happen all that often anyway.

'Will I do?' I asked and she didn't even glance up. I went into the living room to check my reflection for the seventy-fourth time. My hair was still fixed in place, precariously pinned around a large mesh doughnut, and I reapplied my lipstick for what I guessed was the third, maybe even fourth time. I was wearing a vintage-style dress covered in sunflowers and cinched at the waist, because I knew how to play to my strengths. I managed one more twirl, admiring the way the dress kicked out around me, at the exact moment the front doorbell went.

'Holy shit.' I forced out a long, slow breath on my way to the kitchen. 'I love you more than life itself and I'll be back soon. Be good.' There only came a "ach-gnaw-ach" sound in response as Daisy carried on working her way through the hide. 'Good, glad to know I'm loved.'

I grabbed my bag en route to the hallway, took another big breath and snatched the door open before I could give myself too long to linger on the action.

'Wow.'

'Good . . . Oh.' I broke off, noticing the bunch of sunflowers Owen was holding.

'You see, I sensed you'd be wearing sunflowers.' He handed them over with a boyish, nervous smile, and I wondered whether it was too early in the night to kiss him. *You've basically been dating for nearly eight months but, sure, start asking those big questions now.*

'I'll just . . .' I took the flowers. 'I'll just rest these in some water. I'll be back.' And seconds later I was. In an act of bravery, I leaned forward and kissed Owen on the cheek. 'Thank you, for the flowers.'

'Any time, honestly.' He turned and offered me his arm and I found something laughable about the gesture, but I went along with it all the same. Once the front door was locked and double-locked, I linked arms with him and let him lead me away from home and back towards the bustle of the city. 'I've booked us a table at Pablo's — do you know it?'

'*Do* I? I've basically got a loyalty card for the place.' Though I only ever ordered through their takeaway menu because I didn't care how good a pizza place was, their food would always taste better on my sofa.

'Perfect, I got the first thing right,' he said, his tone jovial.

'First two things. You brought flowers.'

'Ah, an extra point for the scoreboard.'

'Who do you think you're competing against?' I asked with a smile.

Owen hesitated before he answered. 'Maybe the version of me you've been imagining.'

There was something both sad and sweet about the answer. I squeezed closer to him, pressing my upper arm against his in

125

what turned into a soft nudge. 'I've just been working from this version for months now.' And then I swallowed back vomit because — *how are we being* this *cute with each other already?*

It was the dreaded dislocation again. The awkward angles of being on a first date with someone who I had shared daily life with, every day, for months already. There was the familiarity of asking about work on the walk to the restaurant, coupled with the surprise of Owen holding the door for me, and even pulling out my chair. There was the eye-roll paired with a playful grin when I asked how his family were, as though I already knew them and their oddball behaviours all too well, coupled with the surprise that he ordered red wine rather than a beer. My bank of Owen information was constantly being updated as though learning him anew, when I had only half known him to begin with.

I drained the dregs of my first glass of wine, which gave Owen the opportunity to ask, 'This is weird, isn't it?' I choked on the swallow. 'Shit, sorry.' He rushed for a napkin but I'd already found my own. 'I meant, *good* weird. Weird as in, I'm on a first date with you, but I think I can already predict the pizza you're going to order.'

I widened my eyes at the boldness. 'That's mighty presumptuous of you, mister.' I reached under the table for my bag, pulled out my purse and set a single pound coin on the table. 'Come on then, place your bets. What pizza am I going to order?'

'Hang on a minute now,' he said while rummaging through his own change. 'You might go ahead and *say* that's not what you're going to order once I've said it, just so you can make away with the winnings.'

I looked at our two pound coins side by side on the table. 'There's a good chance of that happening — you're right. Excuse me.' I caught a waiter as he rushed past the table. 'Do you happen to have a pen I can borrow?'

The young man wordlessly handed over the pen that was clipped to his order pad.

'I'm going to write it down . . . here.' I snatched at the napkin that was ring-marked with my lipstick already. 'And then I'll keep it covered until you've said.' I hastily scribbled down my selection and then flipped the note over.

Owen closed his eyes and took in a theatrical deep breath as though he were tapping into some psychic bond, and a dork laugh spluttered out of me. 'You're going to have . . . pesto, pepper and sweetcorn calzone but you're going to add a meat filling to the order.'

'And what meat filling will I be adding?'

Owen narrowed his eyes and stared hard at me for a second, and not for the first time I felt the overwhelming urge to kiss him. 'Tuna.'

I love you. I flipped over the napkin and slammed it down on the table. 'Whatever, it was an easy guess.'

Owen collected up the two pound coins. 'What will I do with my winnings?'

'Evil genius fund?' I said jokingly, and the sound of him laughing made my stomach feel shamefully warm.

'Actually.' He pushed them back into the centre of the table. 'I'll add to it and that'll be the tip for tonight.'

'Are you always this lovely?'

'Yes.' He took another measured sip of his wine. We were both onto our second glasses now and it was clear that the alcohol had loosened our tongues. 'When I was a young boy, a wicked witch visited my parents' village and cursed me to a life of being lovely, and she said I'd be destined to live out my existence as a lonely, lovely boy, until I found someone equally as lovely. And now here we are.'

'Ready to order, kids?'

'Yes,' we both said in unison and the older gentleman standing at our table laughed.

'Aren't you two cute? What'll it be?' He was poised ready to take down our choices. Owen went with something that sounded like it had enough meat involved to feed Daisy for a week, and he took the liberty of ordering mine, too. I gave him a hooded look and then excused myself to go to the bathroom, snatching my bag from the floor as I stood.

'Sure thing. Nell.' Owen called me back. 'Did you want garlic bread?'

The classic love story: *I'll eat something that stinks if you'll eat something that stinks.*

'Absolutely, always,' I answered, then hurried on my way. I'd already pulled my phone free by the time I was locking myself in a cubicle, and scrolling for Lucia's number. I didn't care what she was doing, what the time difference was, I needed best friend counsel. I needed someone to tell me . . .

'Hey, you gorgeous thing, shouldn't you be on a date right now?' Lucia had stayed up late two nights running to talk me through the excited nerves of an actual, three-dimensional date with Owen — that didn't involve dogs. 'Things not going well?'

'Too well,' I answered in a whisper — something we'd considered as a possibility. 'I feel like I already know him, like I'm on a date with someone I . . . know.' I slammed my palm against my forehead.

'That's because you are.' She matched my whispered tone but managed to make it sarcastic. 'Oh,' she said, her voice levelling out to something louder. 'I see where this is going. I *absolutely* see where this is going.'

'You do?'

'I do.'

'And?'

'And I think you should.'

Of course, I'd known that I could count on Lucia for the answer. If I'd wanted someone to tell me *not* to sleep with Owen then I would have called Nan.

'Thank you, babe.'

'Any time. Just let me know you're safe.'

'I will, I'll—'

'Wait, Nell, what restaurant did he book in the end?'

'Pablo's.' Lucia groaned down the phone at my answer. She knew all too well the allure of hand-stretched pizza,

128

caramelised garlic bread toppings, and homemade gelato. 'Right, that's it. It's a definite yes from me.'

I told Lucia I loved her no fewer than three times before hurrying to end the call and head back to the table, lest Owen think I was having a blow-up of irritable bowel syndrome behind the scenes. But of course, he knew exactly what had been happening, and no sooner had I landed back in the seat opposite him, he smiled.

'Lucia, or your nan?'

I barked a laugh. I could hear the wine in me. 'Neither.'

'Liar.'

And he actually *winked* at me. A cheeky, sexy, lovely *wink* and I felt my stomach rollercoaster dip and my chest hummingbird flutter, and I decided there and then that we'd *basically* been dating for eight months anyway — and that was *absolutely* long enough for any girl to wait.

CHAPTER SIXTEEN: OWEN

To be clear, it had been a *long* time since I had woken up in a bedroom that wasn't my own. Nell's room was pale yellow and her curtains the thin veil kind that let in the beginnings of sunlight. And that's how I woke up: curled up, facing a window scene that I didn't recognise, with the start of sunrise on my face. For the first time in nearly two weeks, I let out an easy breath to start the day. There was the ache of Collie — there would always be the ache of Collie, without a wet snout and wild ears to wake up to — but underneath it there was a kind of ease, or a soothing. I took another slow breath and shifted gently in the bed, to try to gauge the weight of another body behind me. As I shifted, I softly knocked against something that I knew must be Nell, and another slow breath drifted out.

It hadn't been more one person's idea than the other's. Somehow, without saying a word, we'd both decided that I would go home with Nell after I'd settled our dinner tab. She'd protested, pushed and shoved to try to reach the card machine, but I'd managed to beat her to the punch. I'd been in the middle of telling her what a beautiful night I'd had — cursing myself for the use of the word "beautiful" in lieu of something *slightly* more manly — and that's when she'd leaned forward and kissed me — a hard, teenager kiss with an *I'll-die-if-I-don't* force. And I remember thinking again, *This is just beautiful.* On the walk back to hers we'd taken regular kiss stops as though feeding something deep and urgent, but when we'd arrived on the doorstep there'd been a sudden hesitation, on my part.

'We don't have to, if you don't . . .'

'Oh, I *want* to,' I said, reassuring her. 'But . . . you've been drinking, and I don't want . . . in the morning, I don't want.'

Nell kissed me again then, catching the unspoken segments of sentence. 'You've been drinking, too. And I've spent the best part of eight very sober months wanting to do this.'

After that everything was watercolour — until now, until waking up with the warmth of another body next to me. I pushed back ever so slightly again, torn between not wanting to disturb her but also wanting to be as close as I could. I didn't know what time it was, what time she'd need to leave for work, or even when she'd expect me to leave. My clothes might already be folded and waiting for me in the bathroom for a hurried exit. And every cell of me wanted to hold on to this quiet closeness for as long as I could. Because I'd been waiting for it for so long.

'Ahem.'

My eyes snapped open. It was Nell, it had to be. But I was equally as sure that the noise hadn't come from next to me. Instead, it was notably further away. Though I didn't quite throw myself over, I made a quick move to roll around all the same and that's when I saw it: the perfectly wrinkled face, the offbeat set of teeth, the squat and twitching ears.

'She's used to getting in bed with me,' Nell said from the doorway, a mug in each hand. 'I'm so sorry.' I could tell she was on the cusp of a laugh. Meanwhile, I was somewhere between bawling my eyes out — for a change — and laughing along with her.

Without knowing which set of feelings happened to be in the lead, I took what felt like a more natural route out of the situation. I leaned forward and kissed Daisy square on

131

the nose, and she woke with such an abruptness that it was a wonder she didn't go cross-eyed at the sight of me.

'Oh, she . . .' Nell petered out as Daisy huffed and puffed and pushed herself up and off the bed. That's when Nell's laugh cracked into a full giggle and I felt a tenderness move through the whole of my body.

Jesus, you are beautiful. Should I tell you that?

'She's not a fan of kisses on the nose.' Nell walked around my side of the bed to set down a steaming mug of something before crossing back round to her own. She clambered onto the spot where Daisy had been lying, but instead of getting back into bed properly she sat with her legs tucked beneath her, her hands cradling the heat of her drink. 'I hope you don't have a special morning tea ritual or anything?'

I smiled. 'Hot, wet and with sugar. That's my ritual through all tea-drinking experiences.'

'In which case, I got it right.'

I struggled upright in the bed, then leaned my head against the wall behind me. 'Last night was . . .' In the moment I spent searching for the right word, Nell's face dropped. 'No, no, not bad! Jesus, *not* bad, in the slightest.' I tried to think, think hard and quicker. 'There isn't a word for it, I don't think. But you're the wordy one, maybe you can find a word. But it was . . .'

'Worth the wait?' Nell asked.

'And then some.'

Nell sipped at her drink, which left too much of a dialogue opening.

I found myself blurting out the thing I'd been nervous to say. 'You're really beautiful, Nell.'

She spluttered hot tea over the covers. There were even a few flecks on my T-shirt, that I made a show of brushing down. 'Even when you're spitting hot tea over me,' I said jokingly.

'I'm sorry. But really? Beautiful? I'm not sure I'm deserving of that on a good day, never mind first thing in the morning. What's beautiful about any of this?'

Nell gestured from top to toe, starting with her wild waves scraped into a messy up-do; her Disney villains T-shirt that I imagined her grabbing in a hurry; the shorts with a too-busy pattern; the tattoos that I hadn't known existed until last night. I ummed and ahhed over my answer.

'I think the most beautiful thing about the lot of it is getting to see it—' I waved my arm around to broadly gesture at the entire room — 'in this context at all.'

'That's a very smooth answer.'

'I'm a very smooth guy.' But neither of us could keep a straight face when pitted against the blatant lie, and soon we were both back to childish laughter. 'Seriously.' I reached around for my tea as I spoke. 'Are you okay this morning? You don't . . . wish it hadn't happened?'

'No, you crazy idiot, I do not. *Do you?*'

'See above, re. comments about beautiful, worth the wait and so forth. It was . . . everything. I'm just aware it was also a first date.'

'Owen, it wasn't a first date.'

And I knew that she was right. But I also knew that it was a lot of pressure applied *very* quickly while I was nursing an open wound. 'I'm nervous of going headfirst and finding that I can't swim with you, and I *really* want to swim with you, Nell. Does that make any sense?'

She thought about what I'd said for a second and then shuffled forward to close the little distance between us. Her right knee was pressed against the outside of my left thigh and the contact was like static. 'You're grieving and I want to help however I can. We have a . . . strange origin story.' She paused, as though weighing up her phrasing. 'And even though this might be the start of something, I appreciate there's a lot we need to learn outside of our dog walks.' Another laugh escaped her as she added, 'And maybe outside of my bedroom.'

I leaned forward and placed a soft kiss on her cheek. I wanted her all over again, but didn't want to risk undercutting the moment either. I pulled back, but brought her hand with me and gave it two firm squeezes as I spoke. 'Slow and steady?'

'Slow and steady.' She pulled my hand to her mouth and placed a kiss square in the centre of my palm before folding my fingers around it, as though giving me something to hold on to. 'Now drink your tea and get out. Some of us have Saturday jobs . . .'

* * *

Despite having offended her first thing in the morning, Daisy looked to have forgiven me by the time I was getting out of the shower. The door that I'd left closed was now very much open, with a solid twenty kilogram wedge holding it fixed that way, too. I leaned forward and gave her a soft scratch on the head, and she turned her face up towards me in that adoring way that dogs have and — *don't cry while you're at Nell's*. I sucked in a big breath and went in search of my clothes from the night before. They *must* be in the bedroom somewhere — or rather, in the house somewhere, I realised, with a flashback of hardly making it along the hallway before pawing at Nell the night before. Like a perfect hostess, though, when I got back into the bedroom I found my shirt on a coat-hanger already waiting on the door, and my jeans straightened out and waiting at the foot of the bed. I tried to take it as a caring sign, rather than a rushing-me-out-of-the-house one. I'd just dropped my towel and reached for my jeans when I felt something knocking against the outside of my leg: Daisy's head, it turned out. I wrapped the towel around me again and dropped to sit on the floor with her, my back resting against the bed. Daisy scooched in close, closer still, and held a quiet contentment while I rubbed at the spot between her ears, straying down carefully between her eyes now and then, too.

'Collie used to love that,' I said quietly, and I felt my breath catch at the mention of her name. Daisy turned to me, as though understanding what I was saying, and bumped softly against my knee with her wrinkled forehead. 'Do you miss her, too, I wonder?'

'Daisy! Breakfast!' Nell's voice came from downstairs and, somewhat begrudgingly I thought, Daisy pulled away from me and plodded from the room.

I heard the thump-thump of her going downstairs and then the muffled chatter between her and Nell as she arrived in the kitchen. I had missed the footprints of a dog about the place more than I'd realised, and in those few seconds I ached with it. It was only the deep-seated urge to *not* break down in front of Nell, again, that encouraged me up and into my clothes. Once dressed, though, I was the archetypal morning-after-the-night-before. My shirt was shamefully creased, there were small pockets of grey under my eyes, and I had very, very clearly washed myself in a scent that wasn't my own. Nell didn't stand a chance of finding something this floral in the shower at my place, that was for certain.

'I wasn't sure what you'd want for breakfast so I made—'

'Everything?' I saw Nell's cheeks redden at my joke.

'Yes,' she answered, drawing the word out, as though only just realising the mammoth amount of food now spread across her kitchen table. 'Yes, it looks a bit like I made everything.'

'Well, that's great.' I stood with my hands on my hips to survey it all. 'Because I am in the mood for a bit of just about everything that's on this table.' I picked up one of the empty plates that had been left in the centre of the display and stole two slices of toast from the rack. 'I'll move on to the cereal afterwards.'

Nell laughed. 'You really don't have to.'

'I want to.'

And I did. I was abuzz with nervous energy still, my innards vibrating like a washing machine in the final throes of a spin. It was excitement, it was worry, it was — *a little bit of everything*, I thought with a smile, and a little bit of everything combined meant that I could have eaten a horse and chased long after its jockey, too. So I could certainly manage a slice of toast with a second helping of cereal.

Nell took the seat opposite me and I was immediately struck by how *normal* it all felt. Last night had been the first time that we'd sat down for a meal together — or rather, sat opposite each other at a table even — and somehow, sitting together the morning after the night before felt like the only possible way that we could be starting a Saturday. That was, until I saw her spread her first piece of toast.

'You don't have butter?'

Nell froze mid-spread with a splodge of marmalade still on her knife. I'd never seen her look so guilty. 'No.'

'Do you have butter on *anything*?' I kept pushing, unsure of why this was so surprising. Her guilty look collapsed into an amused one, and she carried on slathering condiment directly onto her toast as she answered.

'It's not like you've just found out that I drown kittens on a weekend.' She waved her knife around then and added, 'Poor example. Maybe. I just . . . I don't know, I don't like the taste of butter. I don't mind if stuff is *made* with butter.'

'So you're okay if you don't *see* the butter?'

It had become a rolling joke now, that much was clear from our respective tones. And I took too much delight in the idea of this becoming a continued pun for us. Of Nell and I in a restaurant somewhere in two years' time, me asking a waiter whether the mashed potato on the seafood pie was made with butter or not. The thought was both comforting and a little bit terrifying. *Why am I thinking so far ahead?* It was far too easy to lapse into this thinking around Nell.

'I also don't like Marmite and I think white bread is gross, and I don't understand people who can eat olives. Or drink rum. Though in the case of the latter it's likely linked to some self-inflicted teenage trauma that I'd rather not get into right now.'

I lingered over which thread to pull. 'Drinking game?'

'Ring of fire.'

Involuntarily I took a sharp intake of breath. In my limited experience, any drinking game that involved a deck of cards and a dirty pint at its centre wasn't going to make for a happy anecdote. 'You were bad to the bone.'

Nell smirked, took a deliberate bite of her toast and spoke around the food. 'I still am.'

In the time lull after breakfast while Nell finished getting ready for work and I finished showering Daisy with affection, I took a look around the house, too. I had often wondered where the magic happened — or rather, where Nell and Daisy put their feet up at the end of a long day. Daisy seemed to have beds in every room, toys that had been discarded mid-play in every room, too, and the walls were pockmarked with pictures of the pair of them through the ages: Daisy starting as a small bag of flour and ending at . . . I looked down at her on the floor next to me. *A small sack of potatoes?* It was one of my favourite things about Nell, how much she loved Daisy — but in the brittle aftermath of losing Coll, it was also one of my least favourite things to have shoved in my face sometimes as well. I felt a swell of something then — sadness, grief, anger, a greatest hits of all three — and when Nell hopped and skipped into the living room to ask whether I was ready to hit the road, I found by then that I was. I really, really was.

CHAPTER SEVENTEEN: NELL

Of course, I spent the following weeks frolicking through life with the energy of a newborn lamb in springtime. It felt a little like having tumbled into the stories I'd adored so much as a teenager, and hated so much in my early twenties. But it turned out there was a man who could be nice to you without having treated you a bit like shit beforehand — disappearing act aside, owing to *very* extreme circumstances and all. *Do other women know this?* I wondered. *Should I be telling them?* Though, obviously, I was already telling anyone who would listen, which was mostly Nan and Lucia, with the former already starting to roll her eyes at the mention of my flaming romance while the latter made wild bird noises of excitement at the mention of my new love, so between the two of them they were at least keeping me grounded.

Owen and I shared more dates as the days and weeks rolled on, and for something that wasn't going to be serious, in-at-the-deep-end stuff, it very much felt like that had accidentally happened. Apart from the distant days, that was. They were few and far between, admittedly, but could always be attributed to one thing: Collie. I understood it, because in my own way I was nursing my own quiet grief, while being painfully aware of Daisy's.

138

On the day Owen collected Collie's ashes from the vets, I went as far as shutting the shop two hours early specifically to spend time with my girl. We went home and watched *Beethoven* on Netflix with a pig's ear for company. My snack of choice was toffee popcorn, which Daisy looked at with the same grimace I wore on seeing her snack choice. After the film we went for a long walk at the nature reserve before going home via McDonald's, where I got a large Big Mac meal and the stink-eye from Daisy, who begrudgingly got nothing. I reheated everything in the oven when we got home and I took my burger — and Daisy's equally delicious (I'm sure) dog food — up to bed with us to watch *Beethoven 2*.

Owen and I had already agreed not to talk, him having told me well in advance that he'd want the day to himself. So instead it became a girls' day, and whenever I heard Daisy let out a small and sad whimper, I would hold her especially close until she became too warm with the contact of me and moved away. I couldn't decide which one of us was benefitting more from those hugs.

Hours after we'd both fallen asleep that night, I woke up surrounded by McDonald's wrappers with *Marley & Me* playing in the background. One of us must have rolled over the controls. Daisy was fast asleep on her side of the bed — *see, baby girl, it'll never be Owen's side* — and after I'd watched the slow rise and fall of her sleep-time breathing for nearly a full minute, I took myself into the bathroom for a quiet cry.

* * *

I was wearing my best non-flowery dress for the occasion. It was a loose-fit black number with a high collar. I didn't know whether it screamed "meeting your non-boyfriend's friends for the first time", but it was comfortable and it was — Lucia assured me — stylish. She and I had run through outfit options the day before and we agreed that for a group of men and a pub quiz, this was the best of a floral bunch. Owen had given me a week's notice to get ready for the quiz, too, and I spent that time panicking, planning topics of conversation, and *not* brushing up on popular culture or sport — which was something I definitely should have done.

'Do you know when we last knew a single answer to the literature round?' Owen had said during a late-night phone call where I'd voiced my concerns that his friends might relegate me to the category of "Ditzy and Useless" on meeting me for the first time. 'Alan is the best chance we have but he's a chocolate teapot under pressure.' I felt *slightly* better then, knowing that I was at least bringing some knowledge to the table. *Pray to God that there are questions about books I've actually read*, I thought now, while bouncing on my heels outside the pub where we were meeting.

Owen had texted me to warn me he would be late. He'd had coffee with his middle sister, Louise, after work, and he'd wanted to go home and change from suit to jeans: *better quiz performance clothes xxx* his message said. I'd told him I'd wait for him outside, on account of not knowing a single one of the men I was due to meet and wanting to delay the arduous process of meeting them for a few minutes longer.

It was so evidently quiz night at the spot where we were meeting. People funnelled in in their teams, loosening their shoulders and cracking their knuckles as though preparing for a sporting event. 'We're also shit at the sports round,' I remembered Owen saying and that offered some comfort as well. I didn't want to spend an evening away from my dog for the sake of meeting lads' lads. Though I imagined that Owen wouldn't willingly spend time with those sorts of lads either.

Another quiz team huddle came towards me then — not towards *me* exactly, but towards the door — and I checked the time on my phone to avert their looks. When I glanced back up, two of them had filtered inside, leaving the other three to vape and smoke. They made a heady mixture of something that stank of both cigarettes and fruit.

'We aren't *that* late,' one of them said, checking his own phone. 'Besides, look, he said he's a solid five minutes away still.'

I tried, tried, tried not to overhear. *Is it eavesdropping if you literally can't avoid hearing?*

'We'd better smash No Eye Dear this week.'

'I'm more worried about Agatha Quiztie.'

I swallowed a laugh and in doing so made a weird choking noise that turned into a cough. But they were too engrossed to notice.

'Okay, but can we have a quick chat about the Lisa situation first?'

'What Lisa situation?' the one smoking rather than vaping asked. The third one — the man worried about Agatha — exhaled a plume of vapour over their heads before he answered.

'Lisa got in touch about the dog.'

'Get out!'

My ears pricked up then. I stared hard into the screen of my phone as though reading something, but all that remained there was a picture of Daisy's blissful face staring back — while I listened to a conversation that I already, somehow, just *knew* I wasn't meant to hear.

'I mean, she was her dog as well.'

'Yeah, until she buggered off.'

I wasn't sure which one of them had said it, but I had already decided he would be my favourite.

'Whatever, she just reached out to be sociable.'

'Bollocks.'

'You don't know that there's anything—'

'They've been broken up a long time.'

'So you *genuinely* think it's just about the dog?'

The smoker among them lit another cigarette and I was sorely tempted to lean across and ask for one. But it had been years since that misguided habit had last happened and now wouldn't be the time to start again. I'd be having a stiff gin when I got in there though.

'Whatever her reasons are,' the one I liked said, 'I don't trust her and I don't want her around. Not when there's new stuff happening for him, *exciting* stuff happening.'

141

'Please.' The smoker spluttered. 'New being the operative word.'

'I mean.' The third and final judge-and-jury member piped up. 'It's not really new, is it?' When neither of them answered he spoke again. 'They've basically been seeing each other in one way or another for bloody months.'

'More like minutes,' the smoker said then.

'No, I concur, definitely months.'

'Owen!'

My head shot up at the shout of his name. Owen was strolling towards us all and I couldn't decide which side of the doorway had caught his attention first — where I was, or where they were huddled. He seemed to be waving the three men over while he headed for me, and when the distance between us had folded over he grabbed my elbow and kissed my cheek and my stomach dropped with joy and worry at once.

'Lads, this is Nell.'

I waved and we swapped introductions. 'Nell, meet Luke, Alan and this is Zee.' The men all said hello to me like they hadn't just spent the last ten minutes talking about my non-boyfriend's ex-girlfriend within earshot of me. But I thought I caught a flicker of concern on Zee's face as he turned for the door. *You*, I realised. *You're the one who's on my team.* Though no sooner had the thought arrived, I shook it away. There were no *teams* because we weren't stupid teenagers anymore. And the woman-against-woman trope was tired and tiring in equal measure. *So what, Owen has heard from his ex-girlfriend?* I tried to brush it off with the Cool Girl 'tude I'd been taught to have over the last ten years instead. But then I remembered what happened to pent-up Amy Dunne in *Gone Girl* and it occurred to me that the odd bit of rage mightn't be the worst thing — now and then, in controlled settings.

I glanced around the pub and saw huddles everywhere, heads together and brains limbering up for the questions. At the back table we joined two characters who turned out to be Kai and Sam, but after they'd been introduced I completely lost track of which one was which.

'Don't worry,' Alan said in a low voice next to me. 'None of us are ever completely sure either.'

I laughed and felt something in my stomach — tension, worry, panic — start to relax. 'That makes me feel better.' Owen shuffled into the seat next to me and reached under the table to give my knee a reassuring squeeze, and that made me feel better, too.

'You look gorgeous,' he said in a whisper so the others wouldn't catch it, but . . .

'Owen.' Luke called over to him. 'Don't distract the woman. I want her sharp for the literature round.' He winked at me then went back to writing down the team name — *No Brians* — on the sheet in front of him. 'Ready, lads, lady?'

'Aaaaand for Round One . . .'

The night somehow ran on autopilot from there. And as for worrying that Owen's friends mightn't like me, I needn't have fretted at all. They didn't even have the time to get to know me! Between toilet breaks, drink breaks and smoke breaks, I swapped most conversation with Zee and a *tiny* bit of conversation with Sam — or Kai, who's to say? And then we were flung full throttle into the final round of the evening that I somehow felt would be the real marker of my character and worth, no matter what I had or hadn't said to any of them throughout the night up to that point.

'And Round Ten,' the compère said. 'Everybody's favourite . . . Literature!'

Pockets of groaning sounded from the surrounding tables. I leaned forward, my ears pricked and my mind racing with literature facts — and the occasional worry about Lisa that I was trying to throw into the same box as Diet Culture and things that bad ex-boyfriends had said about me during our break-ups. That box would go into the sea one day.

'To start with, in *Pride and Prejudice*, who does Jane Bennet marry?'

My mouth dropped open but instead of letting the answer fly out, I ushered Luke along to hand me the pen and paper so I could keep my winning knowledge to myself.

Charles Bingley, obviously.

'*I Know Why the Caged Bird Sings* is the autobiography of which American writer and poet?'

Maya Angelou.

'What is the novel *Frankenstein*'s alternative name?'

The Modern Prometheus.

'George Orwell's *Nineteen Eighty-Four* was published in which year?'

1949.

'Name all four March sisters in Louisa May Alcott's *Little Women*.'

Meg, Jo, Beth and Amy.

'And that, folks, is your final question.'

I set the pen down with a mic-drop attitude and it was only then that I noticed the agog expressions on the six men sitting around me. Owen was the first to break the silence with a soft laugh.

'I mean, I told you she was clever.'

I shrugged. 'Books are kind of my thing.'

Luke shook his expression straight, turned to Owen and said, 'We have to keep her.'

And I thought *maybe*, just maybe, I might warm to Luke, too. Zee went up to the bar to hand in our quiz answers and order another round of drinks for the table, and that's when the real Getting to Know the New Girl started. They mightn't have fired questions in the same way that a gaggle of women would, but they certainly had their ways of asking things. Zee was hardly back from the bar with our drinks and Luke had determined whether I was a writer, reader, bookseller or all of the above and what my five-year plan was for life at the bookshop.

'He's also in finance,' Owen said, as though that explained the questions. 'And apparently he's trying to assess whether you're . . . a viable investment opportunity?'

'Maybe Nell has her own questions, lads,' Zee said as he distributed drinks. He pushed a gin and tonic towards me and smiled. 'I've got your back. This lot are like a pack of—'

'Don't mention dogs,' Sam and Kai said at once.

I saw Owen's expression falter, his eyebrows pulling together as though someone had delivered a physical blow, a literal pain, and I shuffled that bit closer to him. Under the table I reached for his hand, laced his fingers through mine and squeezed. He looked up and managed to smile.

'It will be okay,' I said quietly to him, as though I might shield the promise from anyone else hearing it. In the most difficult moments of grief, that promise had sort of become Our Thing.

'Right, room, the results are in!' Attention snapped around to the man at the front who was holding not one but *two* answer sheets. 'And I'm afraid to say, we're going to have to go in for a tie-break question.' There was a chorus of 'Ooh' around the room, rehearsed from years of experience, I guessed. I wondered how many friendship groups were there, how many of them ran along in their busy schedules but made time for these few hours where the only thing that mattered were answers to silly questions. And suddenly, the whole ritual of a pub quiz felt that bit more warming.

'Our tying teams are . . . Agatha Quiztie and . . . No Brians!'

The excitement around the room was infectious. Owen whispered to me that the lads had never won a quiz before, and from their stunned, star-eyed emoji faces that much was clear. But when the compère called for hush around the room, everyone fell silent as if a strict headmaster and a cane were positioned ahead of them, rather than a nice-looking man with a handful of question cards.

'You know the deal, room, we'll be giving these a shuffle and then we'll be asking the question. We'll be accepting the first right answer that we hear. I hope that's clear to every-one?' He waited for a response, but I thought it was more out of politeness. 'Agatha Quiztie, ready?' That time he did wait, and the team captain nodded. 'No Brians, you ready?'

'You bet your bloody arse we are,' Luke said. His hand was flat on the table, as though he was ready to bolt from his seat and run to the front of the room with a winning answer to whatever was coming.

'Ahem.' The compère cleared his throat before he asked, 'How many novels did Roald Dahl write?'

Oh, I thought with a smile. *I think I know this one . . .*

CHAPTER EIGHTEEN: OWEN

The top floor of the office had been transformed into a breakfast haven. There were tables fit for buffets spread across the window wall, offering office attendees both a ridiculous amount of food and an exceptional view of the city. There were bow-tied waiters circulating with orange juice and apple juice while soft jazz played, and the city's elite in the financial sector tried to work out how to eat a toasted cheese croissant while standing *and* holding a conversation. I was on my second pain au chocolat and my first cup of tea when my phone buzzed in my pocket. It turned out to be the first in a *long* series of messages from the lads, one by one voicing their approval of Nell.

It had been two days since the pub quiz and the group chat had been suspiciously quiet in that time. Now my phone was blowing up in my palm, though, it made me wonder whether there was a second group chat, titled *How Do We Voice Our Approval?* One by one and in a flurry of messages seemed to have been their voted-upon option and I wondered which idiot had had that bright idea. I clicked into the group chat proper and typed, *Next time elect a single spokesperson*, before turning off the vibrate feature and pocketing my phone again.

Nell had been quiet since the pub quiz, too. I'd mentioned dinner the night after — last night — and she'd said that she and Daisy had had a long day and could she raincheck? I'd agreed, obviously, on account of not being an arsehole and all. But there was a nagging missing-her feeling all the same, and I couldn't decide how I felt about that. *Is it too soon to miss someone this much?* I'd wondered this *many* times the night before and throughout this morning, too, while I'd been swallowing back on the urge to text her first. Though eventually I'd caved, on account of life being too short and me not being a trainwreck of a teenager with nerves. *Only a trainwreck of an adult with nerves.* I nodded hello to yet another person I half recognised from the last time Douglas had done one of these events.

They happened periodically throughout our corporate calendar. Far from being something we were invited to, it was something that was simply blocked out in certain individuals' online calendars instead, to make it *absolutely* clear that we would be there and nowhere else. It was the first time it had happened to me, though, and I'd be lying if I said there wasn't the tiniest pang of satisfaction in being accepted as part of this fold. Still, the whole thing was in part only a networking opportunity for the lot of us, and it worked. I'd seen this tactic before elsewhere and I knew that the company as a whole would leave here with a wad of new connections in its back pocket. In part, it was a pissing contest. Douglas had definitely invited advisors from competing firms and that was nothing to do with sourcing new business and everything to do with whipping his wang out in public and saying, 'Look at me, look at me,' like a small child who had just learned to pee through the thing.

'Douglas!' I tried for a warm greeting as he crossed the room to me. 'How are you? How's it all going? Are you happy?' The questions knocked into each other like poorly lined-up dominoes, and I tried to swallow back down some of the obvious social anxiety that I was nursing.

'Owen.' He slapped my shoulder in that forceful, alpha way of his. 'Thought you'd cash in on the free pastries?' He laughed, but there was also a very deliberate pause left after the question, too, one that I thought was left hanging for my answer.

'Oh, it was in my calendar?'

'Oh.' He matched my curious tone. 'It shouldn't have been.'

Oh, fuck my life. I willed for the floor to open its hidden jaws and swallow me into the depths of the building. But instead all that happened was another long and uncomfortable silence, worse than the first, too, that I knew I was expected to fill.

'Do you know.' I tried my best for level, cool, non-plussed even. 'I thought it was weird when it appeared in my calendar for today? I should have double-checked with someone. I'll just . . .' I pointed to the direction of the lift. *Go up to the roof and jump right off, shall I?* 'I'll just head back to my office for the rest of the morning then.'

'Here.' Douglas turned around to the buffet table behind me, grabbed a plain croissant and thrust it into my hand. 'One for the road.'

He chuckled like he'd said something hilarious and I tried to match his amusement, all the while thinking, *What the hell is funny?*

I threw the pastry in the nearest bin on my way back from the dizzying heights of the lofty tower and decided that whether she'd replied to my text or not, I was going to call Nell when I was plonked safely back at my desk. It wasn't her job — or anyone's, for that matter — to fix things, but I knew that speaking to her would certainly lessen the load.

Though of course, my expulsion from the breakfast haven wasn't the end of my wearisome burden. I'd also by then got two missed calls on my phone, one from Hattie and one from Dad. *Arses* . . . Dad seemed like the lesser of two evils. I called back, hit speakerphone and rested my head between my palms with my elbows balanced on the desk. It felt like a quiet defiance against my father who would repeat, 'No elbows on the table,' at dinner when we were children, as though doing so was to commit a cardinal sin of sorts.

The phone rang and rang and rang. And *just* when I was about to take an easy breath in and praise the voicemail robot for cutting in, there came . . .

'Owen.'

'Dad. Is everything okay?'

'Absolutely. Is everything okay with you?'

It was the conversational equivalent of having a tooth pulled with poorly administered anaesthetic. At least there was some numbing agent with Dad. By contrast, Mum not only didn't believe in anaesthetic but rusty pliers were her preferred metaphorical conversation tool. I sucked in a deep breath and answered on the release of it.

'I'd got a missed call from you?'

'Oh, yes, *that*, righto, I see. Hattie said she'd call you, too?'

'She did. Dad, is everything okay?'

'Of course, of course. Did Hattie leave a message?'

I grabbed at another thirsty inhale. 'No.'

'Ah, well, righto. She's the best person to talk to about this.'

'About *what*?' I winced at the sharpness of my own voice. There would be a reprimand, I felt sure of it. But instead, Dad sidestepped the snap of my tone and answered with his own isn't-it-obvious pitch.

'Your mother's birthday, of course.' I managed a noise that was equal parts laugh to sigh. But when he added, 'Though you won't be able to bring the dog, you understand?' a strangled noise fell out of me instead. It felt very much like he'd wrapped a telephone cord tight around my neck and knotted it in a neat bow that I couldn't escape.

By way of reply I managed to say, 'I'm actually at work, Dad. I'll call Hattie and get the details from her.' I disconnected the call while he was in the middle of his goodbye and then dropped my head against the flat of my desk with such a force that there was a very real chance I might have self-administered a concussion — not that there would be anyone around to notice for most of the morning, if any of the offices on the way back here had been anything to go by. I lifted my head and then dropped it again, three times and in three hard knocks. So much so that for a second or two, I could believe the other voice was a hallucination.

'They don't know about Collie?'

Maybe I do *have a concussion.* I managed to lift my head and angle it to the door, and there she was, leaning in against the frame like some sultry character from a black-and-white noir film — which was exactly how she was dressed, too.

'Lisa.'

She was wearing a pencil skirt in black with a cream shirt that puckered in at the neck with a black ribbon tie. Meanwhile, I was wearing a shirt that I hadn't had time to iron and trousers that were so old there was a very real possibility that Lisa had actually bought them for me. It was the archetypal "Why must I look like shit when I see the ex" moment, ripped straight out of a bank of bad clichés. Still, appearances aside, I tried to steady my breathing — and my rising irritation.

'Owen.' She smiled. 'May I?' She gestured to the visitors chair on the opposite side of the desk.

'Are you here for financial advice?'

She managed an insincere laugh. 'No, I'm—' She motioned upstairs. 'I'm meant to be at the breakfast club but couldn't resist a peek down here to see whether I could spot you hard at work. You never were one for socialising when you could get away with it.'

Sure, let's pretend I'm meant to be upstairs.

'You were invited as part of Doug's brunch?'

Lisa nodded. 'My firm was invited, as a whole, but we can't actually take *that* much time off as a collective. Neither can you guys, right? If you're still slogging away down here, does that make you the hero manning the ship?'

Lisa had always had . . . a way. It wasn't with words, or with expressions, or even with the way she looked at someone. It was just a way, about everything. The comment, the tone, the lopsided smile that came along with it: everything was archetypal Lisa. And suddenly, her Lisa-ness made me want her hurried out of my office.

'I'd love to catch up but—'

'You didn't reply to my message about Collie.'

I hard-swallowed and heard the glug of it hit my throat. After Collie had passed, I hadn't even contacted Lisa, spiteful single parent that I was. But someone — I still had no idea who — must have got in touch to tell her what had happened. When she then messaged me — *Is it true? About Collie? Xoxo* — I couldn't bring myself to answer, for more reasons than I could bring myself to admit.

'No, I . . . honestly, Lisa, I didn't much know what to say to it. It was a horrible, sudden end and, well, frankly, you weren't around for a huge chunk of her life, so I didn't see why—'

'But I should have been.' I was fast reminded how interrupting was a tendency of hers that I'd really never liked. 'I *should* have been around for her.'

I rubbed at the back of my neck and dropped my face to avoid the sincerity of her expression. 'If you had, then we would have had the faff of working out custody arrangements, blah blah . . .' I waved away the end of the sentence and managed to look at her again, though it crossed my mind that I really might turn to stone if I held the stare for too long. 'It worked out, you know? I made sure she had a good life.' But then came the hideous flashback of the end, and the all-too-familiar prickle of feeling behind my eyes and the worry that maybe I hadn't done everything after all. 'I like to think I gave her a good life.'

I cut the train of thought off before it could gain momentum, otherwise I'd be carrying it for the rest of the day. Lisa set her hand on the table then, as though calling for mine, but I didn't match the gesture. Still, she left it there, an open door through which I could walk at any time, and it crossed my mind Lisa thought that's what *I* was. *Are you trying to open a door?*

'I'm sure you gave her the best life,' she said softly. 'But that's not what I meant.'

Her smile was meek, as though she hadn't just implied something major. *Wait, what* has *she just implied?* I narrowed my eyes to a squint to inspect the edges of the sentiment, to see whether I could catch a clearer meaning but . . . *What the hell is happening here?*

'Anyway.' She stood and smoothed down her skirt. 'I've taken up enough of your time.' She paused, as though waiting for me to dispute what she'd said. But I was too busy working out what she'd implied two seconds ago. I was operating on a significant time delay. 'Call me, if you want? We can talk about Collie, or . . .'

'Lisa, I . . . I get that she was your dog, too.' And just like that, Nice Guy kicked in. 'If there's anything you want, of Collie's, I still have everything, I haven't . . . I'll never throw anything away, so, if you decide that you want something of hers, well, you know where I am.' I didn't have anything against Nice Guy, necessarily. More often than not he was a cool enough guy to live with. But there were times, Christ alive, there were times, when he would open his mouth and what would come out of his autopilot-politeness trap would inevitably, invariably, be something I might later regret. Though when I saw Lisa backing up towards the door with tears in her eyes at the offer, I thought maybe, *maybe*, it hadn't been a terrible offer to make. I knew she wouldn't escalate to full-blown tears though. To start with, she would never cry at a work function. And second, she would never cry while she was wearing fake eyelashes, which she definitely was.

'In which case, I'll call you.' She smiled again and flicked her hair over her shoulder. 'It would be really good to catch up with you, Owen, really good.'

And just like projectile vomit spilling from a child who has over-eaten strawberry pencils and then spent the afternoon on the spinning-teacups ride, it poured from me in a torrent: 'Lisa, I'm seeing someone now.'

'Lisa!'

Fucking hell. Douglas closed in on her, stepping into my office just enough to cup Lisa's shoulder and then unleash her again in a practiced technique taken straight from an HR seminar, no doubt. Lisa flashed a smile that was reality-television-show fake, but Douglas wasn't the type of guy to notice that about her.

'We were searching for you upstairs. They've just brought out the warmed scones and Keith tells me you're a fan.' Then, as though *only just* noticing that I was in the room, too, Douglas looked over to me and back to Lisa. 'You two kids already know each other?'

She opened her mouth to answer but I beat her to the punch.

'We did, once.'

CHAPTER NINETEEN: NELL

The last picture I had uploaded was an action shot of Daisy as a puppy with her jaws clamped around the corner of a hardback book. I had been horrified at the time — though not horrified enough not to take a picture of the scene. And I'd banked it for times when her Instagram following looked to be lagging, which it had in the last couple of weeks. I say *her* Instagram when really I mean the bookshop's. As far as the internet was concerned, Daisy was the proud owner of a pre-loved bookshop here in Green Fields and I was merely the human who brought opposable thumbs to the deal. I had a back catalogue of images saved to my laptop stretching all the way back to when Daisy was just fifteen weeks old — when the book-eating picture was taken — to as recently as two days ago. Unfortunately, happiness and generally being blissed out on life meant that I hadn't been posting as regularly as I used to — which is why I'd gone back to the puppy stash to save the day. Her follower count — *our* follower count — had jumped up by nearly two hundred and fifty people since that last image had been shared, which could only mean it was about time we posted another.

I was sitting in front of the counter on a slow day, cross-legged with Daisy napping next to me. Her head was balanced on my knee. I'd needed the toilet for at least thirty minutes but I was also sure that it was against UK law to disturb a sleeping dog once they were lying on you — there's actual legislation on it in animal-cruelty guidelines somewhere, there must be. That said, I was nearing the point where I would *have* to disturb her.

I tweaked and edited a picture of Daisy sitting inside a box that had recently held a donation of Folio Editions. The books were piled up around the outer edge of the box, perfectly displayed for anyone who might like to zoom in and browse, and I'd captioned it: *Part of the unpacking process.* I was in the middle of listing out thirty meaningless hashtags — #dogsofinstaworld #doggram and so on — when the shop bell rang, causing Daisy's head to snap up and inspect the visitor.

'Oh, thank sweet Jesus for that,' I whispered without looking up. The rush to the toilet was finally within reach. But when Daisy went waddling in the direction of whoever had entered, I chanced a look across while I started to awkwardly stand — all the while trying to hold my bladder in place!

'Who's a lovely girl, who's a lovely, *lovely* girl?' Owen was on his knees in front of Daisy who was wagging her tail with the force of a wind turbine — which of course, meant wagging her entire body along with it. 'Who's the best girl?' he asked then, and I saw the flicker of guilt that came afterwards. Owen forgot himself sometimes. Not to be confused with forgetting Collie, though I knew that's what the pang of guilt was for.

'This is a surprise,' I said, with a too-wide smile that I hoped Owen wouldn't spot as a fake one. It wasn't that I didn't want to see him, of course. It was more that I didn't want to see him until I'd decided whether or not to mention the L-word. Lisa, not love. While Owen and I had talked — via text, and one sleepy late-night phone call — since the pub quiz, we hadn't been in the same space yet and I worried that the close proximity without time to plan might lead to word vomit of epic proportions. *How do you keep something in when you're this nervous of it coming out?* I shifted from one foot to another. Though at least I could pass the fidgeting off as — 'I'm so sorry, she's been asleep on me for *ages* and I really need a wee.'

'Understood,' Owen answered with his face scrunched up against Daisy's.

By the time I was in and out of the bathroom, Owen was sitting on the floor of the shop in much the same position that I'd been — only Daisy wasn't asleep on him.

I laughed. 'You're allowed an actual seat.'

'Well, I figured if the floor was good enough for you two.' Owen flashed a winning smile then and I resisted the urge to swoon a little, for fear of actually turning into a storybook character on the spot. He tapped the space in front of him in welcome and I settled there — 'We need a talk, if you have the time' — with a nest of wasps in my stomach.

'That doesn't sound good.'

Owen focused on Daisy, not me, even when he started to speak. 'It's about Lisa, which I think is something that's probably on your radar already?' When I didn't answer he looked up. 'Alan said you might have overheard some stuff at the pub?'

I swallowed hard and nodded.

'She came to the office today, this morning.'

And now you're breaking up with me on your lunch? I tried to stop a strangled sound from coming out of me but there was no halting it, so I managed to disguise it as a cough instead.

'Look, Nell.' He stopped stroking Daisy and reached for my hand, and I felt the nerves of him in the heat of his palm. 'I only wanted you to know, okay? Collie was her dog, too, but nothing has happened, nothing happened today. It just . . . I don't know, it felt . . . *icky* somehow, not to tell you.'

I waited for more but there didn't seem to be anything coming. I hiccupped a nervous noise then, and moved my free hand to my mouth as though I could catch the sound. 'Sorry, you're *not* calling things off with us then?' I asked

157

pointedly, bringing Daisy into the situation, too, though I knew it was unfair. After all, who could possibly want to leave that wrinkled face?

'Are you mad?' Owen asked the question like it was a completely sincere and serious one, his tone flat, concerned even. But then he broke into a laugh and added, 'Sorry, there was probably a better thing to have said there. But, Jesus, Nell, no, I . . . I *really* like how things are going here. And I *really* don't have an interest in rekindling things with Lisa. It's a cliché and all but exes are exes for a reason, right? I'm sure you have an ex that you wouldn't touch with someone else's ten-foot pole?'

I thought of the misguided affair. He and I had tried to be friends and it had failed catastrophically, owing to the fact that every time I checked his Facebook it made me die a little inside. Dramatic, maybe, but after months of someone telling you that they were going to leave their life to start a new life with you, seeing them go right ahead living a new life with someone else altogether carried a bitter sting. *And no*, I thought with a spasm in my belly, *I wouldn't touch him with someone else's.*

'Lisa and I have history.' He carried on when I didn't answer. 'But it's *history*, very much past tense.' He squeezed my hand and smiled. 'I just needed to be clear, and honest. I hope that was okay?'

A novel concept was what it was. 'It's more than okay.'

Owen leaned forward to kiss me, a slow and soft one that made Daisy grumble at the sudden lack of attention, owing to no one stroking her for a fraction of a second. His hands were either side of my face as though cradling me and with the sudden influx of happy hormones surging, I thought I might just melt right into his palms. When he pulled away, I kept my eyes closed for a second longer and let the kiss work through me like an adrenaline shot, small sparks clinging onto my veins and jumping one to the other. I was convinced that no one in the world had ever kissed me like Owen.

'You look much calmer than you did at the start of this conversation,' he said jokingly and I laughed along with him.

'Funny that, given that at the start of this conversation I thought we were having a break-up talk.' No sooner was the comment out, I rushed to correct myself. 'Not a proper break-up talk, obviously, because you have to be *together* together to break up at all and I realise we haven't really had that discussion yet.' A nervous laugh crept out between words. 'But we *are* sleeping together, which I think is pretty bloody serious so I suppose we'd need some kind of talk if—'

Owen kissed me again, and any word vomit that would have come after the first blurt of word vomit was swallowed between us. I even found, to my shame, that my nervous chatter had been replaced with a soft moan.

'I'm sorry,' I said as Owen pulled away again. 'That sound slipped out.'

He guffawed. 'Okay, absolutely not a thing to apologise for.' He pressed a hand against my cheek and I was suddenly painfully aware of the flush of heat that was there. I imagined my skin as bright red or midsummer pink and imagining that only *worsened* the colouring, I knew, because I could feel the embarrassment rising and — *woman, get a grip of yourself!* I forced out a long, slow breath. 'Back in the room with me?'

I laughed. 'Yes, I absolutely am.'

'Good, because I have another thing.'

'Owen, I'm still reeling from the thing two seconds ago,' I answered, though I kept my tone light. Owen was smiling and there was no hint of nerves, so I reasoned that whatever was coming could only be a good thing. *Right? Right, Owen?* I wanted to hurry him along, which felt rude, but so help me I was only seconds away from it.

'So, Dad called me today, to tell me that Hattie would be calling me, to talk to me about my mum's birthday surprise. For context, *every* year we try to plan a surprise party for Mum and *every* year she works out what the plan is and . . .' I raised my hand with a question.

'Did you ever think that she works out the plan for the surprise party because you plan a surprise party every year,

159

so, it would actually be *more* surprising now if you just didn't plan a surprise party at all?'

'I love how you think.' He leaned over to kiss my forehead. 'But that's also not acceptable.'

'So, she doesn't want a party, but she also doesn't want *not* to have a party?'

'Got it in one. So we always plan something. Different venues, different themes, different . . . just different. And *somehow* she figures everything out and says something to the effect of, "Oh, well I knew what was going to happen but that didn't lessen the impact."'

'Is she actually that formal with it, too?' I smiled

Owen kept a flat expression though, and nodded. 'So, now that I've really sold the entire thing to you and I'm sure you're intrigued to see it all play out in motion . . .' *Oh.* An arcade machine's worth of pennies dropped at once. *Oh, I see.* 'I have no idea what the surprise is, but would you like to be a part of it?'

'You want me to meet your family?' I answered, my voice heavy with the shock of his offer. It wasn't that I didn't want to! Although, it may have been a *little* that I didn't want to. It's more that . . . my thoughts faded and I found myself laughing. 'Sorry,' I said when I caught Owen's cock-eyed expression. 'It's just, again, I started this conversation thinking we were going to have a break-up talk and now—' The hum of my mobile cut me off. It had been in my pocket on silent and the only person it would be ringing for was . . .

'I'm sorry, this must be Nan.'

I ferreted the handset out while Owen said, 'Of course, of course.'

'Hi, Nan, I'm working at the moment, so can I give you a call back?'

'Nellie, you don't need to worry, but I'm in the hospital and—'

'What happened? Are you okay? Which hospital?' I felt the questions knock into each other, like cars in a pile-up, and the analogy made stomach bile turn over in me as I moved. In a synchronised motion Owen and I were both upright from the floor.

'I told you she'd faff,' I heard Nan say to someone in the background.

'Nan!'

'It's only Green Fields bloody General. But, Eleanor, look—'

'I'll be there in fifteen minutes.' I pocketed my phone, rushed to the other side of the counter, moved to power down my laptop, pressed the button for the till, which would need emptying, and . . .

'Nell.' Owen reached across the counter to lay a hand on mine. 'Just go.'

'I need to close up, and take Daisy home, and—'

'I'm owed some time. I can handle the shop, and the . . .' He looked down at Daisy who was staring up at him with fairy-tale adoration in her eyes. I heard him huff, then he faced me with a smile. 'I can handle the Daisy. Just go.'

I fished the keys out from under the counter. 'You don't have to keep the shop open. Everyone will understand. This is for the door, and this is *my* front door if you just want . . .'

Owen eased the keys away from me. 'Daisy will tell me. Just go.' He craned across the countertop space between us and softly kissed my lips, just once. When he pulled away, I felt as though he'd sucked the air clean out of me. 'Please call me if you need anything? I'll be, well, *we'll* be here.'

And something in me really believed him.

CHAPTER TWENTY: OWEN

It was that disconcerting moment — that's actually a solid two minutes at least — of waking up somewhere, having forgotten that's where you'd fallen asleep. The room smelled of cinnamon and something else that I was too heathen to recognise. There was a soft glow coming from a table lamp beside me, and a salt lamp on the fireplace directly in front. The sofa was comfortable, accommodating, having moulded itself to the shape of my side, and there was a dead weight on my legs that made it impossible to move. I pushed the blanket away further down from my face — *did I grab a blanket before I crashed here?* — and looked down to see Daisy precariously nested on, around and between my legs, such was the malleability of her bulk. She was letting out gentle snores that made her seem like a cartoon character — that big breath in followed by the choo-choo-choo sound on the exhale. I didn't have it in me to disturb her, but I was also low-key concerned that there would be permanent nerve damage if I didn't.

Besides which, I was sure that I could hear something beyond Daisy's slow snoring, coming from a different downstairs room in what I had now determined must be Nell's house. If the soft furnishings, lighting and pleasant smells hadn't given it away, the floral wallpaper on the wall directly opposite us really sealed the deal. And then everything from earlier in the day came *whooshing* back in and, carefully, trying not to disturb Daisy in the process, I felt around for my phone. It wasn't in a pocket, or under me on the sofa either, as far as I could feel, so I leaned forward to check the floor and . . . *Ah! There you are.* I thought I might tumble free of the sofa entirely when I leaned forward but it turned out that Daisy was enough to counter my moving weight.

It was 1.32 a.m. and I had a text message from Lisa: *Was good to talk earlier. Let me know when to stop by xoxo.*

She'd called and, because I'm an idiot, I'd answered. It wasn't that I'd forgotten everything that Nell and I had talked about — or rather, it wasn't that I didn't *mean* everything that Nell and I had talked about. Only that Nice Guy was a strong pull to resist and, if I was uncomfortably honest with myself, he'd been in the driver's seat for most of my relationship anyway. It wasn't that she walked all over me or anything, only that . . . that . . . *that she'd mostly walked all over me.* There had been compromises along the way, sure. But I so often thought of them now as Lisa throwing me a bone, or buying herself a bargaining chip for the future.

I ran a hand through my hair and clicked out of the message.

I hadn't spoken to her because of an undeniable pull or anything quite so worrying as that. It wasn't like that with Lisa anymore. Any pull was more about everything we'd shared. The majority of the phone call had been about Collie, with occasional tangents into the trials and tribulations of family life, which was something Lisa and I had both struggled with while we were together — and still struggled with now, if our conversation was anything to go by.

But there'd been an awful lot of Collie packed in. And whenever I'd tried to end the call, Lisa would pull out another memory that would start the cycle of talking all over again and — I clicked to lock my home screen and saw Collie's bright and brilliant expression glaring out as my wallpaper. Closely followed by a pang of something that reminded me of guilt. *Guilt over what, though? Isn't that just the million-pound question?*

Of course, the real million-pound question was whether there actually was an intruder somewhere in the house or whether it was simply the shake of the structure when facing Daisy's snoring — which seemed to have gone from cartoonish and endearing all the way through to full-blown sinus problems in the space of my shifting a leg.

'Daisy,' I said softly, reaching down to scratch her head. 'Come on, girl. We need to make a move.' Continuing in her cartoonish ways, she opened one eye and took a quick, sly look in my direction before closing the eye again and feigning sleep, as though I mightn't have seen her. 'Nice try.'

With a huff she eventually moved, shifting her body like it was a deadweight burden she was forced to lug about from sofa to bed, to kitchen bed, to wherever else Nell might have a bed for her. Honestly, seeing the comforts of Daisy's sleeping, napping and resting arrangements made me question whether I'd been that much of a good dog dad at all. Then a memory fluttered in of Collie sleeping on a pile of clothes that I'd thrown on the landing with every intention of taking them to the local charity shop. She'd spent so much time napping either on or in that pile. And for once, the memory of that was a warming thing rather than something that tore through me, and I marked that as progress.

Daisy left the room before I did and it crossed my mind that she was having a delayed reaction to some intruder. As it turned out, it was more like a homing beacon for having realised that, yes, there were other noises elsewhere in the house and, yes, it was her mum. Nell was sitting at the kitchen table eating macaroni cheese straight from the oven dish that I'd baked it in. I'd served myself a portion earlier, but I'd left the rest in the oven for when Nell got home. I didn't know what else there was for me to have been doing.

There was something tremendously wholesome about watching her like that. Her wild waves of hair were tied into a bun that was drooping from the top of her head, the majority of her make-up from the day had gone, and even though I'd seen Nell in all her First Thing in the Morning glory before now, there was something different about this, as though seeing an amended version of intimate.

When she realised I was standing in the doorway watching her, she already had a mouthful of pasta. Not that she let that stop her. 'This was *for* me, right?'

I laughed and crossed the space, setting a kiss on the crown of her head as I walked past her. I paused for a deep inhale, too, the same way parents do with their newborns, though I thought there was probably a better analogy for it. Her hair smelt of cherry shampoo, Jimmy Choo perfume and, somehow, hospital. 'Yes, it was for you.' I pulled out the chair alongside her. Daisy was already neatly positioned directly underneath the table. I half expected to see her with her jaw hanging open and her tongue lolling out, just *waiting* for a chunk of pasta to drop.

'Grab a fork,' Nell said around another mouthful.

'How's your nan?'

'Ha!' It was a jolly ha, not a sarcastic one. 'Heartburn.'

'You're kidding me.' I laughed along with her. 'And she thought . . . what?'

'*She* didn't think anything. She was having coffee with her friend, Ang, Nan started rubbing at her chest and Ang said, "You should get that checked." Waiter comes over to ask if they want more coffee and Ang says, "She's got chest pain, don't you think she should get that checked?"'

'I think I can see where this is going.'

'Through a Chinese-whisper chain of patrons and serving staff . . .' Nell punctuated the sentence with a laugh every few words and I thought the tiredness was likely making everything that bit funnier, which made it funnier still to hear her explanation of it all. 'Nan finds herself in the back of an ambulance with a handsome paramedic who she spills her life story to before telling him, "It isn't a heart attack, you know?"' Nell's giggles erupted into full laughter then. 'And of course, the wise old owl was right.'

'So?' I eased the fork away from Nell and speared my own chunks of pasta, and there was a ridiculous surge of joy that moved through me to think we were already at a point where this was acceptable behaviour. *And this*, this *is why you feel guilty for speaking to Lisa*, I realised, aware of the immediate drop in my facial expression, too.

'Are you okay?' Nell put a hand on my arm.

'Absolutely, absolutely.' It was a half-lie. 'I'm waiting on the rest of this cliffhanger comedy.'

'They hooked her up to all sorts, scanned this and checked that and double-checked the other, and it transpires that she's fit as, well, as a Daisy dog. I suspect she'll outlive us all.'

'From your mouth to God's ears.' I shoved another four pieces of pasta into my mouth in a single go, as though I could chew through the bad feelings in me. I had always been of the mindset that if I felt guilty over something, then there must definitely be something to feel guilty for. That hadn't always been entirely true. In the past — *especially* when it came to matters of the heart and of Lisa — I'd been too eager to take a share of guilt that didn't belong to me, which made it that bit harder now to work out how much guilt was warranted and how much was just . . . me. But given that not twelve hours had passed since my conversation with Nell about my conversation with Lisa, and how she really, *really* didn't need to worry about anything, and given that I'd somehow managed to slip into a Lisa bear trap in that time and have a fifteen-minute phone call with her, during which I'd agreed to a meeting, too, it crossed my mind that maybe, *maybe* I felt guilty because — *I'm actually being an arsehole?* I was suddenly aware of my mouth having dropped open at the realisation. Nell was looking at me like she was worried it was a stroke.

'What the hell was that?' she asked, her tone jovial, but the look of concern on her face was all too apparent. 'Did you drift off somewhere?'

I set the fork down and rubbed hard at my eyes. 'Somehow, despite napping on the sofa with Daisy for however long, I think I'm just tired. You know when you're so tired you forget how to chew?' *Owen, you're an idiot.* I shrugged and managed a laugh. 'It's a thing.'

'Okay, weirdo.' Nell leaned forward and kissed the spot just beneath my earlobe and I thought something in me was going to burst. 'Look, Owen, what you did for me today—'

'Oh, you really don't need to thank me—'

Nell pressed her index finger against my lips to physically bolt the words in my mouth. 'I do. It meant, it means, *so much*, that you would just step up like that. Not just with the shop but with Daisy and . . . honestly, when I came in and found you two asleep on the sofa, I thought my heart was going to explode with something. And, I don't know, especially after the talk earlier.' She rubbed at her forehead and smiled. 'I'm crazy about you, Owen. I think that's what I'm trying to say. Absolutely bonkers nuts about you, actually. Because I know how much men love it when women get crazy over them,' she said, her tone playful. I don't know whether Nell hadn't heard the words until she'd said them aloud, or maybe the words had come out entirely unplanned, but there was something beautifully vulnerable about her in that moment. With her wild hair and pale face, and her absolute honesty that made me crumble.

'I'm crazy about you, too.'

'You are?'

The look of relief on her face was too much. I *was* crazy about her, of course I bloody was. Lisa was a fly on the windshield, a sour raspberry in an otherwise good punnet; she was a dog-eared page, a scratch on a disc; she was one analogy after another where she was only a blemish on something larger. Nell, Nell was the something larger. *Don't you dare say that out loud,* I cautioned myself.

'I am,' I managed to say.

Nell snatched my hand and stood up from the table, and I didn't need a word of explanation for where we were going — or rather, what we were going to do. There was this mass of feeling moving between us, which sounds disgusting and cliché, but there it was. It was electric and tangible, as though if someone were to touch either one of us we would have given off the kind of sparks that inexplicably get thrown out by toasters and light switches. And Lisa was all but forgotten, relegated to the past where she belonged.

* * *

Until she wasn't. Nell was fast asleep next to me. She wasn't a cuddly sleeper, instead opting to keep so strictly to her own side of the bed that there may as well have been a cushioned partition between the pair of us. I didn't encroach on her space, but if I lay with my hand *dangerously* close to that imagined partition, I could still feel the heat of her in the aftermath of our lovemaking.

I'd never used that phrase before. In fact, I'd ardently mocked people who did. But something different happened, had been happening with Nell, where I was sure having sex with her created a timeslip, or a micro muscle tear in the universe somehow, or another similar concept that might be featured in a *Doctor Who* episode along the way. And when we were inside that timeslip, nothing mattered — phones could ring, car alarms blare, in fact I was sure that someone could stand in the doorway flicking the overhead lighting on and off a hundred times a minute and I either wouldn't notice, or maybe would and simply wouldn't care.

But now, with the sex done and the sleeping underway, all I could do was lie and stare into the abyss of Nell's ceiling — and steal her body heat from close but certainly not direct contact. I wasn't thinking of Lisa in a romantic way in those moments. But I *was* thinking of her. She'd said she would stop round this weekend to collect something of Collie's and I'd autopilot-responded that that was fine. And it was fine! Collie had been her dog, too. *Except for when she left us both*, I was reminded by the judgemental and still bitter part of my brain. But I had a point: she ditched us and never implied a want or need of custody of Coll, even after all their quality time together, even after I thought Lisa had come around to the idea of having a dog that wasn't a puppy.

So, why does Lisa matter? The thought was on a loop, like a Groundhog Day means of self-torture . . . Until Nell caught me off-guard, her skin directly grazing against mine even though I was sure I hadn't moved. My eyes widened and I held my breath, waiting for her to snatch her fingers away — only she didn't. She interlinked them loosely with mine so our hands were hardly held — and the partition remained mostly in place — and while she did that she let out a soft moan, full of delight and simple contentment. And she stayed there, just close enough, while I thought, *So, why does Lisa matter?*

CHAPTER TWENTY-ONE: NELL

'The stones on this fella!'

Nan had been shouting various Ted Bundy facts for the entire time I'd been making Sunday dinner, and it was making me thankful that Owen had turned down the invitation to come with me this week. That said, my nose was still out of joint about his declining the offer. It had taken a lot to extend the opportunity to open up Nan's home to him. Whether Owen realised it or not, he would have been the first man I'd brought here. In all the relationships I'd failed to have — *I make it sound like I've managed loads*, I thought, laughing along while slicing carrots — there had never been a single man I'd loved enough to introduce to Nan. Apart from the one who I'd loved enough to *want* to introduce to everyone. Though even that, in a twisty, self-destructive Nellie way, probably wasn't as romantic as I was remembering. There was a solid chance I only wanted to introduce that man to anyone because I knew full well that I couldn't. *Ah, the reverse psychology.* Though given The Wife and The Other Woman — *women*, I corrected myself — it was probably a blessing in disguise that he'd never made it through the door.

I threw the sliced carrots into bubbling water and then turned my attention to peeling squash. The first hour had been spent trying to clean the chicken that Nan had bought, without either gagging or vomiting into it. I'd always hated touching meat — unless it was for Daisy, in which case some latent maternal instincts would always kick in to remind me of the importance of feeding my young. But on that particular Sunday, even the sight of Daisy's drool hanging from her jowls wasn't making it an easy job.

'Nellie, you're missing the best bits!'

I laughed and skinned away another layer of squash. It needed to be peeled and oiled and thrown in a tray, and then there were no other jobs left for me to do. I would have to sit in with Nan, and that likely meant I would have to talk about Owen. I didn't *mind* talking about him, usually. The problem this time was that after Nan's hospital hiccup, I'd called her to see how she was feeling and to ask if she'd mind Owen joining us for lunch this week. It hadn't felt right asking him before I'd asked her. Of course, she'd howled and yelped and made other ridiculous noises of joy down the phone and said yes thirty-seven million times, sandwiched around exclamations about how she'd love to meet him. And then he'd said no.

I sighed and threw the bare vegetables into the pan with more aggression than the action called for, and oil spilled out over the hob in the process. One more check of the chicken after I'd wedged the messy mixed veg into the oven, in among a stuffing tray, roasted potatoes and homemade Yorkshire puddings (grumpy though I was, I'd pulled out all the stops for Nan's week off), and then I could go into the living room and listen in on the lives of serial killers for a while, to take the edge off an otherwise wobbly day.

There were potatoes boiling on the hob — *because how can we possibly have Sunday lunch without three kinds*, I thought with a smile — and they'd need to be checked soon enough. So all I really needed to do was coast through maybe half an episode of . . .

'Let's talk about your man.' Nan zipped the television quiet, pressing pause when my foot was hardly over the threshold of the room. 'Are you okay that it's just us girls here today?' Daisy plonked herself on the floor at Nan's feet and looked up at me expectantly, as though she, too, was ready to play agony aunt in the situation.

'I *love* that it's just us girls.' And I really did! Sunday lunches with Nan had always been, and very much still were, a sincere highlight of the week. Being crazy about Owen hadn't altered that. 'I'd just wanted to share a girls' day with someone who I care about.' I shrugged. 'That's all.'

'Will you invite him next week?'

I shook my head like a child denying a lie. 'No, I won't ask him again.'

'Oh, Nellie . . .'

'Nan,' I answered. 'I am *fine*, but I won't extend the invitation for a second time. Besides, if he'd come this week then I could have boasted about my cooking. Next week, I'd have to boast about your cooking and that isn't anywhere near as fun.'

Nan leaned forward in her armchair and slapped my leg playfully. 'And you didn't need to bloody do it this week.'

'It's not a need—'

'It's a want, yada-yada. I heard you the first time.'

Nan and I had struck a bargain that she could get the food in, as long as I did all the cooking. Even though the hospital scare hadn't been anything serious, it had been a scare all the same. And I wagered that after an afternoon in the back of an ambulance and an offensive amount of hours in Accident and Emergency — on a trolley in a bloody corridor no less — the least Nan deserved was for someone to take care of her for the day.

'Mind you, if I'd known you were getting chicken . . .'

'Do you think you're in the pudding club?'

I blinked hard. 'I'm sorry?'

'You know.' She made an upward motion with one hand, as though that clarified the question. 'Up the pole, duff, bun in the oven . . .' She made a show of thinking and then snapped her fingers. 'In the family way, eating for—'

'Okay, I get it! Jesus, who knew there were so many ways of asking someone that question.' I leaned right back in my armchair, placed a hand either side of my stomach and breathed out hard until my belly formed a clear pouch — where a baby would naturally sit. 'Besides which, it's bloody rude to ask that. You're basically asking if I've gained weight.' I was suddenly insecure at the mere suggestion, which I hated. I reminded myself that weight gain isn't a good or bad thing, and that it had absolutely nothing to do with what Nan had actually just asked me.

'For a smart girl you aren't half daft sometimes.' She leaned forward for another swipe at my knee. 'Take a breath and let your belly down, Nellie Belly.'

A schoolgirl giggle fell out of me then. She hadn't called me that for years. When I would spend weekends with her and Grandad — before it all — Mum would drop me off first thing in the morning with Nan bouncing on the balls of her feet with excitement. Even though Mum had always given me a hearty breakfast to start the day, Nan would be there with waggling fingers ready to tickle my tummy and say, 'What are we putting in Nellie Belly today?' before showing off the various baking ingredients she'd bought to keep us busy. I remember Grandad keeping well out of the way until flour had been cleaned off the kitchen ceiling, egg whites wiped from the walls and baked goods were cooling on the table. The memory warmed me right through to the core.

'I need to check the potatoes,' I answered when there was enough breath back in my body for it. 'I'll be a mo.'

Nan rolled her eyes and pressed play. I half heard a snippet of Ted Bundy talking about how absolutely innocent he was as I walked back to the kitchen, with Daisy close behind. The potatoes were bubbling nicely for the mash, and I lifted the smaller ones off their hob burner, with their skins still neat and intact. Now that the chicken was cooking, too, it was that bit more palatable to think about eating it. Daisy surely felt the same, given that she was sat square in front of the oven door looking into it like a lazy teenager glued to

173

the latest episode of their favourite reality television show. I crouched level with her to take a picture, making sure I got equal parts Daisy and kitchen for a perfect Instagram square.

'Perfect, hold it right there.' She reacted to my joke how a teenager might, too, which was to say she didn't react at all. 'I know who *will* appreciate my humour though.' I bypassed Instagram and clicked into WhatsApp. Owen's chat was pinned at the top and I felt no shame about it either. I attached the picture and captioned it, *Someone is ready for Sunday lunch xx*. I couldn't decide if that sounded like a dig. But rather than risk it, I back-clicked all the way to the beginning and opted for a laughing face instead. 'Simple and classic, let the emoji speak for itself,' I said as I hit send and waited for the two ticks to announce its delivery.

I deliberately left my phone behind in the kitchen — and on silent, too — for fear that I would turn into one of those lovesick puppies who . . . The thought trailed off as it occurred to me that I couldn't hear the steady plod of Daisy behind me en route from one room to another, and I turned to check her whereabouts in all this. Of course, there she was, a lovesick puppy just waiting on her chicken dinner.

'It won't cook any quicker,' I shouted back to her and still she didn't move. 'Daisy is going to stay in the kitchen to make sure the chicken cooks,' I told Nan as I slumped back into my chair.

'She's a wise girl, that dog of yours.' Nan paused the television again. 'So you'll really not invite him?'

'Nan!' I groaned. 'I already did.'

'And he's busy?'

I left a long, grumpy, teenager pause. 'Yes.'

'So it's not that he didn't *want* to come?'

'No.'

'I see.' Nan left her own deliberate pause then. 'But we're to punish him for being busy?'

'I'm not punishing him! I agreed to meet his family, I just thought maybe, *maybe* he'd like to meet mine, and I realise he hasn't *said* he doesn't want to meet mine, but, like,

I'm meeting his, that's all. It's equal distribution of effort, or something. And besides which, he's got a *much* bigger family than I have thanks to the broods and the siblings and the . . . God, his mother sounds like a demon already and she's just going to hate me because I'm not Lisa and—'

'Aha!' I was sure Nan leaped from her seat with the outburst. She sounded like a Golden Era detective making a breakthrough in a case. 'So how much of this is about Owen being busy and not being able to make today, and how much of this is about Owen having an ex-girlfriend back on the scene?'

I heard my teenage self answer. 'She isn't back on the scene, she's . . .' I rolled my eyes and threw my hands up in a defeated gesture. 'Lingering. Like the smell that old cigarette smoke always leaves in your clothes. Which makes me sound much more hateful than I actually am,' I said before Nan could point it out to me. 'I understand Collie was her dog, too, but turning up at his office and . . .'

'And? Wasn't she there for a work thing?'

'Whose side are you on?'

'Logic, Eleanor. I'm on the side of logic. They've not spoken since, have they?'

There were two responses to that question: the one I wanted to believe was true and the one that made me sound paranoid. I decided to lean in to the first one. 'Not that I know of,' I answered. 'Owen just said she might call, if she decided she wanted something of Collie's to keep.' The slightly more paranoid answer was that I was a solid ninety-two per cent sure that I'd seen Lisa's name on the screen of Owen's phone the morning after the fright before, when he'd spent the night with me and Daisy after Nan's scare. But I didn't want to be *that* girl. The I've-seen-something-on-his-phone-that-I-shouldn't-have-been-looking-at girl. Though that wasn't a gendered thing by any stretch — *everyone* was guilty of side-eyeing a phone when it lit up with a message. It just so happened that on that occasion it hadn't been *my* phone — and I'd just happened to be standing next to Owen when the screen had lit up, too.

'There's more to that answer.' Nan fixed me with a stare and I shrugged unknowingly, ready to deny any allegations if they were to come flying at me. 'Nellie, if I may?' she asked, but I knew she wasn't really asking. 'You like this fella a lot, yes?'

I nodded, though I knew my expression alone was a loved-up giveaway.

'So, meet his family, Nellie. Meet his family, invite him again, spend time with him without worrying about this Louise.'

'Lisa.'

'Whatever she answers to. Don't worry about her until you have to worry about her.' She leaned forward and reached for my hand. 'You're too young and too pretty a girl to be fretting this much over a woman who your man has told you not to worry about.'

One hard blink sent tears rolling down my cheeks and Nan gave my hand a little squeeze when she spotted them.

'Now,' she said, softly. 'Go back in the kitchen and mash my potatoes before they start to go slick. I can't abide slicked potatoes.'

I laughed and wiped my nose with the back of my hand like I might have done as a youngster. 'Yes, boss. Besides which—' I stood and made my way to the door — 'I'm worried Daisy's eyes will go square if I don't drag her away from that oven soon.'

'It's funny, you know,' Nan said, already reaching for the remote. I was braced for another Ted Bundy fact. 'Your mother couldn't stand chicken when she was pregnant either.'

'Nan!'

'I'm only saying!'

CHAPTER TWENTY-TWO: OWEN

I sat cross-legged on the living room floor with a box of Collie's belongings in front of me. Metaphorically, I was holding a limb like I might lose it and my heart was breaking at the thought of forever being encumbered by the loss of something so necessary and precious, and it was the most apt comparison that there was for the dog-shaped hole that I thought, if I had energy to move to a mirror, I might be able to physically observe carved into me.

And it was made that bit worse by the utterly glorious picture from Nell that showed Daisy staring longingly into an oven that I guessed must be cooking meat. *Find someone who looks at you how Daisy looks at Sunday lunch xx*, I replied, and then I threw my phone at the box in the weakest of gestures. It clipped the corner and then landed screen up, so I saw when another message arrived, but I couldn't bring myself to reply to it. I knew then that it wasn't just Collie. It was Collie and Nell — or rather, Collie and Nell and Lisa, which was a disgusting combination of factors that made my stomach turn over with bad feeling. I dropped my head back on the sofa behind me. I don't know how much time I lost staring at the ceiling, but I do know that the next time I came up for thought or air it was because my front doorbell was ringing — and it could only be one person waiting on the other side.

Though that in itself made me a schmuck — a word that I had used with startling regularity while referring to myself over the last few days. But the reason I had taken a rain check on plans with Nell for today was because I'd already made plans with Lisa. And captain of the autopilot-politeness system — also known by his trusted moniker, Nice Guy — had *very* strong feelings about backing out of one in favour of the other. I had too-vivid memories of Wini scolding me for picking one friend up while putting another down when I was a kid. She was always trying to tap morals into us like that, as though having realised earlier that it wasn't necessarily something our parents were all that fussed about.

'You can't cancel on people because you'd rather be with someone else. Little Owen, the whole world would fall apart in a day if we all did such things.' I could remember her throwing her hands into the air in a sincere gesture of defeat, which felt a little overstated for the life lesson she was trying to instil in me. 'Honour your plans.'

And that's exactly what I'd done when I told Nell that I already had plans for the day. But because I'm a schmuck, I didn't tell her what the plans were. In my defence — because isn't that the theme tune of guilty people everywhere — I hadn't invited Lisa over for anything more than a look through Collie's things. She was welcome to a blanket, or a toy. But not the bedtime crackle of broccoli that Collie took to sleep with her every night. I had already decided that that needed to stay firmly in place at home where it belonged.

Because vanity knew no limits, I took a cursory look in the mirror between the living room and front door. Lisa was my ex, after all, and there were rules about not looking like shit in front of your exes, the same rules, maybe, that taught us clichés are clichés for a reason. I straightened out my shirt and then pulled in a ridiculously big breath and, on the exhale, yanked open the door.

And there Lisa was, wearing skintight jeans, a brilliant red blouse and a smile. 'You've made an effort.'

I laughed then, like an involuntary spasm of amusement. 'Hello. That's how we normally greet other humans.'

'Sorry.' She was flustered and I wasn't used to seeing her like that. 'Hello. Are you okay?' She saw my eyes drift down to the bag she was holding, though really it was the smell that I'd noticed first. She held it up, made a happy shrug and smiled again. 'I brought Chinese. I hope mushroom chow mein is still your favourite because I still hate the stuff. But I got chips to share and vegetable spring rolls. Actually . . .' She paused and peered into the bag. 'There's probably not much on the menu that I didn't get, so I hope you're hungry.'

I was, as it happened. I'd known Lisa was coming just after lunch and, sick with nerves and guilt and nerves some more, I hadn't eaten a thing. It wasn't until the waft of warm Chinese food hit me several times over, with Lisa lifting and lowering the bag under my nose, that I realised I was actually bloody starving. But my immediate hunger was elbowed out of the way by the realisation that answering yes to Lisa's question would not only mean she hadn't *just* come over to look through Collie's things, but that she'd also come over for dinner — which was, clearly, exactly what she'd planned.

It felt cruel of her to have engineered a sit-down dinner together. And there was her super-duper smile that she only fixed in place for what she deemed to be a special occasion — which initially was absolutely *not* what I would have classed this afternoon's plans as. I rubbed at the back of my neck and tried to answer quicker. And in applying that mental pressure I wound up giving her an answer to an altogether different question.

'I'm involved with someone,' I told her for the second time over.

Lisa looked as though I'd slapped her — but only for a fraction of a second. Then her stage-presence smile took over again. 'I'm a bit lost. Does that mean you're not hungry?'

'No, I . . . I'm just telling you, so you know. You know, where you stand.' I muddled through, now feeling like a total idiot as well as an absolute schmuck. *Who knew you could be both at once?* But I had done the right thing, I told myself. In that small act of . . . something, I had done the right thing. Though of course, some might have argued that "the right thing" would have been saying no to Chinese. 'It feels weird, not mentioning it,' I added when she didn't say anything back.

'Okay. Well, you've mentioned it twice now, and as we've established that you've got a girlfriend—'

'She's—'

And there it was, the trademark Lisa-laid bear trap. *I* hadn't used "girlfriend", she had — because she wanted to see whether I'd correct her or not. *And look at what you nearly went ahead and did* . . . I wouldn't ever have called Lisa manipulative. But the lads often had done. This felt like one of those occasions where they might have rolled their eyes and played the manipulative card a few hands over, and told me that I'd gone ahead and strolled right into in her plans.

Added to that, like a sharp tap against my cheek, one thought quickly knocked into all these others: *isn't Nell my girlfriend?* Man alive, I *wanted* her to be and had wanted that for months. But we hadn't actually talked about it. *But aren't we too old to talk about it?* I wondered whether I needed to officially ask her, or whether after these many months, she was essentially my girlfriend by default — which felt like the least romantic way of wooing a woman by anyone ever. And if there was one woman in the world who definitely deserved to be wooed, it was Nell . . .

'Whatever,' she said after my long pause. 'Are you hungry or not? Because I definitely am and whether you're eating or not, my Chinese is out here going cold on your front step.' Doubt bounced back and forth before I eventually stepped aside, on a twofold sense of reasoning: firstly, she now knew that I was involved with someone, so *everyone* knew where they stood on that, and, secondly, whether I ate with her or alone, she still needed to come in. 'You always were such a worrier, Owen,' she said as she scooted past me, though she paused on the way to cup my face for a hot second and I didn't much care for that.

'I'm trying to be a decent guy.'

'Decent men were never my type,' she answered as she peered through one doorway, then another, in search of the kitchen. It had been one of my big changes after Lisa left, to up and move to a new house, a fresh space. She hadn't commented on my décor decisions yet, and I wondered whether that was the sort of thing she still felt comfortable doing.

'Ah, well, that'll explain why you up and left me then.'

She shot around and there was that look again — that gentle slap to the face, only this time it was harder for her to shift.

'The kitchen is straight ahead of you,' I said when she didn't move to answer the comment. And when she didn't move, full stop, I scooted past her in the hallway and made a point of grabbing the bag of Chinese as I went. It might have been a harsh card to play so early in the afternoon, but at least it did something to redress the balance between us. Sort of. I hoped.

'Do you feel that you've got that out of your system now?' she asked when my back was facing her, as though not looking directly at me made it easier for her to snap back — not that she'd struggled all that much when we'd actually been together. That was another part of being with Lisa I could remember all too clearly. 'Or can I expect another couple of those comments over the course of the afternoon?'

'They're a bit like hiccups when it comes to you,' I said, opening a cupboard and retrieving plates for us both. 'You never quite know when they're going to come on, and they usually come in a flurry. Take a seat.' I handed her a plate, which she took with a raised eyebrow and a smirk.

'The thing with hiccups is they usually clear with a good shock.'

I was hunting out cutlery for the various containers that Lisa had started to unpack across my kitchen table. 'You're capable of anything as far as I'm concerned. You're never *not* shocking me.'

'Ah, shush, once upon a time you knew me well enough to predict my next move in a chess game.'

'Mmhmm, and then you left. Do you want a drink?'

'What have you got?'

'Coke Zero, orange juice, lemonade . . .'

'Orange juice, please.' I pulled it out of the fridge just as she added, 'Any chance you want to throw a splash of vodka in there for me?'

Sure, because booze is about the only thing missing from this trashcan fire, I thought as I topped up a glass for her. 'I don't have any alcohol in at the moment.'

Lisa frowned. 'Is everything okay?'

And somehow that was the comment that broke the tension. A laugh fractured across my face as I sat down opposite her. 'Yes, Lisa, everything is fine. I'm just out of alcohol.'

'Your girl's a big drinker?'

The mention of Nell made my stomach feel as if it was in a vice-like grip, and I must have worn the discomfort on my face because Lisa soon reached over to lay her hand on mine, as though the deliverer of pain could also be the thing to provide comfort from it — which had been another one of her specialist skills, too, I supposed.

'I was playing,' she said.

'She's a good woman and she means a lot to me.'

There was a long pause while she unloaded hideous amounts of duck onto her plate. I huffed, laughed, and felt the ache of a memory then, and Lisa finished what she was doing before she answered it.

'Duck always makes me think of her, too.'

Collie.

I smiled. 'Do you remember that time—'.

'When your dad left the table for all of *two* seconds—'

'Yes, and Collie was right in there, her jaws clamped around that duck leg like she'd never known food before.' I was laughing hard enough for my eyes to dampen.

'And she slept for basically a whole day?'

'And we always called it—'

'The meat hangover!' Lisa completed the memory and let that one roll into another. For every food container that was on the table in front of us, there were as many memories carefully laid on the table. Some only I remembered and some that only Lisa did, but many that we could piece together with the help of the other as though whipping out rolls of masking tape and taking a careful eye to the broken crockery of our history.

That was how it had happened on the phone, too, and in the handful of text messages — slipping into that muscle memory. Not that I could blame Lisa, *exactly*. It would have been just as easy for me to say no, this walk down memory lane isn't happening. But thankfully, with enough time, the inevitable happened and a roadblock set up between us anyway . . .

'Do you remember the time we took her to the beach and she basically did a bunk with that man's body board? She had the . . . what do you call, the strap thing, for the ankle? She had that in her mouth and she was tearing along the sand and . . . Man, I was trying so hard to shout her back and *so* hard not to double over with laughter.' My face ached for smiling at the memory of the ticked-off man, standing with his hands on his hips, as though a stern expression might encourage Coll to bring his property back. It wasn't until my laughter had settled that I realised Lisa hadn't joined in with it.

'I don't think I was here for that.' She flashed a sad smile and lowered her eyes back to the food that was left on her plate, pushing one piece of duck around, then a cluster of noodles, then a stick of broccoli. 'But it definitely sounds like something Collie would do.'

'She and I—' I started to push my own food around then — 'we got big on beach trips, in the month or two after. It was weird for both of us, being at home on our own. Well, not on our own, obviously, we had each other. But you know . . .'

'I know.'

'Are you done?' I asked, suddenly desperate for something, *anything* else to do, apart from sit opposite Lisa and feel the weight of her watching me.

I reached over to lift her plate away but again she grabbed my hand, again she stopped me in my tracks. The afternoon had had a too-comfortable feeling of déjà vu already — even though we were talking about Collie not being there when she so should have been, and we were doing it in a house that Lisa had never even visited before. But somehow, there was something here that I knew. *Does everyone feel like this when they sit down for dinner with an ex?* I huffed in the face of the thought. *How many people are mad enough to sit down for dinner with an ex?*

'Owen.' I could tell from the tone where she was going. 'I am sorry, for how I left. For leaving at all. I shouldn't have let things get so out of control, how they did. When I realised I was unhappy, I should have said, I should have actually spoken to you. I just . . . I got so tired of *nothing* happening with our life, do you know? The feeling of having settled and I felt so much like you weren't *doing* anything anymore, just letting things happen around you and . . .'

I pushed back from her handholding and grabbed the plate instead. I'd taken careful note of how it was *my* inaction, *my* unwillingness to do things that was the problem suddenly. Even though at the time the problem had been less to do with my inaction and more to do with the fact that I wasn't Zac from the accounting department in Lisa's office. But even with that glaring accusation in my face, I found that I couldn't push back against her. I just couldn't work out whether it was not feeling able to, or simply not being arsed.

'You really don't need to do this, Lisa.' I stood from the table then and scraped her remainders into the bin before throwing everything in the sink with perhaps a little more force than it called for. 'I'll Tupperware the leftovers for you. The living room is back through there, first door on the right. I've left out a box of Collie's things. You're welcome to one or two things, if there's anything you want.'

184

And even though it was uncharacteristic of Lisa's steam-roller personality, she didn't fight me on it. She only thinned her lips and slumped her shoulders, and pushed away from the table.

'Don't take the broccoli,' I added when she was nearly out of the room.

There was a long pause ahead of her answer. 'I wouldn't.'

CHAPTER TWENTY-THREE: NELL

It was the first month of Green Fields Books' own book club — and I had no idea how many people were going to come. It had been Nan's idea in the first instance, two months ago now, when she'd suggested getting a book club in to see what it did for regulars and making regulars.

Sparks had caught and I'd decided to make it book-club-meets-modern-day — despite Nan's loud opinions on the evils of "Instabooktweet" as she scornfully called social media. Still, my plan had been that I wouldn't wait for an established group to come to us, but instead I'd try to make my own. I'd put out an announcement on Daisy's — *the shop's* — Instagram, to say she was starting a book club where all humans and their canines were welcome. On the shop's Facebook page, I'd posted something similar, too, and we'd occasionally reshared the news, complete with the Book of the Month that we were inviting people to read with us to get the ball rolling. Book club members would be welcome to make their own suggestions as the months went on — assuming we would get any readers in the first month, and assuming, too, that they would stay for any months after that. But it would also mean that we could offer discounts on each Book of the Month as an added incentive — and as a way to shift some extra stock.

I'd explained the whole thing to Owen in bed two nights ago. We'd mostly recovered from the hiccup of him not coming to Nan's and instead we'd moved on to the hiccup of me meeting his entire family — which he still seemed to want me to do. I'd introduced the book club into our pre-bedtime conversation to sidestep getting too drawn into the plans he and Hattie had been making. "You're quite business savvy when you set your mind to things, aren't you?' he'd said. "Make sure you mention that to Dad,' he added jokingly. 'He likes a business mind.'

'Maybe you could mention it to him?'

Owen made a quizzical face at my answer.

'I'm not planning on giving my business CV to your family the first time I meet them.' I tried to keep my tone deliberately light even though the edges were already tinged with panic.

'That's a shame.' He settled further into the pillow, pulling the duvet up around him as he did. 'That's the sort of thing they'd find impressive.'

It was about then that I decided if the book club's first month turned out to be a success, then I'd mention it in passing to Owen's entire family — and sans much else that might impress them, from what I knew of them already, I *really* needed this to be a success.

So, on the second Wednesday of the month, Daisy and I set out finger sandwiches and carafes of grapefruit squash at the end of the working day, before we took our best art skills to the shop's sandwich chalk board. I used my best cursive to write BOOK CLUB THIS EVENING, then tried and failed to roll chalk over the underside of Daisy's front paw and print it on the board.

'Well.' I assessed the damage. 'It was worth a shot.' I smudged the failed attempt away and started again, this time relying on my limited drawing ability to fashion a paw print in the bottom corner of the board and a small dog's face — that could easily have been a teddy bear, or even a lion with the right squint — in the opposing corner.

187

'That's that.' I brushed chalk from my hands and onto my jeans, where it left a stain of pink fairy dust down my thighs.

I carried the board out to the pavement and placed it for easy viewing outside the shop front — it sat neatly between the two huge windows that were now adorned with orange and dark green leaves, bunting that I'd rolled out already to welcome knitwear season — and then Daisy and I went back in.

A solid five minutes rolled by before I found that I was nervously eating my way through the finger sandwiches, only realising exactly how many I'd eaten when I moved from tuna into cheese and tomato. But of course, I knew myself damn well enough to know the finger sandwiches would be the first things on my hit list once the nerves arrived. So I trod my way back into the small kitchenette and pulled the emergency tray of food from the fridge. I couldn't have been gone longer than a minute — stopping to shove three Pringles into my mouth in a single go, too, which admittedly held me back on time — but when I returned to the main shop with the sandwiches, Daisy was sitting staring out of the full-length window that formed part of the shop door. Outside, there was a woman waving frantically at me — and she had a French bulldog on a bright pink lead.

'Hi, hi,' I said as I opened the door for them both. 'Come on in. Book club?' Daisy and I both stepped aside to welcome the newcomers, though it wasn't long before Daisy and the Daisy miniature fell over each other in excitement.

'Yes, sorry, I didn't know whether we could just come strolling right in. I'm Jennifer.' She held out her free hand in greeting. 'And this is Coco.'

'Jennifer, Coco, lovely to meet you both. I'm Nell, and this is—'

'Daisy.' She flashed a nervous smile then. 'Sorry, that was weird, but we follow her on Instagram. That's how we heard about the book club.'

I stared down lovingly at Daisy, who was trying — and failing — to inspect something inside Coco's ear. *I knew this dog would be the making of me*, I thought, and not for the first time in her brilliant life. I welcomed Jennifer into the shop proper and encouraged her to grab a drink and a sandwich. 'Before I eat them all myself,' I said and she laughed like I was joking.

No sooner were Jennifer and Coco settled, I found that Daisy and I were greeting the next visitors, and the next, and . . .

The book club was due to start at 6.30 p.m. and by 6.15 p.m. there were five readers already seated and introducing themselves to each other. And to add to that joy? All five of them had brought their dogs . . .

* * *

I had not banked a single name from the many humans who turned up at the book club that evening. But I could happily introduce anyone to Truman the Husky, Archie the Chihuahua, Diane the Doberman, Peter the Pug, and many more besides. Whether it was the book club or the gloriously beautiful face of my dog that had pulled people in, I had no idea. Whatever the reason, though, Green Fields Books was *packed* with pets and their humans, and we had a riot of an evening talking through *Fifteen Dogs* by Andre Alexis. I wasn't sure whether "novels about dogs" was enough of a subgenre to keep us going through the entire lifespan of a book club. That said, by the time everyone was leaving we had at least three months' worth of titles decided — much of which had been ordered and reserved by my new clientele already, which made for a double-hurrah — and I was fairly certain that I had somehow found a niche in the world of dog-owning.

Owen had texted me halfway through the evening to ask how it was all going, but it wasn't until the door was locked and I was sitting cross-legged with Daisy awkwardly napping in my lap — exhausted from her social excursions — that I had the time to reply. Even then I only managed:

AMAZING. Was so busy. Nearly home time. Am STARVING.
Xxx.

I let my head fall back against the door behind me and a hearty sigh escaped. Daisy looked about as done in as I felt, her thick eyebrows moving now and then as she looked up at me. I wasn't sure whether a walk was a good idea for either of us, but owing to my indecision, I thought I'd let Daisy make the final call.

'How about it, babe, should we go home?' I asked, to no avail. There was no reaction at all to that one. But when I was only halfway through the follow-up question — 'How about a . . .' — Daisy was already up and scuttling in the direction where her lead lived. 'Okay, walk it is.'

I left the shop in a semi-mess for Future Nell to contend with. She'd hate me for it, but I was riding too much of a high from the book club's success — and the many happy sales that had gone through the till over the course of the evening, too — to feel too worried about duping my future self when it came to some cleaning. I left the plastic cups on one side of the sink, dumped the crusts from sandwiches in the bin and called it a night. Daisy was waiting at the door again, just like she had been at the start of the evening, only this time she was facing me. I imagined her with her arms folded, tapping one foot impatiently and waiting for signs of her lead.

'I'm coming, I'm coming.'

And we were off. It was a beautifully light evening with a breeze that carried with it some warmth still, even though autumn had definitely let herself in the side-door of the house while summer wasn't looking, a welcome houseguest you weren't expecting. I didn't need a jacket, so held on to that with one hand while Daisy tugged me along with the other, and without prompting she gravitated towards Green Fields dog park — creature of habit that she was.

I let myself be carried and promised both of us that we wouldn't be staying long, but when I saw the lush green landscapes and heard the quiet of it all, too, I knew that I had in fact lied, and we'd both be walking as far as our feet could carry us that night. I let Daisy off the lead and wandered ahead of her, leaving her to stop and literally smell the roses — though the sight of her with her head buried in the undergrowth of a bush made me think of Collie, her backside wagging as she tried to burrow underground. A sad sigh escaped me and I checked my phone for signs of Owen: *Pizza hungry or snacky snacky hungry? xx*

I laughed and tapped out my reply — *ALWAYS pizza hungry xxx* — before pocketing the handset and turning to check for Daisy. And that's when I saw him, balanced down on one knee as though proposing marriage to her when in reality he was giving her a chin scratch.

'Benji.'

He stood and smiled in a shy and endearing way. 'No need to make it awkward,' he said, making things immediately awkward. 'I just saw Daisy and thought I'd stop to say hello.'

'I'm sorry I didn't call,' I said with embarrassing abruptness, verbal vomit running down the small sloped space between us. 'I should have. Well, I shouldn't have, I . . . I'm involved with someone, I think.' *I think?* 'No, I am.' I corrected myself. 'I definitely am.' Owen and I hadn't talked labels — *did anyone when they got to our age, or did it just happen?* — but I thought "involved" covered the majority of whatever was happening between us. 'God, now *I'm* making this awkward.'

Benji laughed and something about the sound caused a chill over me. Not an unpleasant feeling, only an unexpected one. 'Nell, it's lovely to see you both, but if you're seeing someone then you were right not to call. Heck, I should have actually asked whether you were seeing someone.'

Owen and I had been in a strange stasis when Benji had visited the shop, obviously. But explaining that seemed like overkill so instead I graciously accepted what I took to be kindness and pity on Benji's part, and only smiled and nodded along as he spoke. 'It's nice to see you,' I said instead.

'Likewise.' He reached down to scratch Daisy's head again and I tried not to get too caught up in the fact that she was sitting so comfortably next to him. 'You're heading towards the city, rather than . . .' He gestured behind him. I hadn't even registered that Daisy and I were heading towards Owen's half of the city, so ingrained was the walk there now, I guessed.

'It looks that way. Come on, babe.' Daisy promptly left Benji then, and I felt comforted that she hadn't exactly taken much persuading. 'You take care now,' I said over my shoulder as we started the walk away from him.

'You too, both of you.'

We were so far along the path to Owen's that it hardly seemed worth turning around. He hadn't replied to my message, but I reasoned that a surprise visit from me and Daisy couldn't be a terrible way to end the day. *Right?* I tried to reassure myself the closer we got. As the sun started to dip, my sunshine confidence was turning into early evening doubt, and I couldn't decide whether a surprise visit might actually be a bit weird.

'What do you think?' I asked Daisy as I slipped her lead back on. I buried kisses in the folds of her face and felt comforted by that, even if she didn't feel moved to give me an actual answer. 'Come on, no turning back now.'

And there wasn't. We were already nearing Owen's house and I decided that at that point it would be weirder still if I turned around, started to walk home, and then wound up bumping into him anyway — which, knowing my luck, was a distinct possibility. His car was outside, which I took to be another sign that this was totally okay behaviour, even if I couldn't join the dots between those points.

I pulled in a greedy breath, hit the bell and let myself nervously bounce on the balls of my feet while I waited for an answer. When I looked down to check on Daisy, I thought she was shifting uncomfortably from one paw to the other, too.

Owen answered wearing a loose-fit T-shirt and jogging bottoms, neither of which were things I'd seen him wear before. His eyes widened and my immediate thought was, *Well, bugger, apparently it is weird.* But when Daisy set a single paw on the lip of his doorway, he crouched down to greet her with a baby voice and kisses like he would have done at any other time so — *maybe this isn't weird?* I still couldn't tell. He looked up at me — having dropped to Daisy in the same way that Benji had — and smiled.

'What are you two doing here?'

'Is it weird that we are?' I asked, my eyes scrunched up as though braced for the force of his answer. And the sheer length of time it took for him to answer was a crushing force, too. When I looked, I could see that he'd disappeared into the house and was now heading back to us with his phone in his hand.

'It's not really a good time . . .'

Whatthehellwhatthehellwhatthehell. 'Oh?'

Owen turned and waved a pizza-delivery app in my face. 'Only because there'll be a large vegetarian supreme on your doorstep in about fifteen minutes.' I thought my eyes might have filled with tears then — and I tried to remember a time when I'd ever cried over pizza before in my life. But Owen only shrugged and added, 'You said you were pizza hungry.'

CHAPTER TWENTY-FOUR: OWEN

We were days away from Nell meeting my parents and both of us were getting increasingly nervous about the whole thing — albeit for very different reasons. Nell was nervous that they wouldn't like her, that they would think — in her words, *not* mine — that she was some artsy-fartsy type who didn't have her head screwed on and spent her days pissing around with books.

Meanwhile, I was nervous that Nell would think my family was formed of emotionally inept robots — or rather, I was nervous that Nell would see my family for exactly what they were. Hattie was fine — better than fine. In fact, she was quite lovely most of the time, except for when she was around her husband. In those moments, her entire personality dribbled out of an escape valve hidden in her somewhere and she became so beige that I wondered whether it wasn't Hattie at all, but whether she was in fact at home, locked in a basement, while this Hattie 2.0 ran around after Eric, whom my parents loved.

Then there was Louise, who had blossomed into a miniature version of Mum. Which was to say that every coffee or phone conversation with her felt less like a catch-up and more like a job interview. She came complete with her own husband, Fritz — whose actual name was Artie Fitzwilliam — who was similarly inclined to conduct every conversation as though it were a formal exchange, even with me, the man who had once rubbed his back while he upchucked red wine into Mum's white porcelain bath, as though Fritz and I had *any* need for formalities after that.

Then, finally, there was Simon, the light of my parents' lives. He was the archetypal firstborn who was so perfect, so wanted, and so loved, it often made me wonder why my parents bothered themselves with the trouble of another three children at all. I could only assume they'd thought poor Wini hadn't had her hands full enough already, walking around and bit by bit picking up after my parents and their first offspring, that they'd assumed *multiple* offspring would be the thing to make her working days more complete.

Still, while Hattie, Louise and I always managed to bumble along with a baseline pleasantness, Simon and I had no such relationship. He was the first boy and all, and I was the mere second, and I had spent much of my life occupying that secondary role against him. He was older than me, so it made sense, to me, that he'd accomplished more already. But every time my parents gave me Simon's CV of life, it still left me with the aching dread that I was running too far behind to ever catch up — as though there was a need for me to. Simon also worked in the financial sector, but he was part of the investigatory body that monitored the work of registered accountants in the field — making him the Top Dog Everyone Wanted to Impress. I think that may have actually been his official job title. He worked sixty-five hours a week, made double and then some what my take-home was. He drove a car that must surely be a penis extension, and he had a wife that had been carefully peeled from a marketing ad for luxury fashion. I had never seen Magda, or their nuclear children, with so much as a hair out of place — just how Simon liked them.

And these were the people I was going to throw my beautiful, wild, free Nell towards. Never mind her impressing them. I would frankly be more relieved if she and I just got through the experience without someone trying to swallow her whole.

'They can't be as bad as you're making them out to be.' She laughed along with my explanations of them while she was wiping down the kitchenette in the shop. 'What makes them so . . . what did you call them?'

'Robots?'

'No! Emotionally stunted?'

'Inept. There's just no feeling there, Nell, there's a black hole where feeling should be. Do you know I haven't even told them about Collie?' I heard my voice catch as I said her name — and I thought it always would. Of all the things I'd told Nell about my family so far, this was the one that caught her off-guard.

She spun around with wide eyes and an O-shaped mouth before trying for a more neutral expression instead.

I huffed a laugh. 'It's okay, it *is* shocking. You're allowed to be shocked.'

'But you had her for so long, Owen, wouldn't they . . .' Nell let her eyes drift down to Daisy who was looking up at her with so much love that I thought I might melt under the warmth of it, too. 'Wouldn't they want to know that something had happened to her?'

I frowned. 'I'm not sure they would, no. But that's okay, you know?' I lied. It wasn't okay in the least, but I'd already made so many issues out of so many family things, I worried that a further moan about this might look like I was actively trying to deter her from coming. 'They're not dog people and they never were. Whenever Lisa and I went over we always had to leave Collie at home. It was only when it became just me and Collie that that rule lapsed, slightly, but even then there were times when Mum just wouldn't stand for her being there.'

Nell nodded along and then turned away, back to the cleaning that I thought if anything she had overdone by this point, just for something that would keep her busy through our chat.

'Hence, Daisy needs to stay at home. . .' I added.

'Probably for the best. I mean, she's one of the chillest dogs around but it's not like she doesn't take up her share of space.' She turned and spoke to Daisy then, using her best baby tones. 'Which you're absolutely entitled to. Yes, you are, yes, you are, Daisy Doo.'

Then, while I didn't have to look Nell in the face, I probed carefully at the one question that I'd been dying to ask — despite being terrified of it. 'Nell, is it weird that you're meeting my parents, when . . .'

She looked up at me, waiting for the end of the question to come. I struggled.

'You know, with your . . . loss?'

'Oh.' The sound popped out of her, a penny dropping down a well. She turned around and went back to the excessive cleaning. 'I mean, it's not weird, as such, only . . .' She paused mid-action and shrugged. 'It's sad, that's what it is. But it isn't weird. Of course I wish you could meet my parents, and get grilled by my dad and overfed by . . . But I'm glad I can meet your parents, whether you can meet mine or not. Besides.' She paused to clear her throat. 'You'll get to meet Nan at some point, too.'

I couldn't stop myself from closing what little distance there was and wrapping my arms around Nell from behind, letting my hands settle in the pockets of her mom jeans. I kissed the base of her neck, up to where skin met hairline, and I felt her breathing change as I moved over her.

'You're quite brilliant, Nellie — anyone ever tell you that?'

She laughed and tipped her head back to rest against my chest, her crown sitting just beneath my chin, which may well have been my favourite place for her to be. 'Where on earth did that come from?'

'I am dreading you meeting them, make no mistake.' I felt a soft shudder of a laugh move through her again. 'But you are a wonder and I cannot wait to show you off to them.'

Nell turned around so she could face me. I leaned a hand on either side of the counter behind her. She opened her mouth as though she was going to say something. But instead she placed a hand on each of my cheeks, pulled me towards her and kissed me. It started soft and tender, but the longer it went on the harder we both pressed — into the kiss, and into each other, until I had her pinned back against the kitchenette countertop. I moved my hands down to join behind her and waited for her to brace herself against the countertop before I lifted her. She sat with her legs around my waist and all the while we carried on the kiss without so much as a pause for breath. It wasn't until there came a small whine — a whimper, grumble, grimace, even — that the kiss became a smile and, as the unwanted soundtrack continued, it became a laugh.

'Are you feeling left out, babe?' Nell asked Daisy who was busy pawing at my calf by then. 'This isn't your sort of thing, sweet pea, I don't think. And even if it was, it would be weird.'

'Really weird.'

Nell looked back at me, her arms around my neck and her fingers playing with my hair. A whimsical sigh fell out of her and then she said something that caused a vice-like feeling around my ribcage. 'Owen, I really love . . . this, with you two, with us. I really love it.'

There wasn't the same hesitation the second time. But I had a nagging, nagging feeling that somehow what she'd said to begin with maybe hadn't been exactly what she'd planned to say. Still, I only smiled and told her the feeling was all too mutual. I would wait until she'd met my parents — and until I'd had at least two drinks — before I started to think about confessing my undying and ridiculous love for her. *Even though it's there all the livelong day . . .*

'I have a favour to ask you,' I said, lifting her back to ground level.

Nell began rinsing through the washrag she'd been using. She didn't even turn, she only made a murmur of encouragement and carried on with her duties for closing up.

'Could I walk Daisy tonight?'

'Like, now?'

I paused before answering. *Do I want to back out of this?* But I managed to answer, 'Yeah. I was wondering if . . . I don't know, I thought maybe I could take her over Green Fields if . . . I know it's your usual walk with her, after work. I just thought . . .'

Nell turned around and gave me a smile before she kissed my cheek. 'You're really asking permission from the wrong person.'

I dropped to my knee in front of Daisy then, deciding that if I were going to do this, I was going to do it right. I took her front paw in my hand and she looked at me a little like she thought that I was crazy, which was not how I'd heard women commonly reacted in these situations but, still, I pressed on. In a hurried, nervous mumble, I asked, 'Daisy, would you do me the honour of letting me walk you this evening?' At the mention of walk her whole demeanour changed. She snatched her paw away and instead wedged her entire head under my hand, nudging it in the air, pawing to get closer to me, before doing an excited lap of the small room and disappearing to where I knew her lead was.

Nell was aflutter with schoolgirl laughter and it was the most beautiful sound going. 'Well, I think that's probably a yes.'

'I'll bring her back by her curfew, I promise.'

'You'd better.' Nell kissed me again and went back to her chores. 'Do you want to have dinner with us?'

'I was thinking we could grab something, actually? There's that new spicy, herby chicken, what's it called? On the bottom of the high street?'

Nell's face fell into disapproval. 'Anything but chicken.'

'Okay . . .' I lingered, waiting for a fuller explanation that must be sitting there.

'It's just this thing my nan mentioned earlier and now . . .' She huffed a laugh. 'I just don't fancy chicken, I don't think.'

'Okay, anything but chicken we can do. We'll see you back at yours.'

And then we left for Green Fields dog park — just me, a dog who didn't belong to me, and my nagging spin of a sick feeling that was curled up in my stomach like a wild animal napping, or biding its time . . .

* * *

It had been an all-round grey day. But as though being given some divine approval for being on the walk at all, I found that as Daisy and I edged that bit closer to the dog park, the clouds parted and the sun made her way out, and I liked to believe that that meant something.

We pushed our way through the main gates and Daisy, in a way that was completely unfamiliar to me after so many years with Collie, kept to the path for the entirety of the first ten minutes of the walk — even after I'd taken her lead off — bar one slight detour off the beaten track to smell a rose bush. I was fully prepared to call her back, or to yank her out of there by her collar, as I might once have had to do on a walk with Coll, but Daisy brought a disconcertingly different energy to the experience. In fact, I found that fifteen minutes in I wasn't even checking for her anymore. Instead, I was strolling along the path, saying hello to people I hadn't seen . . . well, since, and otherwise enjoying a slow and gentle amble, while Daisy enjoyed her own plod through the world as well.

So imagine my shit-my-pants terror when I eventually did turn around to check on her and found her nowhere in sight. 'Daisy? Daisy!' The shouts got louder as I scanned the immediate area and still caught no sight of her — and Daisy was not an easy dog to miss. *Which I say with love and no judgement on her size.* I started to rush back along the path only to eventually see . . .

'Daisy!' I doubled over, my panicked breathing having finally caught up with me. It felt as though I'd been on a five-kilometre run — or rather, what I imagined going on that sort of run might feel like. 'Daisy, girl . . .' I managed to say as I walked closer to her.

She was sitting between the legs of an intimidatingly handsome man on a bench, wearing what I guessed were just-out-of-work clothes complete with an NHS lanyard around his neck — which I had to assume also made him some kind of a hero. He was scratching Daisy just behind her ear, in the spot that she loved, and I wanted to know how he knew to do that . . .

Why has Daisy even gone to him?

The man looked up and — because he was a gent as well as a hero, apparently — he waited until I had a steady breathing rate again before saying hello.

'You're not Nell.' He smiled, laughed then, and even *I* melted a bit. 'Sorry,' he said, leaning forward to reach out a hand. 'I'm Benji.'

'Benji.' *Isn't that a dog's name?* I thought with derision and judgement. *I mean, it's obviously jealousy. Look at the bloke.* 'I'm Owen, Daisy's minder for the evening.' I tried for my own laugh, too, but my chest hadn't quite recovered and instead it was an awkward and embarrassingly high-pitched noise that came out instead. 'It looks as though you two know each other?' I was trying to keep my tone neutral while steering the conversation towards the big-money topic.

'Yeah.' He laughed again. 'Sort of. I bump into Nell and Daisy sometimes when they're walking. I work at the hospital over there.' He turned and gestured, but then plucked at the lanyard, too, as though just realising it was still there. 'I walk through here sometimes on the way home.'

'You don't have a dog?' I fought the urge to raise an eyebrow with suspicion. 'Or you do . . .'

'No, no, I don't. I just borrow other people's.' There came another laugh, a light, easy sound that made his smile widen in a way that I absolutely didn't approve of. 'But I'd wager I've borrowed yours for long enough.'

'Well, I have her on loan, too, so I'd better . . .' *Be any-where other than here.* I autocompleted the sentence but gave myself points for using my inside voice. 'It was nice to meet you . . . Benji, right?'

'Right.'

Of course I remembered the man's name. But I'm not going to let *him* know that.

When he stood up, Daisy moved away, too, and I was pleased that despite the disappearing act she'd now come back to me without my prompting her — and she didn't look about ready to follow Benji, thank goodness, because my ego absolutely would not hold that weight.

'Nice to meet you, Owen,' he said and just before he turned, he added, 'Tell Nell that I said hey.'

He didn't wait for an answer — which was probably good, because I wasn't sure I had one. There were too many other thoughts lapping away at me instead. I trusted Nell, *of course* I trusted Nell. But the handsome man was, well . . . *handsome.* He was a doctor! He liked dogs! He probably had a family made up of other doctors and saints which I absolutely did not. *I bet he spends his free time volunteering at homeless shelters, too.* It took less time than it did for me and Daisy to finish our walk than it did for me to *entirely* fabricate a list of the ways in which The-man-with-a-dog's-name was better than me. And that wound up being the biggest and loudest of the thoughts I carried home . . .

CHAPTER TWENTY-FIVE: NELL

No sooner had Nan opened the front door, her mouth fell open as though a hinge had broken. She lowered her glasses, looked me up and down, and let out a low whistle.

'Which I'll take to be a good thing?' I asked.

'Oh, Nell.'

I was wearing a vintage black dress that was cinched at the waist by a bright pink belt. My hair — resisting the urge to be its usual wild and chaotic self — had been styled by my local guardian angel and hairdresser into loose waves and occasional curls that dropped down over my shoulders. The make-up was understated, too, with just a lick of foundation and blusher, and mascara to make the eyes pop. I had tried *very* hard to look like a woman who didn't have to try very hard to be beautiful. I wanted to *be* that woman when I walked into the party on Owen's arm. And I hoped to God that he saw that, too, when we were together.

'I really want to make a good impression,' I said, hopping from one foot to the other as though I were a kid again, about to clamber on stage for a school play.

'My lovely girl.' Nan leaned forward and cupped my cheek. 'Owen's family are not important, but they will love you from top to toe.'

I blinked hard and pulled in a deep breath to stifle what I thought was the beginning of tears.

'Don't you bloody dare.' Nan moved her hand away from my face and gently slapped my bare arm instead. 'Now, give me that gorgeous girl.' She reached for Daisy's lead and I reluctantly handed it over. Leaving my girl behind for the night was my least favourite part of the party deal. But Nan had been all too delighted when I'd asked if she'd Daisy-sit. 'There's a steak in the oven, my darling girl, yes, there is.' She spoke to Daisy in her usual baby tones.

'Please don't give her the whole thing?'

'You mind your own.' Daisy sat down next to Nan in the doorway then, and gave me a huffy look as though she was entirely on Nan's side — which was fair, I supposed, given that I was abandoning her for the night.

I promised Nan that I'd be over first thing in the morning to collect Daisy, even though she told me to take my sweet time. I think she not-so-secretly enjoyed the company. After saying an emotional goodbye to both of them — with a thousand soft kisses showered over Daisy's face — I hurried back home to find Owen already waiting for me. And by the grace of God, his reaction was markedly similar to Nan's: eyes popped, jaw dropped, and a long, drawn out . . .

'Fuuuuck.'

'Good fuck, or . . .'

'I "can't wait for you to meet my family" fuck.'

I laughed at the awkwardness of the sentiment, though it still felt like a whopping compliment, too. Owen hadn't been himself the last couple of days — he was . . . in his head more, away with his thoughts somewhere, though he never said where — and I'd largely put it down to his own set of nerves about introducing to his clan. But as he held the door open, and gave me a light tap on the backside as I clambered into the car, I thought — or hoped — his nerves might finally have gone.

He spent the majority of the drive from my house to the venue reminding me of everyone's names and giving me brief but hilarious physical descriptions that might help me to spot them in a room, in case Owen wasn't there to introduce me to them.

'Why wouldn't you be there?' I asked with a sudden flare of worry.

Owen softly laughed at my reaction. 'I'm going to have to pee at some point during the evening.' He reached over to set a hand on my knee and gave me a reassuring squeeze. 'It's going to be fine, I promise.'

And I really, *really* tried to believe him.

* * *

The venue was, in no uncertain terms, a castle. The amount of people that Owen had introduced me to within the first five minutes of walking into the building totalled the amount of people I knew, full stop. Whatever he had to say about his mother, she was obviously a popular-enough woman to fill a foyer, a reception room, half a bar and then some — and I hadn't even caught a whiff of a family member at that point. We ordered drinks while Owen carried on pointing out friends of the family. He was midway through describing a cluster of his dad's old business partners when I felt a hand latch around my elbow and yank me in the opposite direction.

'Oh my goodness, you must be Nell.'

The petite woman threw her arms around me, forcing my face into a mass of tight curls that smelled all too familiarly like hairspray and perfume knocking together. When she'd finished with the tight embrace, she held me at arm's length for a second, her palms cupped around my shoulders, which gave me time enough to get a good look at her face, too.

'You must be Hattie?'

'Yes! Oh goodness, I'm *so* delighted to meet you.' And to her credit, she seemed it. Though she also seemed a little like she was sizing me up for something. 'Gosh, we're all just so delighted that you're here. Hang on, let me get Louise.'

'Bloody hell,' I heard Owen say next to me in a part-groan, part-laugh. He wrapped an arm around my waist and I was especially glad of the contact. But it also meant that he could tell that at some point during the confrontation with his sister, I'd stopped breathing. 'Nell, you're going to need to exhale at some point.'

When I did, it came out in a burst, as though I'd been underwater swimming for too long — and there was a noise rushing through my ears that matched that analogy, too. Once that big breath was out the way, though, I managed a few smaller ones, and then I managed a laugh. 'This is so ridiculous. Why am I so nervous?'

Owen kissed just beneath my ear and a creep of something wonderful moved down my spine. 'Because you care and I love that about you.' I softened at the comment, my whole body loosening as I leaned closer to Owen and enjoyed whatever blissful moment was passing between us. 'Right.' He kissed my forehead. 'Louise is coming over. Keep breathing.'

'Nell.' Hattie took up the mantle of introductions. 'This is Louise.'

Louise didn't quite have the same bounce as her sister. An older woman, she gave me a practiced smile and extended a hand in greeting rather than going all out for a hug. Though she did say it was nice to finally put a face to the name — which made me wonder how much Owen had told them about me, or how much time he'd spent talking about me, both of which happened to be things that made me feel that bit better about the situation. It must have made me feel braver, too, because as though tumbling into some wild mode of autopilot I found myself saying, 'Is Simon here or . . .'

Louise and Hattie swapped a look.

'Oh shit, did something happen with Magda?' Owen asked, suddenly much more interested in the chatter than he had been. He'd forewarned me that if there were going to be sparks, they'd likely come from Simon's corner of the ring.

'No, he's . . .' Louise nodded behind us and Owen turned to look. 'He's just over there.' I turned then, too, and saw a tall and offensively chiselled man who looked a little bit like he'd come out of a Barbie's companion box. Simon was easily six foot tall with a jaw made of marble and a suit that I wagered must have set him back more than my monthly takings at the shop. I could see already why Owen didn't much care for his brother — they may have shared genetics, but it was clear from looking at them alone that they were cut from different cloth. He was talking to a woman who wasn't his wife — that was clear from their body language, the way she threw her head back when she laughed and softly slapped his arm, as though to underscore that whatever he'd said was definitely the most hilarious thing she'd heard all day, even though it likely wasn't. Still, they were a good-looking pair. The woman was wearing a red wrap dress, which she absolutely had the figure for, and her hair was a beautifully messy updo that must have taken her, or her stylist, an offensive amount of time.

'That isn't Magda?' I asked then because everyone had been quiet for too long and it was starting to become unsettling.

'No.' Louise only flashed me a tight smile, without offering anything more. Then she politely changed the topic entirely. 'Owen tells me you run a bookshop?'

'Own, she owns a bookshop,' Owen corrected, and I squeezed against him in thanks. 'It's Green Fields Books, in—'

'Oh my goodness.' Hattie burst in. 'That's *your* bookshop? My friend literally just went to a book group, club, thing you hosted. With dogs, right?'

I was *beaming*! For days now I had been trying to work out how to seed the shop's successes into everyday conversation with Owen's family and now, I didn't have to. Instead, chatter naturally unfolded like a flower showing one petal at a time, with Louise and Hattie both asking questions and looking genuinely interested in my answers, and I was desperately hoping that any responses I gave them would cross-pollinate with the rest of Owen's family members, too.

'Anyway.' Louise eventually shifted the topic. 'We've hogged you long enough. Have you even met Mum yet?'

I shook my head. 'Not yet. But I have a little . . .' I gestured to the gift bag I was holding. It wasn't anything big, largely because I didn't know the woman well enough. But it was a vintage, cloth-bound edition of Emily Brontë's *Wuthering Heights*, which Owen had tipped me off was his mother's favourite book. I'd tried not to judge her too harshly for it, and had gritted my teeth to the point of nearly causing a fracture when I'd ordered it into the shop, wrapped it in tissue and wedged it into the bag. 'It's just a little something.'

Hattie reached forward and squeezed my forearm, and with a shocking amount of sincerity said, 'Nell, that's tremendously sweet of you.'

'Owen, why don't you take Nell to the gift room?' Louise suggested, and I tried not to balk at her use of the phrase "gift room", which she seemed to have used in an entirely serious and not at all piss-taking manner. 'I think Dad was up that way, too, so you may manage some introductions?'

Owen nodded. 'Of course. We'll see you both later?'

'Lovely to meet you both,' I added as Owen led me away. He held my hand as we swerved through the room, moving at such a speed that I didn't even have the chance to ask how I'd done with his sisters! Then, thanks to a shuffle of an older gentleman who seemed unwilling to move for anyone, we wound up heading in Simon's general direction. *Two siblings down, one to go*, I thought, sucking in a deep breath to ready myself. But Owen swerved us again, taking us out into a hallway then up a flight of stairs. 'We missed your brother,' I said, not realising how out of puff I was until I tried to get the sentence out in a single breath.

'Hm?'

'I thought we were heading towards Simon?'

'Oh, we can catch him later.' Owen's pace slowed once we were on the upstairs landing, where everything seemed altogether calmer. I wondered whether we could hunker down here for the rest of the evening. But I was also buoyed by having met two out of three siblings, and a part of me was desperate to rip off the plaster of meeting a third. *Where are the parents? Let's tackle them!* The cocksureness absolutely did not suit me in the slightest.

'I'd like to meet your mum,' I said, having dropped her present on a whole table full of presents. 'Is that . . .'

Owen leaned forward with a soft smile and kissed my cheek. 'It's more than okay. Come on, let's tackle the madding crowd.' I took his arm and tried not to swoon at the literary reference — one so good that I'd definitely used it myself before. 'I hope I get points for that nod to Hardy,' he said jokingly.

'Oh, you get *points*, don't you worry.'

Once we were downstairs, we managed to steer back towards the bar without running into another member of Owen's family. Though Simon —the Jolly Green Giant, as I'd already come to think of him — had waved at us from across the room, before beckoning us towards him. He seemed like the type who was used to summoning people. Owen ignored the call, though, and instead ordered a drink for me, a drink for himself and a drink for his mother — 'She'll soften quicker if she's given alcohol' — before we braced the wave of suits and swanky dresses, in an attempt to find where the birthday girl had bunkered down.

Seconds into our journey through the ocean of guests there came a confused, 'Owen?' as though the speaker was surprised to see him there.

But Owen answered with a less confused, 'Dad!'

Owen's dad moved in for a handshake — *a handshake?* I tried to keep any reaction in check — but when he spotted a drink in either hand, he changed the gesture to a light bump on his son's shoulder instead. 'You must be looking for your mother.'

Owen laughed. 'Yes, with reinforcements in hand. But, Dad, look, while I've got you—'

'She'll be around here somewhere.' His dad looked over the heads of the crowd. 'Have you tried the . . . oh, of course you've tried the bar, you have drinks. Oh!' The final eruption was accompanied by wide eyes and the smallest of steps away from us both. 'Goodness, you have company.'

'Dad, this is Nell. Nell, this is my dad, Theodore.'

Clearly on firmer ground this time, Owen's dad looked notably relieved that he could shake my free hand — and in return, I gave him my best businesswoman's shake. 'It's a pleasure to meet you, sir.'

'And you, dear, and you. Now . . .' He was looking over our heads. 'Where's Mother?'

He gave Owen another light tap on the shoulder before he wandered off into the crowd. As meeting the parents go, it was the most understated interaction I could have imagined. In fact, far from needing to impress Owen's dad, I felt grateful that I'd even registered on his radar. The man seemed to have the attention of a magpie.

'That was . . .' My words withered when I realised I didn't really know what to say.

Owen snorted. 'That's Dad, yes. That also means we're one parent down, one to go. Mum's usually not this difficult to find at a party.' Owen spoke over his shoulder. 'I'm surprised we didn't bump into—'

And then Owen and I came to a literal bump. He stopped short in front of me and I collided into his back, spilling a streak of my gin and tonic down his jacket. *Bollocks*. I rubbed quickly at the spill but tried to pass it off as gentle contact while craning to ask whether he was okay. Owen's stare was fixed ahead on an older woman — *is that his mum?* — talking to the same red-wrapped woman that had been with Simon earlier.

'Do you know what—' he turned abruptly — 'let's have these drinks and then see her?'

'But we got her a drink?'

'Well, I'll have it.' In two thirsty mouthfuls he downed half of the orange juice and vodka that we'd bought — despite the fact that he was drinking gin and lime. 'See, it won't go to waste.'

'Owen, what's going on?' I tried to laugh but there was a turn of nerves in me. 'Is . . . Have you changed . . .' *Has he just realised he doesn't want me to meet her?*

210

The turn of nerves became a revolving wheel of them, knocking into my insides, rattling around in the spaces between each rib. I tried to form a sentence but I couldn't push any words out. It felt as though every ounce of worry that I thought had dissipated had instead bubbled to the surface, and even the sight of my gin was turning my stomach. 'I think I could do with using the bathroom. Do you know where it is?'

'Yes, excellent idea! Okay, yes, it's this way.'

Owen dropped me off in an actual queue for the women's bathroom — *a whole castle and we're queueing for the loo?* — with far too much enthusiasm. He told me he'd be outside when I was ready, getting himself a burst of fresh air, and I nodded along like all of this was fine. Inwardly, though, I felt like I'd lost track of something. Everything *had* been fine, but then there was a spin when . . . *was it seeing his mum?* I leaned against the wall for support and lowered my head slightly, taking deep breaths as I went. I'd never known a sickness like this, not one quite so violent or so sudden, though I didn't feel like I was going to be sick, only that the threat of it was in me. I was forcing out another long breath when I felt a hand between my shoulder blades.

'Are you okay, hon?' I looked up and into the face of the red-wrapped woman. She was even more beautiful up close: neat white teeth, perfect make-up, red lipstick that made her look like she could take the throat out of something. She smiled widely when she saw my face as though recognising me — which apparently she did. 'Oh, oh, you're Nell?'

With a sudden clarity of mind that only comes in hideous, ugly moments of panic, I realised *it's you, you're what Owen is steering me from . . .*

She held out a hand as she introduced herself. 'I'm Lisa. I've been so looking forward to meeting you.'

And then, in a move that went against every British bone in my body, I jumped the queue for the bathroom. But at least it stopped me from upchucking on the floor.

CHAPTER TWENTY-SIX: OWEN

This is why people smoke.

I paced from one side of the patio to the other. There was nothing else for it. The only thing that steadied me was to keep moving. It felt as though Nell had been in the bathroom for at least a month and a half — *but isn't that what women do?* — and I started to doubt what I'd said to her as I left. *Did I say that we'd meet out here?* I tried to replay the last of the conversation but everything was smoke and mirrors — and then literal smoke, as Simon appeared through a cloud of vapour like a poor magician's token trick.

'How's it going, kid?' he asked, in his smug bastard tone, and in my schmuck panic I opted for a physical response to the question. Despite our painfully obvious height discrepancy, I found that I was gripping onto the lapels of Simon's suit jacket and tip-toeing as tall as I could manage to lessen the distance between our faces.

'Did you invite her, you pillock, was it you?'

I saw my spittle land on the collar of his unbuttoned shirt, and when Simon looked down with a disdainful expression I guessed that he noticed it, too. *Don't back down now*, I told myself. *Let the spittle underscore the point.*

With me still hanging from his lapels, Simon click-click-clicked his vape to turn it off and pocketed it. Then he grabbed my hands and, in a swift, and frankly quite embarrassing, lifting motion, loosened me from my hold over him. Once there was a reasonably healthy distance between us he brushed his suit down, as though I might have left more than just spittle on his collar.

When he eventually spoke it was with a level tone and a raised eyebrow that reminded me far too much of Mum. 'Look, milksop, I'm not sure who you think you're talking to, but you'd be wise to remember it's me.' He pushed into my shoulder with his index finger then, and between that and the orange juice and vodka I'd necked, I was instantly unsteady. 'But if you're talking about the new girl meeting the old girl, no, that's *nothing* to do with me. Coming from someone who's rolled in their share of relationship shit, I wouldn't ever sink that low.' He brought his vape out again, and it seemed as though his argument was over. Meanwhile, I was back to pacing, running my hands through my hair as I went — having exhausted the action of fumbling about for nothing in my pockets, which had kept me busy to begin with. If Nell took any longer in the sodding bathroom, though, I may well have ripped my hair out entirely by the time she came back. Though of course, that worry soon slipped to one side when Simon the Pillock, as he would henceforth be known, delivered his final blow. 'Now, Mum on the other hand . . .'

'Mum? *Mum*?' I was in his face again, albeit fuelled by shock this time rather than rage. 'How the hell did *Mum* invite her? It's meant to be a bloody surprise party!'

Simon shrugged. 'Mum always knows about these things.' He pulled in a long drag and exhaled a dragon's worth of vapour. 'I think it's Dad, you know, who tells her. Ever since the cheating incident all those years back, it's like he's terrified to keep anything from her.' He shook his head, inhaled again and spoke through the plume. 'Shocking, it really is. But, no, while I appreciate you giving me credit for being quite such a twat towards you, it's credit I'm undeserving of.'

'Did you just call Mum a twat?'

He let a long pause pass before he answered. 'Don't you have a girl to chase? Tick, tock, tick, tock, which one, which one . . .' He moved his head to the beat of the words as he turned to walk away — and that's when I saw her.

Nell was standing in the doorway to the outside patio with smudged make-up. It mightn't have been noticeable to someone who hadn't seen her at the start of the party. But there was something different about the mouth, and a slight smudge to the make-up around the corner of each eye, too, and I was trying to read her expression for signs of rage or disappointment or — *it's shock*, I realised then, deciphering the paleness, the blank-slate look on her face. *She's in shock*.

'Nell . . .' I took a step towards her and even though there was a solid two metres between us still — me in the open air and her still safely tucked inside the building — she held her hand palm up to stop me. 'Nell, I don't know whether you heard *anything* that was said between me and Simon just now, but I didn't invite her to this. *I* didn't even know that she'd be here.'

Nell shook her head slowly. 'Then why . . .'

'Mum invited her. I have no fucking idea why. But you have to believe me, *I* didn't invite her.'

'Why would your mum . . .'

It was like she genuinely didn't have energy enough to finish her sentences. I wanted more than anything to close the gap between us and to pull her into the perfect hug, one where her head sat beneath my chin and I could kiss her and tell her everything would be fine. The fact that you simply couldn't offer that comfort when you're also the cause of the distress physically winded me. I found that I was reaching for my stomach in expectation of feeling a kick of pain there.

'I have no idea, honestly, no idea. But, Nell, listen . . .' I tried my luck and took a step towards her. She didn't stop me, which I took to be a sign of something positive. *That, or she's getting ready to slap me*, though at least a pinch of anger would have been better than this stunned version of her. 'Nellie, think about it. Logically, why would *I* be the person to invite her? I brought you, I wanted to introduce you — why the hell would I engineer a crash collision when things are so . . . just so, Nell . . .'

'She said the two of you have been talking. That you . . . Did you have dinner together?' Something ticked over in her expression then, as though the shock had finally given way and there was something terrifying underneath it, and quite suddenly I wished we were back in shocked land because in anger land, Nell was *definitely* not using her inside voice — at a party, with my family and my family's associates. She managed a few tentative steps forward then, too, placing her firmly on the outside patio with me, where people were laughing and smoking and . . . *Listening?* 'Have you been seeing her, is that true?' she asked, louder than I would have liked, but how do you shush a woman who's just found out that you have in fact been acting like a bit of an arsehole?

Of course, the answer was you didn't shush them at all. Instead, like a cornered chimp, you started to fling your own shit into the situation and hope that it somehow counteracted the shit that's already there.

'Okay, well, why don't we talk about the time *you've* been spending with *Benji?*'

Nell's face screwed up in confusion as though she'd never heard the name before in her life, and it crossed my mind that I may, *may* have made a colossal balls-up in mentioning the handsome doctor at all.

'How the hell do you know who Benji is?'

Aha! I felt somehow vindicated, until a slither of sadness hit at the thought that she may actually have been spending time with this man.

'Daisy and I bump into Benji on walks, he's been in the shop, like, one time? How the hell did Benji become involved in this?'

'Well.' I huffed and fidgeted. 'All I'm saying, Nell, is that we've all got our own people . . . in our lives . . . who we may or may not spend time with.' *Fucking hell, what am I admitting to here? Or am I trying* not *to admit to something here?* Even I didn't know where I was going with the argument anymore. I only knew that it was killing me to see Nell look so confused. She still hadn't explained the Benji situation, though; after all, once upon time, she'd just bumped into me and Collie on walks, hadn't she? And then the flare of indignation rose through me again. *Don't do it, Owen.* The logical bit of my brain put up a good fight. *Do not turn a* you *thing into a* Nell *thing.* 'Besides, you were just going for walks with me once, weren't you?'

And there it is, you bloody idiot . . .

Nell's mouth opened but whatever sound may have escaped was imperceptible. She looked as though I'd wet-fish slapped her around the face with the accusation — and worse still, a growing crowd of people had heard it. There might have been the background bustle of conversations on the patio when this confrontation started, but now we had an open-air theatre space to ourselves and I had literally stunned Nell into silence in front of *everyone* within earshot. And still I waited for the comeback, for the defence. Though of course, Nell's defence would inevitably mean that I had to provide my own — which I couldn't, on account of having been a bloody liar for all of five minutes. But then there came something worse than accountability. An option I hadn't been at all prepared for, although I absolutely should have been. Instead of snapping back, defending herself, repeating or redrafting the Benji explanation, Nell only shook her head and shut her eyes tight for a second. I suspected it was to hold in tears. I recognised the look from times when we'd talked and cried over Collie together, and that memory made this moment all the more horrific. Because instead of saying anything at all, Nell only turned and moved through the crowd of onlookers — and then she was gone.

* * *

And after that, life became really shit.

I was screening calls constantly, from Lisa and from various members of my family. But I was simultaneously *terrified* of putting my phone on silent in case I missed a call from Nell. It had been three days now and there hadn't been so much as a "*typing . . .*" on WhatsApp, though I had started to type once when I saw her online, on the off-chance that she might see me typing and feel inclined to message me to ask what I'd been typing. *Because apparently, who knew, but I am thirteen years old.* I clicked into my conversation window with her again, and saw her online.

There came a knock on my office door then, and Douglas stepped inside without waiting for a welcome. He'd always struck me as that sort of person. 'Everything okay in here, sport?'

It was the first time he'd ever called me by an affectionate nickname. Ordinarily, I would have taken this as a sign of something positive. In the late afternoon of another Nell-less day, though, it meant nothing. 'Of course, Douglas, absolutely.'

'Only . . .' He looked at his watch. 'You should have clocked off forty minutes ago, and you've been staring at that phone of yours for at least thirty-nine minutes.'

I managed a laugh, and in the nerves of the moment I rubbed at the back of my neck.

'Woman?' he asked, and I hesitated before nodding. 'Want some sage advice?' Something told me the sage advice was coming whether I wanted it or not. 'Tell her that you're sorry? It goes a long way, it turns out.'

It was the sincerest that Douglas had ever been, and it threw me for a loop. I opened my mouth for a thank you, or a . . . anything! But there was nothing I could give him apart from a joyful kind of surprise. And then, just when my silence was about to become awkward for the pair of us, my phone rang — and I leaped on the handset like a kid would leap on a caramel-coated chocolate bar.

Douglas laughed. 'I'll let you get that.'

'Thank you, Douglas, just . . .' But he'd already buggered off — maybe to impart wisdom elsewhere, maybe to enjoy some water-cooler talk with "one of the boys" to counteract the sage wisdom and all. I answered the humming handset. 'Hiya, mate.'

'Come on, dickhead, I'm downstairs,' Alan answered in turn. I thought I could hear Luke in the background, too. 'We've come to escort you.'

'To the pub quiz?' I turned off my computer and grabbed my jacket from the back of my seat. 'I think I probably could have made it there on my own, lads.'

'That's what I said but Zee has been bleating on about being supportive and I don't know, some other bull, what with . . . everything. So, Luke and I are here to give you a support either side. But if you take any longer to get out of that friggin' office—'

'Then I'll come up and bloody get you,' Luke finished in a much louder tone.

'Give me three to five minutes and I'll be with you.'

'Okay, you've got two or I'm sending Luke up.'

'If you could start googling literature facts on your way down, that would also be—'

There came a kerfuffle down the phone line and the muffled sound of Alan saying, 'Don't be a dickhead, mate, he's really hurting here.'

I disconnected the call and pulled up a fresh page in my browser. After inputting *20 literature facts for a pub quiz*, I took a cursory look through the first two results while I waited for the lift to arrive on my floor and carry me to ground level. The lads were waiting there, both with open arms, but to my surprise it was Luke who got to me first.

'I am sorry, mate,' he said as he held on to me in an awkward hug. 'You don't think there's any chance of . . .'

'Luke.' Alan cautioned him.

'No, it's okay,' I answered. 'I'm okay. But I don't . . . I honestly don't know. I might call her.' Though I mostly said it to test the waters for their reaction. I hadn't quite expected Luke's reaction to be as it was.

'I mean, if you called her now . . .' He checked his watch. 'She could probably make it down to the pub in time for the lit round, I reckon.'

Alan backhanded him across the arm. 'What did I literally just say about being a dickhead?'

'Come on.' I paced off, leaving the pair of them bickering behind me. Going straight from work would mean that I'd have to tackle a thirty-five-minute walk there the following morning, but I wagered that might be worth it for the distraction of a night with the boys. 'Maybe getting my arse battered by Agatha Quiztie can be my penance for this whole sodding mess.'

'Now, let's not be hasty.' Luke rushed after me. 'I'm not sure an arse-battering is necessarily a road you want to go down in the situation.'

'Are we still talking about the quiz?' Alan asked then, and it was the first time I'd laughed in three days. *Nell would have laughed at that, too*, I thought and then I was checking her WhatsApp again, typing a fake message again . . .

When we were still a ten-minute walk away from the pub, Alan confiscated my phone. 'You can have it back when you can be trusted to use it responsibly.' He slipped the handset into his back pocket.

I didn't even fight him on that. Not only did it seem like a fair comment, but it was also a relief. At least now I had three blissful hours of not knowing, not checking. It was Schrodinger's text message. A small gas canister that could go off at any time, or not. Even though I knew that it wouldn't. After all, Nell wasn't the schmuck.

CHAPTER TWENTY-SEVEN: NELL

Eloise had stepped up for Daisy and shop duty for an extra hour, though the former took infinitely less work than the latter. I'd had to schedule a doctor's appointment and of course, the doctor could only see me at the most inconvenient time imaginable. Eloise said she didn't mind, though, in fact, 'I'm glad you're going to see a doctor, Nellie. You've looked dreadful for days.'

I muttered a solemn thank you before telling her I'd see her later and hanging up the phone. She, like Nan, was of an age where she could say whatever she bloody liked, and, while it cut sharp to be on the receiving end, I personally couldn't wait to arrive at a point in my life where I could say whatever I liked without the worry of a sour face or a comeback. And at that, I thought again of Owen, slinging accusations and generally acting like an all-out crazy person, over a man whose surname I didn't even know without looking.

I thumbed Benji's business card again, before putting it back inside one of the drawers behind the till at work. Over the last few days I'd carried it around with me, not through the temptation of calling him, but through the temptation of ripping it in two and forever swearing off all men.

'You're not Bridget bloody Jones,' Nan said when I shared that intention with her, and I thought she was probably justified. 'Keep it. It may come in handy if things don't work out with the other chap and all.'

But I couldn't guess at the likelihood of things working out too well with "the other chap", given that it had been nearly a week now since the argument — in front of his entire family no less — and I still hadn't heard from him. Of course, I'd committed the shameful sin of intermittently checking his social media channels, but the only things posted there were two memories of Collie — both of which had made me want to reach out to him, though I'd managed to resist. Still, I couldn't imagine the hurt those flashbacks brought him and it was strange to think I was no longer the person providing the comfort.

But maybe Lisa is.

Aaaaand just like that, Lisa was back in the room making any intended reconciliations on my part curl up and die in a corner of the stockroom. Speaking of which, I found myself again — by mid-morning, which was at least slightly later in the day than this usually happened — steadily lowering myself onto the shop floor so I could sit next to Daisy, who was napping in one of her many beds. I didn't speak to her, only stroked the rough of her fur and took deep inhales and exhales. And soon, as she always did, she would shift a little closer and a little closer still, until the weight and warmth of her was pressed into my thigh.

'Oh, Daisy, what are we going—'

The question broke off when I felt the hum of my phone in my back pocket. I shifted awkwardly to free the handset. *Lucia?* I checked the wall clock opposite me and answered with a measure of suspicion.

'Are you just getting home from a night out?'

'No, you cheeky cow.' Her voice was thick with sleep. 'I'm just waking up. I've got a shoot on-set at five a.m. and if I don't get up at this godforsaken hour then I won't have a chance of coffee. Need I say more?'

221

I laughed and agreed with her. I knew Lucia well enough to know that getting along with her at any time in the morning without a coffee was grim, never mind if they actually expected work out of her.

'But I wanted to call and check in, to see how you're doing.'

'I'm fine, honestly.'

'Sitting on the shop floor again?'

I let too long a pause pass before I said, 'No . . .'

'Daisy looking after you?'

'Yes.' That was an easier one to answer. Now, she had schlumped the full weight of her head on my knee, meaning that by law I couldn't move anywhere even if I wanted to. 'I have the doctors today, for . . . you know.'

'Oh, boy, okay.' Lucia suddenly sounded more awake, as though my announcement had given her a gentle tap around the face. 'What time?'

'Midday. Eloise is covering so I don't have to close, so that's something.'

'Mm. You're doing the right thing, babe, getting stuff checked out. You can't just bury your head and wait it out, can you? Well—' she huffed a laugh — 'I mean, you *can* . . .'

'But I definitely shouldn't.'

'But you definitely shouldn't,' she answered in agreement, and I was glad of the reassurance. 'Will you let me know how you get on?'

'Sure, I'll text though, I don't want to distu—'

'I'll be sincerely insulted if I get anything less than a phone call. I just want to know how you get on. I don't need the gory what-have-you.'

'Jesus, I hope there won't be any gory what-have-yous.'

'You know what I mean.'

The shop bell rang ahead of me and pulled my attention up. Alongside answering every phone call like my life depended on it — in case it was Owen calling to apologise — I had now developed a Pavlovian response to hearing the shop door open. Whenever it went, wherever I was, my head would snap around

222

to stare down the visitor — on the off-chance it was Owen, turning up on my doorstep again, just like he had done the first time. But of course, it hadn't been — *and it won't be*, I reminded myself sullenly. I was trying hard to get used to the idea.

'I've got a customer, Luce. I need to go.'

'I love you, babe. You'll be fine.'

'I love you.'

The swapped sentiments made my eyes prick with feeling. It's a tired and ugly old cliché to say that absence made the heart grow fonder. Maybe it did, maybe it didn't. But I knew what absence *did* make you do: it made you realise in the quiet dead of night, in the hectic afternoon of a workday, in the calm of an after-work dog walk, whether you loved someone or not. *Oh, and I did, I do*, I thought with more than a measure of sadness as I struggled up from the floor and tweaked my theatre-mask frown into a smile instead.

'Mr Gentle!' By name and by nature, he was the softest-spoken customer that I had — and he was about all I could take that morning. 'Here for your order?'

'Oh, Nell, is Daisy okay?'

I looked across to her where she was belly up and exposing herself to the world. 'I think so?'

He smiled. 'Only because you were sat down there with her.'

'Oh!' I managed a laugh then, while I ferreted around under the counter for the man's order: *Yellowface* by R.F. Kuang. It seemed an unlikely read for him. Mr Gentle had never told me as much, but I suspected he was part of a book club in the city somewhere, because at least once a month he would order something like this — a book that I absolutely couldn't marry to him as a reader. I sealed it in a brown paper bag and placed it on the counter. Bought and paid for already, as Mr Gentle always insisted on. 'We're fine.' I lied to the kind man opposite me. 'It's just, I suppose sometimes you just need to sit on the floor with your dog, don't you?'

Mr Gentle let out a low, lullaby chuckle and the sound made me truly happy. 'Yes, yes, I suppose you do.'

The door was hardly closed behind him when I clambered back on the floor, back to kneading the soft dough of Daisy's tummy. Customers came and went but this spot was our safe space for much of that morning — that was, until I had to leave for the least-wanted doctor's appointment of all time.

* * *

The waiting room smelled of illness. Doctors' surgeries had forever been a place where I worried I would leave sicker than when I arrived. Though it wasn't exactly sickness that had brought me. On this occasion there was a nagging nausea in the pit of my belly that I hadn't been able to shift for at least a week. It was impossible to know whether that was down to everything that had happened, or whether it was actually down to—

'Eleanor Cobalt?'

'Yes!' I leapt from my seat like an excited bingo player calling for a full house. 'Yes, that's me,' I said more quietly, before following Dr Thompson into her office, leaving behind the swill of sniffs and coughs.

'So . . .' Somehow she managed to sit down and immediately start typing something into my notes, even though neither of us had swapped a full sentence. She punctuated whatever she was writing with a final hard tap on her keyboard before she turned around to me. 'Last period?'

'Five weeks ago.'

'Sexually active?'

'Yes.'

'Being careful?'

'I thought so.' I laughed as I spoke. 'But given that I'm here . . .'

Her round face softened into a smile. I could see Dr Thompson as a mother. In fact, I had seen her as a mother, more than once when she'd been out with her own two children, a boy and a girl. She'd brought them into the shop

224

once, too, and we'd both smiled and pretended that she hadn't been the person to perform my last smear test, while her well-behaved children kindly asked whether it was okay to touch Daisy. There was something of the maternal in her in the way she looked at me then, too.

'You said you've taken a test at home already?' She turned and looked at the screen then. 'Ah, two tests at home already — is that right?'

'That's right, yes.'

'And they were both positive?'

'Well, no.'

When she faced me again her smile had bunched into something more inquisitive. 'Inconclusive?'

I sucked in a greedy breath. 'This only started because I told my nan that I'd gone off the smell of meat, or just handling meat, really, and then she started talking about my mum and how *she'd* been really weird about . . .' I petered out when I realised I'd been answering a question that she definitely hadn't asked. And I wondered whether she was as trained for this — for this incoherent spill of feelings — as she was for physical ailments. It seemed likely, given the hideous things that people happened to share with their doctors. Pregnancy scares included.

'I understand,' she said softly, and I wondered whether she did. 'And the results of the tests you took at home?'

'One of them was a sad face, to show negative, which I think is mighty bloody presumptuous. The second one was . . . I don't know, the window was all watercolour. It was basically a frown.' I let out a nervous laugh. 'In the result window, if they'd put an emoji there it would have been a shrugging face, I think. So, it wasn't positive.'

'But it wasn't negative either.' She autocompleted my worry. I found myself wondering whether Dr Thompson had always wanted to be a mother, or whether it happened for her through expectation or accident even — though it probably hadn't been an accident twice over. Maybe the first was an accident and then she decided she liked it? Maybe being a mother wasn't anywhere near as bad as she thought it would be and in fact, she found she was quite good at taking complete responsibility for another human's life even though it was absolutely something that she never wanted as part of her own life and — *did someone turn the air off in here?*

'Eleanor, take a deep breath for me, okay?' Dr Thompson was closer to me then, rubbing my arm softly and speaking so gently it was almost a whisper. 'That's it, keep breathing for me.'

Is this a panic attack? I pushed and kneaded at a spot on my chest where I'd suddenly grown a pain.

'Whatever happens, this is going to work out,' she said and I was immediately comforted by the lie. If it had been Nan talking to me I would have asked her to promise, but I thought that might put the doctor in a tough spot. 'I'm going to get a sample jar. Do you think you can manage a wee for me now? The bathroom is just around the corner, into the next corridor.'

I nodded along. I would have agreed to anything that meant easing my anxiety that bit quicker. The doctor handed me a ridiculously small pot for my urine sample and all I could think of then was how I was ever going to be able to aim well enough, and how much easier bloody men must have it, by having something to aim with. But at least it tore my thoughts away from the pain in my chest and the potential orange seed in my stomach because *of course* I'd gone ahead and googled the sizes of babies.

'Bring that back in when you're ready.'

'Thank you.'

I tried to hide the pot up my sleeve on the walk from the doctor's room to the bathroom. Once there, I pulled everything down like a horny teenager who'd just got lucky at a summer party. My pants were round my ankles and I was clenched with an all-too-familiar "this is going to hurt" nervousness. 'Get yourself together, Nellie,' I said in an inside voice while I tried and tried to let pee out. And seconds later, when it did come, so did a fresh wave of tears. The feeling that bubbled to the surface in the doctor's office was pouring out of me then and, as though the two things were somehow a part of the same bodily function, I sat there on the toilet with pee filling my small and ridiculous sample pot and mascara tears dripping off my chin.

CHAPTER TWENTY-EIGHT: OWEN

It felt as though, while I had been idly and ignorantly looking the other way, someone had crept into my life in the middle of the night and rearranged its defining features. There were no more dog walks. Scratch that, there was no more dog. There was no more romance, no more pizza nights, no more winning the pub quiz.

In place of all these things, was far too much time. I found I was leaving work every day and taking myself on a walk that I didn't especially need, for the sheer bliss of not having to be home alone. I avoided the dog park, obviously. But I made sure that every walk took me past or at least close to Nell's shop. Not that I had balls big enough to actually go inside.

I spent my days oscillating between "Yes, I am the one who needs to apologise" and "Who the fuck is Benji, anyway?". Managing the two made it increasingly difficult to decide whether I should visit the shop during actual opening hours. And after those long and tortured walks, I would come home to an empty house. I'd look at the many spaces that used to be occupied by the three most important women in my life. The scratches on the hallway wall from when Collie's pre-walk excitement was simply too much and she took it upon herself to try to reach her own lead. The patio doors that Daisy would nap against, having decided that literally anywhere else in the house was too hot for her. The armchair that Nell would sit in and read, dangling her legs over one arm in a display that was somehow graceful and not all at once.

That was what I did every night now. I played Spot the Grief in my home until it was time for bed. Most nights I sandwiched dinner between the self-pity, but I'd reverted back to microwave meals and toasties, having decided cooking for just me wasn't worth the inevitable hassle. Besides which, cooking is a lot less interesting when there's no dog lying at your feet while you do it.

Of course, after the torturous weekdays there came the equally torturous weekends. This was my third without Nell and Daisy. I had lost track of the weeks since Collie, though it felt like forever since I'd felt the soft nudge of her cold nose and the fading memory of that alone was enough to cause a physical ache. To honour that, I decided — *foolish, foolish man* — that the best thing I could do would be to unpack the photograph albums from the box where I'd previously stored them, and unload photo after photo of Collie in various states of cuteness and hilarity across the living room floor.

I was a mess by the time I found the picture of her wearing a wafer cone as though it were a fashion accessory for the face. She'd buried her nose in it only seconds before the picture was taken, trying to reach whatever ice cream was left. Two tears landed with dull thuds on the picture. I hadn't even realised the crying had started again. *I need digital copies of them all*, I decided then. *That'll give me something to keep busy with*. I struggled up from ground level and went in search of another distraction. There must be something in the house that needed cleaning or clearing. Though one heartache soon led to another when I opened the cupboard where the hoover lived, only to be faced off with one of Nell's favourite cardigans. I buried my nose in the wool and thought of her, Collie, her — and there was a physical ache in my chest that I knew, logically, was likely a fresh wave of feeling. But

229

illogically, I wondered whether it might be a literal fracture. And that's when the front door bell went.

'Good God, Owen, you look terrible.'

My mother. I sighed — the heavy, weighted sigh of a man who had in the last week googled what the UK protocol was for divorcing one's family. 'Mum, what are you doing here?'

'That's rude,' she answered flatly. I expected there to be more, but it seemed that that really was all she had to say in answer to my question.

So I matched her tone with an, 'Okay.'

She looked around the outside of my home, where my hanging baskets were much in need of a rainy downpour and my front door was no doubt in need of a lick of paint, too. It wouldn't have surprised me if she suggested with some sincerity the possibility of burning the place down and just starting afresh.

'Again,' I said when the silence became too much to stand. 'What are you doing here?'

'You won't answer your phone to me.'

'Because I don't want to speak to you.'

'Good God, Owen, stop being so petulant.' And then, in an uncharacteristically rude manoeuvre of her own, Mum pushed her way past me and into my home, marching down the hallway as though she knew the layout of the place.

'By all means, come in.'

'Will you offer me tea or will I have to make my own?'

I closed the front door with a forceful click and turned to face her. 'I didn't realise you knew how to. Isn't that the sort of thing Wini takes care of?'

She drew in such a pronounced and deep breath that I saw her chest rise with it. But she didn't actually grace me with an answer. Instead, she finished her route to the kitchen and there came the rush of water and the slam of the kettle being dropped back onto its stand. I realised then that the living room looked a little like those dramatized scenes you find in films where the stalker man has taken picture after picture of the same girl — albeit a dog version — and suddenly the mess of that room became much more of a priority than the mess awaiting me in the kitchen. I hurried back in, dropped to my knees and started to collect together the snapshots of Collie as though herding a splayed deck of cards.

'What are you . . .' Mum must have done some mental maths then: Owen, evidence of crying, pictures of the dog. Even she had the emotional capacity to understand those elements combined, I was sure of it. That, and she'd managed to get this far into the house without being attacked by excitement.

'Why didn't you tell me?' she asked, in a tone that sounded markedly softer than her earlier one. If I hadn't known better, I would have thought the woman was hurt.

'You always hated her, Mum.' I carried on collecting the photographs, only now I took my time, adding them back into their respective folders that formed a timeline of Collie's short and brilliant time on earth.

'I'll make tea.'

By the time Mum had clunked her way through the tea-making, all of Collie's photographs were back in their folders, the folders back in the box. I pushed them to the corner of the living room and took a seat in what had become Nell's armchair. It wasn't until Mum was sitting on the sofa, cradling her own mug of tea — a mug that, I noticed, had Collie's face printed on it, and I couldn't help but wonder why she'd had to choose that bloody mug out of them all — that I tried again at deciphering why exactly she'd crawled out of her lair and into my own.

'Why are you here, Mum?'

'Look, Owen, what happened at my birthday party—'

'Do you mean Lisa being there?' I cut across her. 'I just want to be sure that we're talking about the right thing.'

'Yes,' she answered stiffly. 'Though we'll come to the fact that you made an absolute show of things with that girl of yours in a moment.'

'I think maybe we should *start* there, on account of that show only happening because you invited Lisa, and that girl of mine no longer being that girl of mine, *because* you invited

Lisa.' I felt a flare of real anger in me then — lane-hopping-in-traffic, queue-jumping-at-the-supermarket, not-picking-up-your-dog's-mess-level anger. 'Can we start there?'

'Let's.' She answered like she had something hidden up her sleeve and I felt a deep roll of sickness move through my gut. 'To be clear, you lost that girl of yours because you lied to her about having seen Lisa, a fact that I am privy to on account of it having been announced to everyone within earshot at the party.' *Shots fired.* I resisted the urge to physically knead at my chest in case there was a real bullet wound there. 'You're your father's son, Owen. You and Simon are, as much as you mightn't admit it.'

'What does that even *mean*?'

'You think he and I haven't had our share of battles?'

I narrowed my eyes to look for the hidden meanings, stashed between syllables, or in the difficult breaths I heard her take throughout the short question. 'Dad . . .' I began to say, not knowing altogether what sentence might form after it. But a flashback came then of what Simon had said at the party. *That cheating incident?*

'Anyway.' She sipped her tea and went back to cradling the drink. 'This isn't about me and your father. My point here is that couples row, Owen — it happens. You work out who was in the wrong and you apologise. Failing that, you apologise anyway. I find the latter option tends to speed things along.'

My head snapped back at the — *is this even advice?* 'So, is that what you're here to do? Apologise, whether you think you're in the wrong or not?' Of course, she'd applied the logic to couples and in that moment, as far as I was concerned, we were hardly even family. But still, I wondered whether she'd given her game plan away.

There was a lengthy and considered pause before she answered, 'No. I'm here to actually apologise.'

Collie could have walked in backwards on her hind legs with a rugby ball balanced on the end of her snout and I would have been less surprised. 'I'm sorry?' I wondered whether my mother wasn't actually there at all then and whether, in the deep pit of despair I'd made for myself with Collie and Nell, I'd imagined the whole encounter so far. I even went as far as taking a sip of my tea to see whether it burned my mouth — which, of course, it bloody well did.

'I shouldn't have invited Lisa.'

'Then why do it?'

'Lisa and I have always got along. She and I bumped into each other in the city one day, had a coffee, and I invited her. It was that innocent, and, I'm afraid, that thoughtless. Of course, once asked, I couldn't un-ask.'

'And you didn't think to at least give me a heads-up?'

'No, no, it would appear I didn't.' She fidgeted with her mug and stared into the drink as though it were a wishing well that might undo the fuckwittery she was apologising for. 'I didn't,' she said again. 'And I'm sorry.'

'I . . . Mum, I . . . thank you.'

It was all I could manage. She gave me a firm nod in response. I suspected that was all she could manage, too.

'Now, the girl. Nell, is it? Your sisters said she's charming.'

'She's also not my girl anymore.' I set my mug on the floor. I suddenly didn't have the stomach for it. 'I haven't spoken to her since.'

'Flowers?'

'I'm sorry?'

'Have you sent flowers?'

I laughed. 'I'm not sure she's the type to be won over with flowers.'

'It isn't about winning her over, Owen. But you have to start somewhere. Flowers can often be a good start, and a heartfelt apology is often a strong follow-up.' She huffed a laugh then, an actual smile breaking out across my mother's face, and I tried to remember the last time I'd seen a beam that looked so sincere on her. 'I must have forgotten my own advice. I should have bought you tulips.'

'I'll . . . I can try flowers.'

'Owen, I'd like to ask you something and I'd like an honest answer before we move forwards. Is that . . . manageable?'

Suddenly I was seven years old and caught stealing biscuits; seventeen years old and caught stealing booze; twenty-one years old and caught having pranged the side of Dad's car against the wall of the driveway. Now, I was thirty-two and — *what can I have possibly done?* Still, I nodded in agreement to her terms.

'Are you in love with her?'

Like a movie-scene montage, I imagined the many moons of knowing Nell and the things that there were to love about her: the way in which she always ate strawberries standing over the bin to catch drips; how she never dried her hair on Sundays because she could afford natural mess when she wasn't at work; the way she split custard creams in half to have the filling just on one side; how she would make a special journey to a cash point to give money to the homeless man outside Tesco; the fact that she always gave spare poo bags to dog walkers who needed them; how she stocked my favourite foods in her cupboards — Christ, the fact that she even knew my favourite foods! *How could anyone in the world* not *be in love with Nellie Cobalt?*

'Yes,' I admitted with a laugh. 'Irrefutably, undeniably, unconditionally, I am in love with her.'

Mum nodded and leaned forward to set her own drink on the floor — an action that must have pained her deeply — before she fell back against the sofa and appeared to make herself more comfortable.

'Get yourself a pen and paper, Owen.'

'I . . . Okay . . .' I looked around the living room hastily, as though one or the other might just be lying around, before rushing to that drawer in the kitchen where everything got dumped. I came back with a pencil and a Chinese takeaway menu, the best I could do at short notice.

'If you love her, undeniably, irrefutably and so on, this is what you'll need to do . . .'

CHAPTER TWENTY-NINE: NELL

The flower market was an assault on the senses. I could practically hear the crackle of open fires and catch the whiff of spiced pumpkin *everything*. I tugged my cardigan a little tighter around me and I wondered whether it was the actual temperature drop catching up with me, or only the signs of the seasons that were dotted around the market making me come over all autumnal. This area was an add-on to the county's flea market, rather than the main attraction, but it made for a colourful scene to walk through on my way to traders and book dealers, both of whom were my actual reasons for visiting. That, and the fact that if I spent another Sunday wondering what Owen was doing at that exact moment in time then my brain might just dribble out of my ear and land in a sad pool on my kitchen floor — which was where I was doing the majority of my moping these days, so it could coincide with sad snacking, which was another thing that I needed a break from. Still, I stopped to peruse the flower stalls en route, pausing here and there to drink in the sights of coppertips, marigolds and sunflowers before eventually stopping at one stall covered entirely with white flowers: pale tulips, carnations and peonies, all of which were bursting with such smells that I wondered whether the stall holder was periodically stepping out from behind his stand to spritz the air with perfume.

I thumbed the corner wrapping on a large bunch of lilies. Nan didn't want any kind of compensation for taking care of Daisy for the day, but I reasoned the least I could do was take a token bouquet of something home with me. It was this or two whopping cream cakes which, admittedly, we both probably would have enjoyed more. But still, this would brighten up the living room a touch more than icing sugar. And I reasoned they would double as a thank you for having put up with quite so many toddler tantrums and snappy comments dealt her way in recent days and weeks.

The most recent of which had been that morning when I'd dropped Daisy off. Nan had opened the door with a smile and I answered with,

'I'm not pregnant, by the way.'

It was an announcement she looked taken aback by, shortly followed by relief, and then more confusion. 'Did I say that you were?'

'Nan! You said all that stuff about Mum and chicken!'

'Oh, Nellie.' She waved her hand and reached across for Daisy's lead. 'That was just an observation.'

I huffed and tutted and near-on threatened to blow the house down for a second before realising that she was, of course, entirely right. Nan had only made a throwaway comment or two to kickstart this, but somehow they had seeded their way in. I thought they'd probably given me somewhere proactive to put my panic and upset though. Panic and upset that were not welcome bedfellows with being overworked, anxious, and being diagnosed with anaemia. I was taking iron tablets and needed to include a few more greens in my diet — but I wasn't about to go admitting that to Nan. Instead I only grumbled a thank you for having Daisy, and Nan, in an overtly cheery tone, told me I was very welcome.

'Try to pick yourself a good mood up if you can find one while you're out?' she shouted after me when I was five steps down the path to her front gate. And even though I turned to throw a smart-arse comment back, I decided to let her have the free shot on account of the comment being entirely justified.

'You can mix and match flowers, if you'd prefer?' The stall holder pulled me out of the morning memory and back into the moment. 'Put the lilies with something else, maybe?'

'The lilies are perfect, actually.' I fumbled to free my purse from my satchel as I spoke. 'I'll just take those, thank you.'

I bought and paid for them, and cradled the flowers in the crook of my arm where a baby would sit — or, a more appropriate comparison, where Daisy might sit when she was feeling especially cuddly, which she had been lately.

I'd been in two minds about bringing her or not. We'd never spent much time apart but even more so at the moment. As though she were fine-tuned to the delicacy of my injured feelings, I found she was sticking closer and closer, plodding to and from the bathroom with me, nuzzling even nearer when we ended the day in bed with a dog-themed romantic comedy to keep us company. But as two children skidded right in front of me — 'Justin, Clara, slow down! You nearly hit that lady!' — I realised that she was much better off at home with Nan, and would probably be on her third slice of cooked ham by now.

I managed to navigate the last of the flower stalls without buying anything else. There was a houseplant stall that looked especially appealing — *doesn't everyone love houseplants since the pandemic?* I browsed my way along their offerings, but given that I'd managed to kill three in the time that it had taken for Owen not to call me, I thought I'd forgo asking any more greenery to sacrifice itself for me. Instead, I emerged victorious on the other side where there were stalls galore for me to spend money on — on glittery old things that I definitely didn't need but could at least love without killing.

Though of course, the first stall to catch my eye had been a long-time favourite, and the real reason for coming at all. The Mystery Corner was a bookshop devoted entirely to classic crime — a long-standing love — and whenever I visited any market the whole county over, before I'd even looked at the books themselves, I found I was drawn into idle chatter with the owners.

'Nell!'

'Walter!'

Walter was the outlandishly charming older gentleman who owned this glorious mess of paperbacks. He was everything anyone might imagine a bookseller to be. He stepped out from behind the stall to reveal an outfit made up of green corduroy trousers, a loose-fitting white shirt and a black waistcoat. His hair circled his head in great wisps and there was a pair of spectacles balanced on the end of his nose that I was certain I'd never seen him use. I liked to think they were there to complete the aesthetic. He clutched me by the shoulders and air-kissed both cheeks.

'How are you, pet?'

'I'm well, I'm well, and you?'

Walter was back behind the partition of his stall by the time he answered. 'Oh, I'm upright and still have all my teeth — what more is there?'

It was the answer he always gave, but it never failed to make me smile. 'Have you been busy today?'

'We have, as it happens. You've just missed someone walking away with a job lot of Agatha Christie—'

'Walter, stop.' I rested a hand on my chest and looked away. 'You'll break my heart.'

'But we do have . . .' He reached out of sight and came back with a book in hand. 'I wasn't sure whether you had it.'

The Secret of the Wooden Lady, an original Nancy Drew. 'Oh, Walter.'

'Marvellous, I'll take that as a no. It's yours.'

'And the price?'

He held a hand palm up. 'It's yours.'

Years ago, when the love of books was only just settling into me, my mother gave me a falling-apart copy of *The Clue in the Crumbling Wall*. It was her first, and my first, Nancy Drew novel. And I'd been steadfastly collecting them ever since. The offering was enough to make tears prick the corners of my eyes but I tried to hold back on actually crying in front of this kind old chap, who would no doubt panic beyond measure if a woman burst into sobs in front of him.

'You must let me pay.'

'Consider it a gift.' He was already sliding it into a slim paper bag. 'You don't look yourself, Nell. I hope you won't mind me saying. Besides which—' Walter leaned across to hand the book over — 'a little kindness often goes a long way in the world these days.'

'Thank you.' I accepted the book and blinked hard as I did so, trying to settle those tears again. 'I . . . I'll give someone a book!' I said, with probably a touch more enthusiasm than it called for. 'In my shop, I'll give someone a book, instead of letting them pay.'

'Perfect.' He smiled, soft and gentle with it. 'That'll be perfect, Nell.'

'If I was ever going to run into you anywhere, I should have guessed it would be here.'

The strange voice cut through mine and Walter's moment and I turned round to find, of all people, Benji. He was standing at the edge of the stall, leaning against one of its supporting pillars in a very Cool Guy fashion. Meanwhile, I was clutching my book to my chest with my watery eyes and my hair that hadn't known the touch of water or shampoo for a solid four days if not longer.

'Benji.'

'I'll see you soon, Nell?' Walter said then, before another customer pulled him to the opposite side of his set-up. Still, I shouted back my goodbye.

'And thank you for the book!'

'It's a pleasure, dear.'

'Only one book?' Benji said, assessing the weight of my paper bag.

I managed a smile. 'It was a gift. What are you . . .' I wanted to ask what he was doing here, of course. But I wasn't sure whether there was any way of doing that without sounding like an abrasive cow. So instead I scratched out the start of the sentence and tried for something that sounded more sociable, if not disgracefully cliché. 'Fancy seeing you here.'

'We've got to stop running into each other, yada-yada.' He added his own cliché to the pile, which at least made me feel better about the weak effort of mine. 'I'm here with my grandad.' He looked somewhere behind him then but turned back without having pointed anyone out. 'He's disappeared down a rabbit hole of crockery that he doesn't need.' When he laughed, my stomach turned and I couldn't tell whether it was a good feeling or a bad one. 'But what are the odds of running into you here?'

If I consumed as much true crime as my nan did, I'd think the odds were serial-killer-stalking-me high. Though that probably wasn't an acceptable thing to say either, not even if I managed it in a jokey tone. 'I'm sure there's a way of calculating them but I've never had a head for numbers,' I said instead and that at least made him laugh lightly. 'It's nice to see you though,' I added, because it's a thing that people say. But when Benji's look softened — coupled with a, 'Yeah?' — I wondered whether he might have read more into the comment than I'd intended.

'Are you heading this way?' He turned so we could walk together and I went along with it, mostly to get out of his eyeline. 'There's something weird about bumping into each other, though, don't you think?'

I don't like where this is going . . .

'If I weren't a man of science and statistics, I'd wonder whether someone was trying to tell us something.'

Oh, now I really *don't like where this is going.*

'Benji, I—'

'You have a thing with someone, I know.'

When I turned to catch a look at his profile I noticed that he was smiling still, but the note of disappointment in his voice was unmistakable. His comment had caused a sting of disappointment in me too, though, because — *I'm not involved with anyone.* My belly dropped at the thought and if it weren't for the book in one hand and the flowers in the other, I might have reached down to cradle my gut and tried to ease some of the emotional weight that had settled there.

'Yeah,' I said instead. 'I have a thing.'

'The guy who was walking Daisy the other week, right?'

There was a clattering of pennies dropping then, as though a lucky player had wedged enough 2ps into an arcade pusher, and they'd all knocked a load off the first ledge and then another load off the second, and the thunder of them all had collapsed into the tray at the bottom. One or two might have even spilled out onto the floor.

That's how Owen knows who Benji is.

'You saw him?'

'Mmhmm. Daisy saw me and came rushing over. I guess she recognised me, which is very sweet, really.' *And it is sweet of her, little traitor that she is.* 'Anyway, he came rushing after her and saw me and . . . I don't know, he was kind of sheepish when I introduced myself. Owen, right?'

'Right.' I couldn't say much more. There were too many feelings flooding in at once and I found that I was bouncing between feeling sorry for Owen — for being so blindsided by the sight of Daisy running over to another man — and being absolutely bloody furious with him for not just *asking* me about it.

'I can see the attraction.'

I laughed and agreed. 'He's a pretty handsome guy.'

Benji came to an abrupt stop then and I wondered whether his politeness had timed out. 'Look.' He turned to face me. 'I'm sorry if I caused any trouble there? Obviously, it wasn't my intention. I'm not exactly a . . .' He laughed softly and rubbed at the back of his neck, in a gesture that reminded me all too much of the man I was in love with and angry at. 'I'm not exactly a trouble-causing kind of man, ordinarily.'

And of course he wasn't. Aside from the outright weirdness of repeatedly bumping into him at different spots around the local area, Benji had never been anything but respectful and kind. In fact, he was a storybook archetype in many ways

— not least because he was spending what I assumed must be his day off walking around a flea market with his grandad! But I realised, given that life wasn't storybook perfect, bumping into each other repeatedly didn't exactly *mean* anything. What meant something was *choosing* to bump into someone, over and again, choosing to show up for that person because they were *your* person. That's what counted. That's what a relationship stemmed from. That's what Owen and I — *had*.

'Anyway, I've found the old boy.' Benji gestured out towards the mess of stalls and I glanced across to find an older gentleman trying to wave back. He looked as though he was balancing arms full of carrier bags and I couldn't help but laugh at that. 'Christ knows how he's managed to buy so much in the ten minutes he's had on his own. I dare say there's a full tea set distributed across those carriers.'

'You'd better get cake to go along with it.'

Benji smirked. 'I like your thinking there.' Then, in a gesture *so* formal that he may as well have reached out and slapped me lightly on each cheek for the shock it caused, he held out a hand for me to shake. 'Anyway, I'm sorry again.'

I pushed his hand away and gripped him in a hug so tight that he stopped talking mid-apology. I didn't realise the logistical error of the gesture until it occurred to me that Benji was likely getting an earful of crackle or pollen depending on how the lilies had crushed against him. 'We're all good, Benji, but thank you for the apology all the same.' When I moved away from him his expression mirrored what my own feelings had been following his handshake suggestion, and I wondered whether a hug had been too much. But given that I was a mess of feelings these days, a hug had been exactly what I'd needed.

'Right.' He sounded flustered when he spoke. 'I'm off to explain to him who the woman hugging me was.'

I managed a laugh. 'Just tell him I'm a friend.'

Benji smiled in a way that made me think he was satisfied with that answer at least. 'I'll do that.' He moved to walk away, but turned to add, 'I'll see you around, Nell?'

'It seems likely . . .'

Benji's grandad gave me another wave — this one slightly easier, given that Benji had freed him from two of the carriers he was struggling with — and I waved back before casting a quick glance at my watch. The market was a mess of stall holders still but there were only a few that I made a journey anywhere to see. So I decided that a strategic lap around the place would be the best plan of attack. Then I could make it home in good time for Sunday dinner with the girls — and I could catch the bakery before closing time for those two cream cakes . . .

CHAPTER THIRTY: OWEN

It had been nothing short of a mind-blowing experience to receive what seemed to be sincere and heartfelt advice from my own mother — apart from the bit about me needing to have a shave and a shower, which, while fair criticism, was probably something I could have lived without.

Still, by the time she'd finished I was about ready to lie down in a darkened room. I didn't have a clue what sort of big gesture would win Nell back around, especially now so much time had passed since the dreaded argument. And in the days that followed Mum's visit, I couldn't help but feel like there was a massive timer lingering overhead, too, and that any second now it would start harping that hideous tune that an iPhone automatically plays while asking me if I wanted to snooze — but it also felt a little like I'd unknowingly hit that button a handful of times already.

That said, Mum's advice did give me the shove up the arse that I needed to make a big gesture to another woman in my life. A few days after the visit I was wrapping up a day of automatic working — which was how I looked to be getting through most things in life by then, running on automatic alone — when there came a knock at my office door. I looked up expecting to see one of the high-end suits, no doubt readying to dump a pile of last-minute pleas on the corner of my desk, but instead there was . . .

'Lisa.'

I'd been screening her phone calls for days on end. I hadn't even given her the courtesy of a text message either, which was hugely out of character but, given the circumstances, I thought entirely necessary. During the deep and agonising moments of reflection that came in the early hours of the morning while staring at my bedroom ceiling, I'd come to suspect that Lisa had known exactly what she was doing when she'd introduced herself to Nell at the party. And that was fine, I'd decided, too, on account of that being Lisa's prerogative. Resultantly, my own prerogative had been to *slowly* phase her out — as though it were possible to ghost someone after you'd already ended your relationship with them, years prior no less.

'This is a surprise,' I said, pushing back from my desk to highlight that yes, my departure was imminent.

'You're ignoring me.'

'I'm not, look.' I tried to laugh but it came out nervous and awkward — which, coincidentally, was exactly how I felt. 'I just don't have anything to say.'

'Because of the party?' She fidgeted with her fingers, staring down at her hands as she did so, with a scorned schoolgirl demeanour that frankly she was far too mature for now — or maybe I was too mature for it to be effective. 'I really didn't mean to cause any trouble between you and the girl.'

'Her name is Nell, and I think you probably did.' My tone was a firmer one than I usually took, and I think it surprised us both. But I decided then that firm was the only way. 'How did it come up in conversation that we'd been spending time together, incidentally?'

Lisa shrugged and carried on looking at her hands. 'I just assumed she knew.'

'Okay, well, now she does.'

'It's not *my* fault that you hadn't told her.'

'You're totally right.' I stood up from my desk and collected my jacket from the back of my chair. 'It's totally my fault that I hadn't told her, but it's your fault that she found out how she did.'

'Owen.' She stepped into the space, making eye contact for the first time too. 'I would never, ever do something that would ruin your relationship with another person. You *must* know that.'

I thought on it for a second before I answered. 'I actually don't know that, Lisa. I don't know anything about you anymore because—' I shrugged to underscore the matter-of-factness in all of this — 'I don't know *you* anymore. I know we've talked more, and spent some time together, but truth be told if Collie hadn't been a sucker for eating things that she shouldn't have done, then you and I likely wouldn't have got to talking at all. So, why don't we swing back to that?'

She looked as though I'd lightly slapped her and it took everything in me not to rush out an apology.

'So what, we just go back to not talking?' she asked, as though the idea was absurd.

I walked towards the doorway and deliberately stepped around her. 'I don't think there's anything I have to say.' I turned in time to catch Lisa's mouth bob open and then close again. 'I'm not saying this to be a schmuck, Lisa, I just . . . there's nothing here that we need closure on.' I flicked the lights off. 'I think we got all the closure we need.'

'Right,' she said after a long pause. 'Right, I think I see.' She pushed by me then and walked out into the corridor. She was four steps ahead and clearly not about to say goodbye.

'Take care, Lisa, okay?' I said to her back, though she turned and managed a faint smile in response. She only nodded then and went on her way, while I pulled my office door closed and fidgeted longer than necessary with my keys. Getting in a lift with her and travelling down several floors didn't seem like the best way to try to end this kind of conversation. I gave her a ten-minute head-start before I made my own way out. And on the lengthy car journey home I tried to work out whether I'd been a dick, or whether I'd only broken a lifelong streak of being a doormat. But either way, I stood by everything I'd said to her — and the relief of finally having said it was unreal.

* * *

Two days and approximately zero ideas later, I did the only thing that a man in his early thirties can possibly do when faced with a challenge involving women: I called my mates and, under incredibly false pretences, asked them out for a pint — and a pile of advice that they didn't know they'd be giving. Of course, all of them said yes because deep down they're a decent bunch — and not so deep down they've never been known to refuse a drink. Though the fact that Alan's response to the group chat was a message that read: *Are you about to* Sex and the City *us for tips about women?* made me think that at least one of them had me rumbled.

It was a Saturday afternoon and I knew that Nell would be in the shop. But I also wasn't wholly convinced that a drive-by apology on my way to the pub to meet my mates was the grand gesture my mother had been referring to days earlier. Instead, I went for a walk-by in the shamefully desperate hope that I might just bump into her, rush through a very rehearsed apology — after endless run-throughs in the shower, in bed, during work meetings where I'd scripted everything I could possibly say to her — and magically have Nell back in my life. Though, of course, that wasn't going to happen either.

Still, I used the excuse of a dry afternoon to walk five minutes out of my way and glance through the intricate window displays of the shop. What had started out as orange and green leaves earlier in the season had since become leaves, a book tree and . . . *Is that a pumpkin?*. I was hoping to see Nell fluttering around in a floral dress somewhere — because in my mind's eye I had become so accustomed to Nell in flower prints that the two were inextricably bound to each other now. But the shop was heaving. Instead of seeing Nell, I could only see clusters of customers browsing one book-shelf or another and, while I was entirely gutted not to catch sight of her, I was also twofold relieved. Firstly, because it could only mean good things for Nell at the end of a workday if there were that many people buying books. Secondly, because, well . . . *Because you need something better than this*, I reminded myself as I walked another few steps along the pavement opposite. There was a bench just a few yards up the road and, feeling every ounce like a stalker in plain sight, I took a seat there and somehow felt that little bit closer to her just for having settled on the same street.

I'd hardly even registered the presence of another person on the opposite side of the bench until she spoke. 'I'm waiting for it to quieten down in there, too.'

When I turned, I was greeted by an elderly woman — in her eighties, if I had to guess, although I'd always been terrible at that game — and even though I was sure it must be me that she was speaking to, she still had her head nestled in the pages of a hardback as though she hadn't spoken at all. It wasn't until too many quiet seconds ticked by that she looked up and nodded in the direction of Nell's shop.

'Heaving in there, isn't it?'

I smiled and managed a half-laugh. 'It certainly seems to be.'

'Mind you, good to see that the book trade isn't long dead to the screen.'

'You're not a Kindle fan?'

She made a grunting noise that I guessed to mean hard no. 'Give me pages and a strong spine any day.'

'I could never get along with hardbacks,' I replied. 'Anything good?'

The woman closed the book then and gave me a flash of a striking red-and-black cover. It was a Ted Bundy biography — and I was stunned to silence. If I'd had to pair a reader with a read, this might well have been my last coupling that I'd ever make.

'Cheery,' I said jokingly.

'I'm brushing up on my facts.' She lay the book flat on her lap, which I took to be a sign that our conversation might be about to stretch out into something more substantial, and I couldn't tell whether I was relieved at that or not. Ordinarily, this would be the type of encounter that I might immediately text Nell about, and I felt a stab of new sadness that this was yet another thing I wasn't going to be able to tell her. *Unless you move faster*, I reminded myself again. 'What sort of a reader are you then?' she asked.

'I'm a romantic comedy guy, I guess,' I said with some embarrassment. It felt like an uncomfortable contrast with the eighty-something-year-old true-crime buff who I'd found myself seated with. 'I haven't been up to reading much lately though. I'm sort of going through a . . .' The phrase "break-up" lodged in my throat. 'I'm sort of going through a thing, with the woman I was involved with. It makes reading about happy couples that bit harder, you know?' I said with a sincerity that surprised me. I wasn't altogether sure why I was opening up to this woman, unless I was priming myself for the emotions that might spill out when I was two pints down with the lads. Still, she nodded along as though she were interested and that assuaged some of my awkwardness at least.

'Your fault or hers?'

'Mine,' I answered without hesitation. 'Completely and utterly mine.'

She made another noise, then, this time a thoughtful one. 'Maybe the books will give you an idea or two on how to fix things.'

'Do books hold that kind of magic?'

The woman laughed. 'I don't know, my granddaughter would probably say they hold *a* kind of magic.'

'Your granddaughter sounds wise. Fellow bookworm?'

'Bookworm, book hoarder, bookseller. If it involves books . . .'

'That's not a bad way to be.'

'No.' She looked across to Nell's shop and I felt a twinge of guilt that maybe I was boring the poor woman already. But then she turned to look at me, with a squint and another thoughtful noise. 'She's about your age, actually. Though I suspect you'd look younger if you had a shave.'

I spluttered a laugh. I couldn't work out whether it was an insult or an observation, but I was sure it was the funniest thing anyone had said to me in days. 'I've let myself go a little in the last few weeks.'

'Well, that won't win the girl back.'

'That's the trouble.' I swallowed the urge to look over at the shop front, too. I had visions of Nell walking out for a breath of air, glancing around, catching sight of me and — *and what?* I hesitated on sharing any more details with the woman. But she hadn't got up and left yet, so I reasoned that was signal enough to press on. 'I'm not sure what *will* win the girl back.'

'My husband always used to start with my favourite chocolates. Then if that didn't work, he'd say sorry.' She smiled, though more to herself rather than me. 'Whenever I said sorry, I did it with homemade chips.'

I laughed again. 'How long were you married?'

'Not long enough.' Her tone had changed then, the light-heartedness giving way to a sadness that was so heavy I thought the bench might sag beneath us both. 'But I got a beautiful daughter, and a beautiful granddaughter, and a beautiful great-granddaughter.' She paused to weigh the statement after she'd said it. 'A mostly beautiful great-grand-daughter, anyway. I have a lot to be thankful for from that man.'

'It sounds like a mighty good marriage to me?'

'Oh, I don't know. Everyone has their moments. There was one time . . .'

I wondered whether she'd decided the privacy of the memory was something best kept close. But then she added, 'I'm sure you're not interested in the stories of an old crone.'

'I am!' I said with too much gusto. To my shame, I was sure I might have even leaped an inch off the bench. She laughed and I tried to steady myself before saying again, 'I am. It's worth knowing these things. You might be giving me insider information.'

She laughed a hearty chuckle, a long-term smoker sound. 'Young man.' She shuffled along the bench to be within touching distance and I wondered whether she was going to share a trade secret, whether it was worth whipping my phone out and noting down everything she was about to say. 'Do you love the girl?'

I let out another breath. 'Yes, I really bloody love her. And, I don't even know how it happened, from walks in the park to this.' I gestured vaguely in the direction of the shop. 'This pining and hurting and . . . wishing that I'd made better decisions when it bloody well counted. But, yes, I love the absolute bones of the woman and her dog and her wild hair and her . . . her unfathomable obsession with flower-print dresses. I love it all.' I ran a hand through my hair and laughed. 'Sorry, that was probably more of an answer than you bargained for.'

'If you love her, the best thing to do is to *show* her that you love her. Not tell, *show*.'

'I've left it too long, I think.' And of course, that was a concern. For all I knew, Nell could have been manning the shop with help from her superhero doctor friend that afternoon. They could have been going on dog walks together and sharing pizza, and doing all the things that she should be doing with me. 'It's been weeks since . . . since we argued, and she found out some things that upset her, and . . . I don't know, there might even be someone else for her now and—'

'And, and, and,' she interrupted. 'I'm hearing a lot of *ands* for someone who wants the girl back.'

'They're not excuses,' I said, the words brittle with defensiveness.

'No, no, young man.' She reached across and tapped my arm. 'They're things that are holding you back.'

'So what?' I turned to get a better view of her. She was wearing a knowing expression by then. From this view of her profile, I thought there might have even been signs of a smirk. 'I just shouldn't let these things hold me back? It's that simple?'

'One big shove, one big *show*. It's that simple.' She turned to me and smiled. 'And, and, and, if it doesn't work out, I can at least promise you that when you're my age you'll be glad you gave it a mighty go.'

I let the words sink in. *One big show*, I parroted back silently. *One big show*. Though I still didn't have a clue what a big show might be. I had to assume it was the same or a nearby thing to the grand gesture that Mum had mentioned, but people seemed to throw these descriptors around without any set meanings! How would I know what one big . . . My ringtone hummed in my pocket and cut off any reply. 'I'm so sorry,' I said as I pulled the handset out. The woman waved away the apology and only shifted back to her side of the bench. It was Alan — probably calling to point out that I was thirty minutes late, and I'd promised them the first round. 'I'm meeting friends, I . . .' I waited for the call to time out before I stashed the phone away. 'I'm sorry.'

'Save those apologies for the girl.' She winked and nodded. 'One big show.'

I smiled and stood up from the bench. 'One big show. Thank you. I . . . thank you.'

'You're welcome.' She opened her book again and buried her face between the creases of Bundy's story, which I took to be her goodbye. But just as I stepped around the bench and back onto the main pavement, she turned. 'I didn't get your name?'

'Owen.' I held out a hand, which she didn't take. Instead, she smiled again and turned back to her pages.

'I wondered . . .'

I smirked. 'Me too . . .'

CHAPTER THIRTY-ONE: NELL

I didn't make a habit of crying in Green Fields dog park. But every now and then, it was inevitable. While Daisy was busy scampering in among rose bushes — a behaviour that I had come to think of as her homage to Collie, even now as the bushes were wilting with the season change — I found myself a bench and a patch of quiet. It was my favourite thing to do during those days, find quiet. Nearly another week had passed without Owen in my life and in that time I had learned the following: Nan was dating someone, a revelation that led to my needing to lie down in a darkened room before asking her twenty-one questions about the man; Lucia wasn't only planning her trip home, but planning to stay for even longer than expected, a revelation that made me cry over FaceTime, and I missed Owen, unfathomably, undeniably, in a way that caused my entire body to hurt at times, and that was a revelation that wasn't a revelation at all.

There had been so many long days since the argument at his mum's party, something that still left me red-faced with both embarrassment and anger if I thought about it for too long. And it was killing me quietly that there hadn't been an apology — or even a text! I might have waited it out longer for an apology if there had at least been a phone call in its place. Admittedly, I hadn't called either but — I groaned, and dropped my head back to stare into the clouds. Despite the weather having been grim all day up until now — grey-scale clouds with a threat of showers, leaves carried on a crisp wind — the sky had turned over into a brilliant clear blue, pockmarked with cloud coverage still, and I hoped it might bring me something like clarity, too. Especially as life had now become a classic will-they-won't-they, and nothing about it felt enjoyable. In fact, for the sake of knowing one way or another, I had decided, begrudgingly and grumpily, a "they won't" was going to be the tragic ending to our story, as though losing Collie part way through hadn't been tragedy enough.

And that afternoon, having decided that we wouldn't, I decided to let myself have that cry, too. It wasn't a wail. I saved those for when Daisy was asleep and I was in the bath, because no child should have to see their mother like that. Instead, this cry was a soft, several-tears-down-each-cheek-type of affair. There was no shoulder-shuddering, there was no heaving or struggling for breath. There was only the quiet sadness of admitting privately to myself that the person I loved was no longer in my life. Because of course, I did love him.

On my seventh day of missing him, Nan had outright asked, 'Nellie, are you in love with the chap?'

And I answered without hesitation, as though it were the easiest question in the world to answer, even though it was also the first time I was admitting the information aloud — or to myself, for that matter.

'Then why don't you call him, hm?' My eyes widened and my mouth bobbed open slightly, and Nan chuck-led heartily at that. It wasn't the suggestion of calling him that did it, but more that the suggestion came from Nan, the woman who once boycotted her local corner shop just because the cashier was rude to her once. The woman knew how to hold a grudge like a relieved mother might hold a newborn, nurturing it well into adulthood. 'I know, I know, I'm a fine one,' she said. 'But, Nellie, my girl, isn't life a bit short for it all?'

It didn't feel short, of course. I realised that when you were nursing a heartache, days were incredibly longer than they might be when you were otherwise fit and well. Workdays at the shop stretched out too long, evenings alone lasted for whole days. The only moments of respite from it all were here, in the dog park where it all started, where I could gulp in huge mouthfuls of air and fill my body with something other than ill-feeling for a short while. Although here there came the interruptions, too: the other dog walkers who would always stop to say hello; Benji, who had reduced his contact with me to a friendly nod as he walked by, and, on that afternoon, while I was midway through my teary out-pouring, an interruption came in the form of a woman wear-ing a concerned expression and shaking my shoulder until I tipped my head away from the clouds and back upright.

'Excuse me,' she said, with another shake. 'Do you own a bulldog?'

Oh, please, don't take Daisy from me, too. I was scan-ning the area for her before I could even answer. 'Yes, I do. Did you see her? Was someone taking her?'

When life was already fractured, it's so easy to assume that a larger crack would appear at any moment. In the two seconds it took for the poor woman to form an answer, I had already imagined the ways in which Daisy might have been dognapped and sold into a doggo slavery circle, convinced as I was that such a thing must exist, even though Daisy — Daisy, who was spayed as a puppy — would be fruitless in such a situation.

'Oh, she's fine, she's fine,' the woman said, obviously thrown by my flare of panic, which I took to mean that she couldn't possibly be a dog owner herself. 'It's just that she's sort of gone wandering off on her own? I saw her over there, behind the rose-bush cluster. She's fine, merrily toddling away and all, but, yes, she's obviously on her own.'

'Thank you so much.' I collected my cardigan from the bench behind me. 'Thank you, really.' I spoke over my shoulder as I rushed in the direction the woman had gestured towards — the dreaded rose bushes that always caught Daisy's nose as she walked past them. I was hollering her name — 'Daisy? Daisy!' — in my best neutral tone, because anything more would have likely panicked her, too. I rounded one cluster of flowers and then another, worry rising in my chest like water pressure when I didn't immediately spot her. Though of course she was fine, because it turned out she was with . . .

'Owen.'

He was kneeling down in among the rose bushes, with Daisy sitting alongside him as though the whole thing had been perfectly staged between them. I was suddenly so painfully aware that there were likely mascara tracks down my cheeks, and I tried to do that thing where you convince yourself it doesn't matter how you look when you see an ex, because they're an ex and you don't have to impress them anymore. But obviously that was a great big lie, made all the more awkward against the fact that Owen looked offensively handsome. He wore his usual dog-walking jeans, but he'd paired them with a crisp white shirt that gave him a cleanness I appreciated. It was like looking at a blank slate and I so desperately wanted for his clothing to be a metaphor. Meanwhile, I was wearing mom jeans with two rips in — neither of which had anything to do with Daisy, which made the tears infinitely less adorable — and a T-shirt that said Point me to the library with a massive bloody thumbs-up on it. I couldn't have been any less prepared for seeing the ex for the first time if I'd actively tried for it.

Owen smiled when he saw me though, a nervous, boyish smile that made me wonder again how staged this meeting was.

'Nell,' he said with a shake already in his voice. 'I miss you.' If I hadn't known better, I would have guessed there were tears in his eyes, too. 'I miss you like an ache, Nell, and it's terrible and horrible, and . . . losing Collie has been horrific, but finding you, finding you two—' He reached forward and kneaded at the skin rolls on Daisy's neck. 'Finding you two has been one of the best things that's ever happened to me in my decidedly normal life.'

Why is there a necklace box on the floor?

'I know that what I did was shitty. I'm a schmuck and a liar and I absolutely should have just told you that Lisa turned up with food. She was meant to be there to get a thing or two of Collie's, and before that, yes, we'd spoken a handful of times but it was nothing. It could never be anything.' His shoulders sagged with the weight of the sad explanation. 'That's honestly all it was, Nell. I'm over Lisa, I was over Lisa long before I met you, and then I met you and realised that Lisa was never . . . she was never sustainable, she and I weren't, because we didn't have this.' He threw his arms open and gestured to the whole world around us, and I felt something like delight tug at my insides. 'She and I didn't have everything that you and I have, or could have, if we just tried, or tried again. And the Benji thing . . .' I rubbed at my forehead. 'On my life, that was a me thing and that's my thing and . . . I should never have accused, or implied, or doubted, even! He's . . . he's a handsome guy and I'm just . . . Me. And somehow that got all the way in my head, and I shouldn't have listened to it, never mind even said things about it and . . . Nell, I'm never going to be able to say sorry enough times for everything that's happened — sorry, by the way, sorry, sorry, sorry, over and again — but I need the chance to at least try to fix this.'

Why is he reaching for the necklace box?

'This is a wild and crazy thing to be doing, I know, but I honest to God in my absolute gut believe that it's also the most sensible decision I have ever made in my entire, beige life.' He laughed along as he opened the box and I held my breath for a dangerous amount of time. 'I hope that what's in here is okay, for you both, but if it isn't that's okay, too. Whatever happens on the other side of this, Nell, I need to know. I need to know that I gave it absolutely everything, because that is nothing shy of what you deserve, every day of your life.'

Is that . . . Is he clipping a collar on . . .

'Daisy and I have talked about this, and I asked her whether she was comfortable with it . . . there you go, girl.' He leaned forward and kissed her head and she looked up at him adoringly in such a way that I thought I might die from it. 'Go and show your mum,' he said before he kissed her again and nudged her along towards me.

The tears were coming again by then, as my beautiful girl followed instructions from this beautiful — albeit ballsy and slightly stupid — man, and she plodded over towards me before setting her rump firmly on the ground and looking up at me with real purpose on her wrinkled face. I realised then — or I liked to think, anyway — that she was looking up to show me what appeared to be a new collar. So I crouched level with her to inspect whatever offerings Owen had brought to the table — alongside this heart-healing, tear-inducing apology of his. And there it was, in leather detailing, a chain of white-and-yellow daisies around her thick neck — with something hanging where her dog tag should have been.

Ohboyohboyohboy.

'Nell . . .' I looked up to see Owen struggling to stand upright and laughing as he did so. 'Been kneeling there for longer than I thought,' he said jokingly as he closed the gap between us. 'Nell, never in my dull and quiet life have I met someone or loved someone as brilliantly colourful as you are, and the prospect of not having that around every day . . . it kills me and it's been killing me.'

He was kneeling again then, level with me albeit a slight distance away given that Daisy was still sitting between us. Owen reached forward to undo the collar and slip the ring free, and Daisy waited, fixed and patient, while he clipped her new accessory back in place again, too.

There was a true risk of my becoming starved of oxygen by then, between the shoulder-shudder of tears that I was trying to hold back and the breath that I had apparently been holding since Owen started speaking. I felt a noise — an answer? — bubbling up from somewhere in my stomach and I put my fingers against my mouth to trap it in, lest all manner of crap and ill-considered responses came out with it.

Owen held the ring out towards me and I realised then that he was crying, too, although he was wearing a wide smile with it. 'Nell Cobalt, you wild, crazy and beautiful creature, will you marry me?'

It was how I imagined a near-death experience might be, insofar as your entire life flashing before your eyes and forcing the ridiculous question of how you arrived here, at this self-defining moment. I thought of Jack Stephens, my first kiss at primary school, which was more spit bubble than kissing but I'd always counted it. I thought of Chris Hand, my first sexual experience who'd thought the way to a girl's climax had been to act like a jack-hammer. I thought of the man whose name I still couldn't speak aloud, and how broken and lonely I'd been when he'd left. And I thought of Owen, my brilliant and hilarious and loving Owen, a man who had made a mistake or two — haven't we all? — but who was, now, right here, waiting for me to say yes.

Yet, when I finally drew breath enough to answer, instead of the sobbing yes that every person who had ever proposed longed for, there came a quiet, squat and sad little, 'No . . .'

And I think it surprised us both equally.

SIX MONTHS LATER . . .

EPILOGUE

It took very little time for me and Daisy to become accustomed to walking into a house full of smells at the end of a Saturday. Owen's new favourite thing seemed to be experimenting with recipes and he was unlikely to get complaints about that from the Cobalt side of the household. It was, I had decided, one of many perks to living with a man — something I hadn't done before in my young and weary life but now, having experienced it, I would ten-out-of-ten recommend. The cups of tea and the commitments to watching Netflix series together, and the vast array of home-cooked meals that adorned our kitchen table, *more* than made up for the fact that Owen complained of a blocked nose whenever I lit a scented candle and he passionately hated sleeping in a warm bedroom, and there was also one occasion where he put my favourite cream T-shirt in with a dark load of washing — counterbalanced by the fact that living with a man apparently meant there was someone there to catch up with loads of washing at the weekend, so there was that.

There was also the whopper of a fact that Owen still loved me, despite me having turned down what was a very cute marriage proposal, even if it was a *totally* misguided one. Though that, of course, had been counterbalanced by my own proposal: down on one knee, fumbling in my pocket for my janitorial bundle of keys, thumbing through them to find my house key, and then holding it up like a fantasy hero who had just unlocked a final quest. Owen had cried for a tiny while longer before he'd realised what I'd been asking him.

'You want to live with me, but you don't want to marry me?'

'Owen.' I reached up to wipe a tear from the end of his nose. 'I don't think I want to marry anyone.'

He wiped his own nose then. 'But you want to live with me?'

Daisy was lingering nearby and I pulled her closer to me and held up the key again. '*We* want to live with you, Owen Winthrop. Will you—'

'Yes.' He laughed and he cried a little more before he kissed both of us on the forehead in turn. 'Yes.'

There was a continued counterbalancing act while we worked out the logistics of living together. Though I was coming to realise that living with someone at all might be one big balancing act — which was maybe what made it work. Still, after some lengthy conversations during some lengthy dog walks — which, even now, was where Owen and I swapped the most detailed accounts of our days — we decided Owen would move into our house, owing to the fact that we didn't live in the grubby financial district, and Owen didn't exactly want to live in the grubby financial district anymore either. It made his journeying into work longer, but it did mean that he was well placed for an end-of-the-day walk with us. Couple that with lazy Sundays, What's-Owen-cooked-now Saturdays, and Your-Family-or-Mine (a game that involved no balancing whatsoever — I always won) and now, somehow, three months in, it felt a little bit like it had always been the three of us. A tripod, and the two of them most definitely kept me upright.

But after another month of life as a trio, I walked into the bedroom one night to catch Owen watching YouTube videos about how to introduce a baby into a family that already had a toddler . . .

'Is there something you want to tell me?'

Owen set a hand on his stomach. 'Nell, I'm late . . .'

Daisy bounded onto the bed then and distracted us both from the gentle comedy of a pregnancy scare, which, now that I knew I most definitely *wasn't* pregnant, had become something I could laugh about again. Still, I'd sensed a larger conversation under cover there, too.

'Do you think you're ready for another dog?'

Owen kneaded at the soft wrinkles of Daisy's back and avoided eye contact. 'It's too soon.'

'Okay, but . . .' I eased the iPad away. 'You're considering it?'

'We're okay, aren't we, Daisy?' Daisy nuzzled into his palm, his hand fitting her like an awkward cap and she looked delighted with the arrangement. 'I don't want to replace Collie.'

I climbed into bed next to them both. 'Like you ever could.'

Owen and I didn't say anything more about it that night, or the night after even. In fact, weeks rolled by without the mere mention of another dog and then suddenly . . . . There was a man at work who knew of a rescue home, and one of their dogs had recently had a litter. It couldn't hurt to look, right? I nodded along with every rhetorical question Owen asked, knowing this was a place he needed to arrive at on his own. Although when we saw the bundle of boys — '*All* boys?' I asked, a little perplexed at the prospect — I felt remarkably like my head and heart would pop open at once.

Daisy met the puppies with total indifference, but I reasoned that was a thing to be worked on. And when we brought Duke home — because *of course* when we'd met the puppies, we'd had to have a puppy — I soon noticed that she started to take him under her wing. Not in a literal way, thank goodness, because she really was only one misplaced sit away from stifling the kid — though there were times when he followed so close at her tail that I thought he was asking for it, just a little bit. But she nudged him in the right directions around the bookshop, kept him busy when there were customers — or let the customers take the reins entirely while she sneaked into the storeroom for a minute's quiet — and in the late, late hours, when we were a family of tired things, I'd caught her cleaning his ears once, too.

'Thank God,' Owen had said when I told him. 'I really worry about those things.'

I looked down at Duke in his bed at the end of our bed and saw that those very ears were still upright and alert, as though he were listening in on us even now. Duke hadn't graduated to the bed yet owing to his size, and the fact that I lived in horror at the thought of him trying to use his fly-away ears to jump off the bed in the night and landing flat as a flat thing, us finding him in the morning, battered, dejected and forever scared of jumping on our bed, even when his big boy legs might allow for it.

'It is normal for corgis to have such massive ears. Apparently he'll grow into them.' Owen was reading reassurance from his phone screen.

I snatched the handset away and dropped it into our amnesty box at the side of the bed. No screens after 10.00 p.m. — it was a house rule that Owen had implemented and I'd begrudgingly adhered to. The shock of having my Kindle snatched away from me during some of my best reading hours had been too much to bear. But given that we'd replaced it with the television screen, with cuddle puddles of pets and soft things, with . . .

'What episode were we on with *Grace and Frankie*? Had we gone on to season two yet?'

I lowered my head onto Owen's chest and scooched over to make room for Daisy, who would come padding up from the bottom of the bed when she'd finished staring over the edge of it to check that Duke was asleep. Owen gave me the controls then, having decided that choosing between season one and two was too much hassle after a long day of making food for us all. *For this, screen time isn't exactly much to give up,* I thought then, not for the first time, as Daisy circled and circled and dropped between us both.

Just look at how much we've all gained . . .

THE END

ACKNOWLEDGEMENTS

There are a lot of people — and animals — who deserve thanks here. Firstly, Benji — my own little life-saver — and his friends: Danny, Frankie, Lola and, most of all, Archie. I know these animals and their owners, without really knowing them, and that gave me the bones of this book. It's one of the few novels I've written where I can tell people exactly where the seed of it came from, and it's chiefly from those morning walks, where we never quite know who we'll run into, but we can often count on it being a friend.

Then, there are my actual friends; a handful who deserve extra-special credit and they know exactly who they are. Without you, I couldn't have written a romantic comedy for dog-walkers — a description that still makes me shake my head in wonder that I managed to write this book at all. Thank you for having read whole chapters, eased worries and encouraged me to tell Owen and Nell's story.

I have to extend thanks to my fantastic agent, Andrew James at Frog Literary, for seeing something in this book and taking a chance on it, and me — I genuinely wouldn't have got here without you. Thank you as well to the entire Joffe and Choc Lit team for having welcomed me with open arms. Your editorial guidance has been amazing, and your excitement for this book is everything I've needed from a publisher. Finally, dear reader, thank you for taking a chance on this book of mine. I hope you've enjoyed reading it just as much as I enjoyed writing it, and I hope we'll meet again soon.

THE CHOC LIT STORY

Established in 2009, Choc Lit is an independent, award-winning publisher dedicated to creating a delicious selection of quality women's fiction.

We have won 18 awards, including Publisher of the Year and the Romantic Novel of the Year, and have been shortlisted for countless others. In 2023, we were shortlisted for Publisher of the Year by the Romantic Novelists' Association.

All our novels are selected by genuine readers. We are proud to publish talented first-time authors, as well as established writers whose books we love introducing to a new generation of readers.

In 2023, we became a Joffe Books company. Best known for publishing a wide range of commercial fiction, Joffe Books has its roots in women's fiction. Today it is one of the largest independent publishers in the UK.

We love to hear from you, so please email us about absolutely anything bookish at choc-lit@joffebooks.com

If you want to hear about all our bargain new releases, join our mailing list here www.choc-lit.com

Milton Keynes UK
Ingram Content Group UK Ltd.
UKHW012248110624
443988UK00004B/280

9 781781 897478